We Are Still Awake

A Cautionary Tale

Billie Nicholas

TIMELINE

2016: A shift in power sent a country into chaos.

2017 – 2018: The Resistance was put to sleep.

2031: A small handful of people were still awake.

2016, WEST VIRGINIA

When he was seven years old, his mama took him to the store where he got to choose from the bubbles or the Silly Putty or the jump rope, which wasn't really a jump rope, but pieces of regretful twine super glued together. He held her hand tightly, never wanting to be too far away from her, looking up at her like she was an angel because she was his whole, big, beautiful, falling apart world. He watched as the lights haloed her unbrushed hair and thought about what he would choose.

There was a definitive moment when his hand lost its grasp of everything.

They were walking toward his prize, and he felt her fingers with the long red nails go limp, and he fumbled for them. *"Where are they going? I can't let go, I can't hold on, where is she going?"* His small hands used their little kid strength to pull at the manicured fingers, then the hands, then the arms, then the whole parent who was supposed to stand upright and lead him through the store. Through everything.

He watched as his mama made a silent thud on the floor almost in slow motion, and one of the fake red press-on nails came off in his hand. He held it tightly as if this small piece of his mom could possibly stop what was happening.

"Mommy," he cried. The first time was a small exhale that came out almost involuntarily as if he had extinguished the sadness he held in his body all at once. But he hadn't.

"Mommy!" He screamed it this time. It was so loud that some people

1

stopped to peer at the young boy and his unconscious mother. But then they kept on walking because, frankly, they had seen it all before.

Every hour of every day of every week and month and year for as long as they could remember.

The boy pulled on his mama's arm, and it was so heavy, and he didn't know how he could ever get her back home to her bed where she belonged.

The store manager was suddenly standing over him, and the boy could hear him talking on his phone. *The police! Emergency!* His beautiful mama with her nine red fingernails was going to get help, and they would walk hand in hand toward his present (he had decided on the putty!) and then to the register, and then he would try his best not to get it stuck on the car seat. Before they drove away, he would remind mama to buckle his seatbelt because that silly mommy always forgot. But he would forgive her this once because she was so sleepy in the store.

So sleepy.

The sweet young boy clung to her limp hand as the ambulance finally arrived (delayed from so many completely identical episodes like hers), and he watched as the medics administered that magical stuff his mom needed to take back the really bad thing she had done to herself. Again.

The paramedics tried and tried, and he knew deep in his little boy heart that this was not going to be like the other times. As her breath stopped completely, he felt his heart banging the saddest song in his small chest.

* * *

It was exactly one week earlier when he had been lying in bed with his mother, bare feet against skinny legs. They were watching the news together as they had done every single night for a year.

"This man!" she shouted, "This is the man our stupid country needs!" She lovingly shoved her son off of her, gently removing his grasp as he clung to her stained tank top. She put her face close to his and said in a whisper, "I'll be right back, my love." Then she disappeared behind the bathroom door.

He knew by now that the person who returned wasn't really his mama. She was a ghost of who he imagined her to be. She was the hauntress of his night terrors. The ghoul that prevented him from shutting his eyes until all

2

his muscles gave out from exhaustion.

November 8th was exactly like any other night. The two of them were curled up in the too-small bed with its dirty sheets in the single room apartment. There was barely enough space to exist. They did not have a kitchen and relied on a hotplate that the boy was allowed to use at will or the twenty-four-hour fast food joint down the street. They did own a car, but it broke down every couple of days, and oftentimes his mom would think it was funny to walk through the drive-through to get their food. Had his mother lived for much longer, he might have stopped finding the humor in such behavior.

A miniature bathroom off the bedroom clung onto a door that was begging to fall off. When strange men came over (they were rarely the same), the boy sat in the bathtub with his blankets and his stuffies (Mr. Beary and Spotty the Giraffe) that were still filthy from being dropped in a muddy puddle. When it had happened, he'd howled and howled until his mom slapped him across the cheek. With a sting on his face and a bruise pressed hard into his self-worth, he had tried to scrub his stuffy friends with a bloodied rag he'd found in the bathroom.

There were bugs with supervillain armor that his mom tried to squish with her bare feet or her favorite boots full of holes, but they always escaped to the recesses of their evil caves. To the boy, who rarely got to go to school because his mother favored "hooky" over the two mile walk, they were his fearless companions.

His mom had left him alone that night to reside in her dream state of which he was not part of nor really wanted to be. Her eyes were both shut and open, and the boy knew better than anyone that such a thing existed. He held onto her hand with so much love, sometimes he believed it could stir her awake. She didn't so much as twitch, so he watched and watched and watched the news by himself. It was a big night, or so it seemed. People were shouting. They were excited. Some people looked worried. Some even looked afraid.

He took on all the emotions, not knowing where to place his tired thoughts, trying desperately to understand what was happening.

The hours passed and the people became more frenzied. Sleep never came, so he stayed up all night long. He watched the energy ping pong around the screen, and finally with great purpose, decided to feel excited too. When he finally found out what was happening, his little feet tucked in between his

3

mama's bony knees, he felt like he might explode with news. And when his mother finally opened her bloodshot eyes and looked into his bleary ones late the next afternoon, he whispered what he'd been holding inside for hours.

"He won."

She stared at him. He could see her pupils focusing, then refocusing. He had never seen her deep brown eyes that held one million terrible stories so big and so beautiful.

"He won?" She whispered it, too.

He nodded.

"HE WON?" She shouted it now.

He watched in disbelief as she jumped up and down, the skin on her legs flapping in little waves of happiness, and her unbridled breasts bouncing all about. It was the most he'd seen her move in his entire seven years of life.

The little boy nodded at her and smiled. He had too few smiles for a child his age. But in that moment, it felt like he had won a giant trophy, like the kind he'd seen on TV. He was the bearer of the very best news: his mother's hero had been elected the President of the United States of America.

"Baby," she leaned down to the end table and shoved two pills in her mouth, then got close like she always did when she wanted to tell him something meant only for his ears. "We have to celebrate. Get dressed!" she whispered.

He pulled on his pants over his too-small underwear, then pulled on a shirt that barely fit over his head. His pants had gaping holes in the knees and were two and a half inches too short. But still, he stood there proudly. He had been dressing himself since he was three.

"Ready," he said standing up as tall as his height allowed. He stared at his mama in her tight purple dress. She looked like a skeleton, but he didn't know enough to be embarrassed by her hollow cheeks or her boisterous track marks. She took his hand, and they walked down the stairs together, stepping over Lou who lived on the first floor, and who they later found out had died of an overdose or sadness or regret or all of the above.

4

They went to the local tavern three blocks away—a place where people parked their bodies at 11am sharp and did not move until they slipped off the barstool or until Lonnie, the owner, kicked them out. The boy's mom marched past a group of impossibly drunk men smoking cigarettes outside and grabbing at her as she made her way to the door. She did not seem to mind.

The boy sat under her barstool playing zombie games on his mom's phone. They were the thrills that let him escape, even if it was for an hour or two or eight or until his mother's phone ran out of power, and he had to sit two feet from a wall hunched over the tiny screen while it charged. Sometimes the games were happy and he was a curator of brightly colored gems, and sometimes they were dark and grey and hopeless, and he was a warrior fighting to survive. He believed at the time that either world was better than the one he was in at seven years old.

He shifted from side to side as she moved around on the barstool, flirting with a nearly incoherent man next to her. The boy assumed that this was the man who was going to give her that day's medicine.

The barstool stopped moving. *I am a statue. I am a statue. I am asleep. I am a zombie.* The boy tried to concentrate on his screen. He watched his mama clip clop away to the grimy bathroom to do whatever it is mamas do to earn their drugs. She was gone for seventeen minutes, and even though he had eaten twenty-three brains in his zombie game, he felt like the world had stopped.

The air siphoned back into his lungs when he saw her walk toward him, tucking something into her oversized purse. She grabbed the boy's hand and yanked him up to his feet. Her hunger for the high could be felt in the very ends of his toes, and he wished he could grab it from the air; put it in his toy chest. Put it in his mouth and chew it slowly, finally understanding the power it had over the only person he loved in the world.

Outside, people were falling down in the streets, a sort of tent revival, and cheering, "America!" "Hallelujah!" Some people were sobbing, joy in its most primal form, and thanking a god they had not talked to in a long time for the new leader he had given them. He would change everything. He would save them. The boy felt the familiar, desperate tug on his arm as his mother pulled him back toward the hell hole where they lived, up the stairs and over dying or mostly dead Lou.

She made a beeline to the small bathroom even though he had told her on the walk home how badly he had to go. He sat squirming on the bed until he couldn't hold it any longer and gently pushed open the door. There she was, lying on the floor with a secret smile on her face. He stared at her and tried to take a picture with his mind.

He watched some protests and people crying on the news, but it didn't seem like the same type of joyous sobbing he'd seen on the street. Finally, his mom crawled into bed with a funny smile and snuggled him tight. He felt so safe.

They watched together for a while, his still-small feet tucked safely between her once lovely legs, until she gently pushed him away, removing his love with her addiction. Going to feed herself (for one of the last times) behind an unhinged door.

2031, PORTLAND, MAINE

The smacking ring of the closing buzzer shocked Elliot out of his waking nightmare. There was an old song coming out of a tinny speaker, and it stirred up some distant memory that was both overloaded with joy and unbridled sadness.

The factory itself was revived from the glory days of the American worker when men came in and punched a card and completed a task over and over again until it was time to go home. Their hands were always rough. Their feet were sore. Their brains were on repeat. But they brought home an honest wage to their hungry families. Many of their wives stayed home rearing the children, sometimes staring out of the window with a wish for a different life that would never come true. But eventually things changed, slowly at first and then at such an astounding speed, the good 'ole American worker had to start running to keep up. Some couldn't. Some panted and then fell down and struggled, and some never got up again. They sat there on the side of the superhighway shaking fists at advancement, technology, the government, themselves.

Before the first Dictator came into power in 2016, factories stood like tombstones dotting desperate landscapes. The worker had been pushed out and replaced. *Progress!* the powers that be called it as they replaced him with machines. He sat at home in his La-Z-Boy with the crinkly plastic and his too-tight sweatpants and a Bud Light in the cup holder covered in potato chip grease. He had only known this one job; he had done it all his life. He hadn't gone to college. He didn't have to.

The Dictator built an army out of his supporters, a militia that served to protect his regime and maintain order across the nation. He created a new kind of factory worker out of the people who resisted him, and a new kind of factory life. Elliot still remembered the broadcast: *"I have singlehandedly brought millions of jobs to this country!"* It had always been true that the Dictator's biggest fan was himself.

Elliot got in step behind the rest of the workers—organized zombies filing out to face the world or what was left of it. He carefully looked out of the corner of his eye to see the people shuffling past him. They had so little life left inside of them that they almost weren't human. He saw signs all around the factory mocking the group of prisoners: *The Working Man is the Winning Man! Get to Work, America! Earning an Honest Wage = Freedom! Dream Pills Achieve the American Dream!*

But it was all a lie. They had been taken.

Workers shuffled toward an open door, almost like that of a dungeon. It was the first time Elliot had felt the outside stench of the air since 7am, and he decided to give himself a small moment to appreciate it. Sometimes, in his darkest hour, he took solace in the fact that they would all die anyway by way of suffocation, so dense and filthy and toxic was the air.

That day had been stressful, but not in a "Bob interrupted my meeting" kind of way. The workplace stresses of today were otherworldly altogether.

He had been in the rhythm of his daily tasks: repetitive to the point of blow-your-brains-out monotony. The assumption was that no one could do much more than a singular task because of the significant amount of dope coursing through their veins at any given minute. To a sleeper—the pet name given to them by the militia—it might have been a relief to do something so repetitive and familiar. To someone who could still formulate his own thoughts, it was unbearable.

Elliot was always careful to keep his eyes down and concentrate on what he was doing. Today, it was pulling a lever that sealed a metal can. He forced his eyeballs to stay fixed on the can rolling into place, a tiny one-man tin orchestra, the satisfying sound of air hissing out of each container, and the triumphant progression to the next worker who would dress it with a label.

Keep eyes forward. Shoulders slumped. Command body to appear limp. Tell eyelids to droop. Will eyeballs to glaze over. He knew all too well what happened if he looked like a real human being whose synapses were still fully firing. In the eyes of the government and the militia who served it, the Resistance was all that had stood in their way of complete and total domination. But everyone believed that the Resistance had been eradicated a long time ago.

Elena waited for one of the guards to walk past before she hissed at Elliot under her breath. It was barely audible. It seemed to travel gleefully along the moving cans and reach up to lightly tug at his ears. But he heard it: *"Cave."*

His two-timing eyeballs shot up in her direction, even after all the years of practicing slow movements, of telling his brain not to think and his body not to react. He felt betrayed by his own pupils, and he thought about gouging them out in punishment. But instead, he quickly aimed them back at his work as another guard walked by.

"You!" the guard nudged Elliot with an assault rifle. The understanding that he had been caught in the despicable act of responding to stimuli was palpable. He could feel Elena's breath change. It was so subtle, only he would have picked up on it. He liked to think that he knew her as well as anyone could know someone in this dark world. For no other reason than they were both still awake, they had become friends.

Elliot looked up at the guard slowly, so slowly, as he had been practicing for years, since he was just a boy, since they had discovered his deep secret. He kept his eyes at half mast and allowed his mouth to hang open as drool threatened to drip drop on the guard's shiny boots. He wished it would; dirtying those boots with his saliva would be a miniscule bomb of victory.

Another guard came over to the first. They both smiled, and their breath quickened. Elliot detected a little bounce in one of their steps. It was the most exciting thing to happen to them in days, and besides: torturing sleepers was one of the militia's favorite activities.

"What going on o'er here, Joe? This here sleeper giving you a hard time?" He swung his gun over his shoulder as if it was a baton, and he the leader of a grand marching band. If Elliot hadn't been playing the role of his life, he would have hit the ground out of fear of being sprayed by a round of ammo.

"Ah, nothin'. I thought I saw this one here move his eyeballs real fast, but he just as doped as can be. They give this one a big 'ole dose, ain't that right?" The guard shoved a hard boot into the back of Elliot's calf, and Elliot told his body to forget it had muscles, bones, thoughts and even a heartbeat as it fell into a pile on the floor.

Guard Two kicked him again, this time in the stomach, but Elliot did not call out in pain because he was not supposed to feel pain. He sucked it in slowly, a giant vacuum of suffering, and allowed it to overflow out of his nostrils. He didn't dare watch them as they walked down the hall cackling and waving their guns. He wanted to run after them and grab their weapons and blanket them with bullets and yell to all the workers, *Run! Everyone get out of here!* But he knew that the only person who would move a muscle was Elena because the rest of them didn't know where they were or who they used to be. Not anymore.

He made himself lay on the ground for a full minute before he slowly pushed himself up and went back to work. His eyes did not leave the cans, counting them as they rolled into view. He tried to think of one of his happy things, one of his waking things. He only had a handful left anymore, and he held them tightly in his rough hands, using them, tuning into them like a favorite movie when he needed to go somewhere else. When the final bell rang, he had reached two thousand seven hundred and ninety-one cans, and he was forced to stuff his memories back into the recesses of his mind. He walked out slowly through the exit with the others, and a scanner read the chip in his wrist, alerting the system that he was leaving for the day.

The rail was waiting to pick them up. It was sleek and modern and went so fast, it made his heart slingshot into his throat as it sped down the coast. Despite himself, this short ride to and from the factory had come to be something he looked forward to each day. He loved the feeling of the soft seats sinking just a little beneath his meager weight as he just barely peeked from below his eyelids to glance at the seaside rushing by. There were abandoned ships dotting the bay—he used to pretend they were ghost ships when he was a teenager. He would imagine he was a captain or even a pirate, and he would take his ship on a great adventure and leave this place behind and maybe even end up in another country across the sea. And maybe everyone was still awake there. He longed to stick his head out of the train window, just to feel how fast they were really going. After being trapped in an archaic, windowless factory, the modernity of the train was a gut punch; it reminded him of what might be happening outside his barely see-through bubble. Even though he was stuck on repeat every day, it was the train ride that made him feel like something was still possible.

Back in the Waking Years, he had ridden on a train once. The daydream was foggy, but he was able to pull at wisps of it to gently jog his memory. He had eaten something in a crinkly bag. His greasy fingers had made beautiful smudges on the window that cast rainbows on the shiny armrest if he looked at them at just the right angle. He had been terrified to jump over the large gap between the train and the platform, but he held his mom's hand tightly and leaped, tugging her along with him to the next great adventure. Then he couldn't remember if it was really his mom or someone else entirely, and he dismissed the whole reverie as a dream he had made up in his head.

The train screamed just a bit as it reached his stop—a high-rise housing complex that was more like a prison than anything else. A buzzer sounded. The sleepers responded accordingly and began to shuffle out of the car. Elliot said a silent goodbye to his seat. He wished he could ride the train forever, wherever it went, eating snacks out of crinkly bags and holding someone's hand.

The sea air slapped him in his face, greeting him home. It smelled like fish guts and burnt hair and profound sadness, but he tried his best to suck it all in before he entered the complex. He reminded himself that he had the meeting tonight and that he only had to endure the sleeping pod for a couple of hours. Ever since that one foster parent who had made him sleep in a too-tight drawer in a dark, dank closet, he had become severely claustrophobic. To a sleeper, such things wouldn't matter. To Elliot, it was near torture to get shut in a coffin-sized space every night as he battled demons that assaulted his leg muscles and made him feel like he was going mad. Every time he wanted to give up, to end it all and destroy the tormented thoughts that smashed around in his head, he stopped right before he went over the edge.

Because there were not many of them. At least not many that he knew about. They barely stood together as a threadbare army. But they were still here, not sleeping at all, always alert. And they were the only chance this godforsaken country had left.

2017, WASHINGTON, D.C.

A small, nine-year-old girl walked through the prison doors holding her father's hand with everything she had. She knew that if she let go of that hand for a second, something terrible would happen, like a prisoner would pull her long black hair or spit on her barely-freckled nose or the Earth would open up and swallow her whole.

She had not slept in four days, staying up late to read about prison life and what went wrong that day at the march. She'd scoured every news article online that featured her mother. They all said the same thing: her mom had started a movement that could have changed everything, but after the staged riots at the march, she was trapped in a prison. She read the articles until her eyes burned, then stared at the red mark on her ceiling, still there from the time she and Amanda had been coloring on her bed. Amanda had accidentally flung her marker up in the air, and the two had almost exploded from their giggles. But Amanda wasn't her neighbor anymore.

Father and daughter sat down in two hard plastic chairs the color of their pool when they first took its cover off in the spring. They waited there for what was probably a couple of minutes, but it felt like decades to the young girl who so desperately required her mom. They had never spent even a night apart until now. Finally, a painful buzz sounded, and the prisoners filed in through a single door. Except for their worn cotton orange suits, they looked normal. They were mothers and sisters and wives. They were not scary. The girl noticed that some of them even had the same tattoo as her mom on their wrists. It made her feel proud.

When she saw her mother, the girl was relieved, the aching worry draining out of her exhausted limbs. Her mom had the same determined face, albeit a few more small lines around her eyes. When she saw her only child, a smile that could replace the very sun itself made the dull prison uniform bearable. If the girl had known it was the very last time she would see her mother smile, she would have traced it with her fingers and shoved the memory of it deep inside her pockets for safekeeping.

"Sarah," the girl's father said. "You look alright!" He was kneading his wife's hands like they were dough, and the girl could see her mother wince in pain from his pressure. But Sarah didn't stop him for a minute, and the girl knew it was because when someone you love is suffering, you let them have everything they need.

"Of course I'm alright, Ben. It's just prison, it's not like I've been put on a carrier."

They were all silent for a second because that's exactly what had happened to many of their friends, neighbors and the people they loved. Removed from their homes like a herd of animals and put on carriers. Taken to some of the most unlivable places in the world. For reasons that still didn't even begin to make sense. The girl still remembered watching the neighbor she had been friends with since she knew what a friend was from a window across the street. Government agents had pulled up and knocked on Amanda's door. Amanda's father shouted and shielded his wife and daughter and twin sons as if he could stop what was happening. The girl watched as they grabbed Amanda's dad by the wrists and as he kicked one of the agents in the shin as a last-ditch effort to keep his family safe. The agents had grabbed the kids and put them (not-so-gently) in the white windowless van and then cuffed Amanda's parents and wrestled them inside. The girl had screamed from her window until Sarah took her daughter in her lap trying to explain all of the irrational reasons why Amanda's family was taken away like fear and war and unthinkable acts of evil.

Sarah leaned across the table at the prison visitor center to grab her daughter's hands. "Oh, how I've missed you, special girl. You doing OK?"

The girl nodded her brave smile. She had barely gone to school since her mother was arrested nearly two weeks ago. The bullying had become too much. It started as food throwing in the cafeteria—a piece of salami on her shoulder, a milk knocked over on her tray. But then it escalated to pushing in the hallway, her books flying as her head hit a locker. To them, to the others, her mom was a radical, a renegade trying to take their guns and kill their babies. But the girl didn't hate them. Her parents had always taught her not to hate them because the world had too much hate in it already.

"How much longer do you think you'll have to stay, mom?" She loved feeling her mother's fingers laced through hers—it was like putting on a favorite pair of shoes, worn-in so much that they could only belong to her. She longed for the mornings when she'd climb into her parents' bed and curl up just right in her mother's arms.

"Eh, it won't be too long now, my love." But her eyes said something different.

"Time!" a guard yelled, and the families all around them scrambled up out of their seats to hug and say their goodbyes.

The girl leaned over the table at the same time as her dad, and the three of them clung together, just like they always did. They scooped each other up and held each other tight. It had been that way since the moment she was born.

The visitors gathered their things and turned to leave as the girl's mother started walking back toward the door.

"Elena!" her mother called out, and the girl spun around quickly to look at her mom with her wild red hair and orange suit. "Don't stop fighting. Don't ever stop fighting! We are the Resistance! WE ARE THE RESISTANCE!"

The other prisoners joined in chanting, "We are the Resistance!" pumping their fists in the air. One of them climbed up on a chair.

Guards flooded in from the door with shields and tasers and pepper spray at the ready, kicking down prisoners and kneeling on their chests as the women screamed out in pain. Elena tried to rush toward her mom, but her dad grabbed her with both arms and held her tight, a parental straightjacket. Guards pushed the visitors out, and Ben fought to keep his footing.

The last thing Elena saw as the door shut them all out was her mom trying to bite a guard's arm and the electrical current finding contact with her mother's neck, finally leaving her limp on the floor.

* * *

It was five full weeks until they were allowed to go back. Ben had called several times a day every single day, and when he wasn't talking on the phone, he was talking to his lawyer or sitting in his wife's chair staring into space. Most of the time, he couldn't get through to the prison and would throw his phone across the room, pounding on the kitchen counter. Other times, the prison operator gave him a vague answer about his wife's condition or her whereabouts. One said, laughing: *That rebel is getting what she damn well deserves.*

Elena spent most of the time in her room, furiously sketching and writing her stories. On paper, she was the model child, pushed to be perfect by her overachieving parents, but it couldn't be further from the truth. From the time she was a tiny girl, her mother saw things in her—sparks, she called them. Her aptitude for music, and her ability to play a song on the creaky piano in their study after only hearing it once. How she could draw, *really* draw, then paint magical creatures and scenes that could have only been carefully extracted from her imagination—a miniature pair of forceps gently pulling at her daydreams and plopping them down on paper. She made up tales taller than her father to go along with her art, and before she could write, her mother would write them down for her in a loopy script, never changing a word because she wanted it to be so completely her.

What she didn't tell her parents though, what she never told anyone, was that she existed in between the pages of her carefully stapled-together books. She did not see the world as everyone else did but rather saw it with blinding colors carefully applied and painterly strokes to accentuate the ordinary. She carried about her day as if she was living the story itself, complete with quotation marks and articulate descriptions of what was happening. Had someone been able to pluck the real-time thoughts going through her head, they would soon turn into a short story, then a novella, then an epic novel about a girl who danced on the precipice of what could have been.

Her parents did not push her to be gifted. They simply allowed her to be.

Elena had worked through twenty-eight stories—some bleeding with her fat teardrops— before her father got the call from the prison.

"What did she say? Is she OK?" Elena grabbed his phone as if she could read the message herself.

"It wasn't her, honey. It was one of the guards. She said we could come up this weekend to visit mom. She sounded...I don't know. Like she was laughing at me."

They rode up to the prison in silence in her father's Mercedes, Elena staring into the side mirror at the pavement they had left behind. In her mind, the road opened up like a giant mouth, and the white lines turned into jagged, sideways teeth dripping with an oily saliva. It munched at them as they sped away, barely missing them each time. With each snap of its enormous jaws, her right leg involuntarily bounced in a quick staccato, a habit that began on that very car ride and one that she battled each day for almost fifteen years after. Sleepers didn't have nervous twitches because sleepers didn't know enough to be nervous, and she forever fought the tick that threatened to give her away.

Ben kept glancing at his daughter as he drove. She knew he was worried about her. She had looked in the mirror that morning and couldn't believe how much older she looked. Her forehead was in a permanent furrow, and her eyes were yellowish with bags clinging onto her face like barnacles. Last week, he had agreed to get her a private tutor so she didn't have to go to school anymore. She had come home with bruises and a look of such despair, and she knew he'd do anything to take her pain away. He was her protector—he always had been. The tutor lasted only a week before she was deported on a carrier and taken back to Iran. Elena had cried herself to sleep on her father's chest and woke up alone and fully clothed in her bedroom.

They walked through the same door at the prison and sat down in the same chairs, but Elena didn't hold his hand this time. Her look was hardened, her shoulders stiff. Her hands were poised on top of her knees, and she was completely still except for the bouncing. Finally, the buzzer sounded, and the prisoners shuffled in.

Sarah was the last one to come out. She was being led by a guard, who almost appeared to be holding her upright, and Elena knew, understood, that her mother would not have been able to walk without assistance. It was her very first feeling of sheer panic—the kind you have when you're driving and you know you're about to hit something and there's nothing you can do except put your hands up to protect your important parts. This imposter of her mother didn't have the strong, powerful stance of a fighter, but rather appeared to be sleepwalking with her eyes open. Barely open.

The guard nearly shoved her mom into the chair, and as Sarah slumped over the table, Elena could see small bubbles forming in the creases of her open mouth.

"Mom?" Elena reached forward and grabbed her mother's hands, shaking them a little. She looked up at her dad, silently begging for his help, but he stared at the woman he had known since he was a teenager as if she was a science experiment gone wrong. He was in shock.

"Dad, talk to them!" Elena was getting louder now, and it caught the attention of a guard who sauntered over.

"Quiet you!" the guard scolded them. "People trying to visit family 'round here."

"Excuse me, ma'am. Why is my wife in this...state?" Elena's father looked as if he might cry. As if this was the thing, even after all the other things, that would send him over the edge. Elena was quite sure that if a single tear slipped over her dad's lower lid, the world would end.

"State? I don't deal with them treatments. No sir." The guard put her thumbs in her belt and swung her authority back and forth.

"Treatment? My wife doesn't need treatment!" Ben was angry now, even though his eyes still shone with a glassy sadness.

The guard leaned forward until her large breasts were pressed against the dingy table and her face was just inches from Ben's. Elena could smell fried food and see inconsolable stains on the woman's front teeth. Had she not hated her more than anyone, Elena would have felt sorry for her.

"Like I said, sir, I don't make them treatments." She lowered her voice so it was almost inaudible above the din of the visitation center. "And if you as smart as your fancy ass clothes say you are, then I wouldn't say another damn word about it. You got me?"

Elena could feel her father suck in all his air, and it was as if she could see the pigment vacuumed from her life all at once, never to return again. She watched as he tightened his fists on the table and was afraid he would take a swing at this woman as she sauntered away. But her dad was not a fighter. He had stood by her mother, an unflinching symbol of all that was right or should be right in the world, as she fought against the injustices of the people. He never looked away; he was always there when she came home. But his stance was different from his wife's, as was his temperament. He plotted and planned instead of resisting.

Ben leaned forward so he could look into what was left of his wife's eyes. "Sarah," he begged. "Sarah, it's me. And Elena." He quickly glanced at his daughter, trying to ignore her brow and her anxiety. Then he looked back at his wife. "Can you hear us?"

Sarah's eyes tried to focus, but could only manage for a moment, then rolled back into her head. Elena had never in her life seen her mother not in control. Ben squeezed Sarah's hand as tight as he could, and Elena was worried that he didn't care anymore if he shattered it. "Sarah!" He said loudly, and Elena put a hand on his arm as if she could help him.

They watched as she finally looked at them and the corners of her mouth turned up a little into what they decided to take as a smile. Elena felt a rush of life stampede back into her body. It was an infinite amount of tiny horses meticulously drawn into the very matter of her body. They rumbled across her bones. *Mom.*

"Ben," Sarah whispered. It sounded as if her mouth was full of sand. It was as if she'd had a stroke or worse, and her eyes desperately shot around the room looking for her words and trying to understand her surroundings.

"Time!" Two guards rushed over and grabbed Sarah's arms, ripping her away from her family, her feet dragging toward the mouth of the prison.

Elena clung to her father's arm, a piece of driftwood in an ocean of sadness, and she stared as her mother disappeared behind the door without a fight. The buzzer rang, and Elena watched as the prisoners all stood up together. It was different from the last time, and she hadn't noticed it until now. Their movements were robotic; she could almost see their metal parts poking out beneath their human ones. There was no hugging or emotion from the women in orange. Their eyes, like her mother's, were either glassy and not seeing much at all or desperately searching for the answer to a question they could barely remember.

They were a slew of fighters, these women. People who had taken to the streets and shouted at the state and waved their fists at the injustice of what was happening to them, to their brothers and sisters, to their country. But now their mouths hung open in paralysis of thought and reason.

Elena understood right then, this young girl of nine, that the woman who had disappeared behind the door was not the mother she knew and loved. And that the next part of her story had just slipped out of her small hands.

2031, PORTLAND, MAINE

One of their meeting places was called the Cave. There were old chairs with green cushions that held years' worth of occasions and tables that were so ornate and beautiful Elena winced when she saw a gash in one of them. Elena had once found a menu in this old dusty basement and allowed herself a full five minutes to imagine what oysters with a mignonette or a lobster roll or tuna tartare tasted like. She pictured her adult self meeting her mother for lunch and the two of them gazing out at the ocean, dreams and plans swirling brilliantly around them, drowning their silly worries in mignonette and chatting about the things moms and daughters discuss. Frivolous things. Happy, joyful things.

Maybe she would have gone to college and studied to be something that her mother would have loved to tell her friends about. Maybe one of her "sparks" would have caught into the most delicious wildfire, and she would have woken up each day so grateful to be alive creating and building and inventing that thing the world really needed. Maybe she would have met someone, and maybe she would have even gotten married, and maybe she would have had a daughter of her own. She felt the dullest stab of pain as she halfheartedly watched it all stack up into what could have been a normal life. She thought about the trillion little moments that might have pivoted this existence into something else. But she knew it was for naught—there she was sitting in a heap of miscalculation, dreaming of extinct menu items in a dusty basement.

When Elena was still small, before everything changed, her parents had taken her to New York City. Her mother once told her, "A person can be precisely who they are here," and Elena didn't really know what that meant, but put countless versions of it in her notebooks the next day. She had sat with them at an outdoor cafe watching people unlike anyone she had ever experienced walk by with that indescribable something about them. They moved with a saunter that one only earned after living in such a thankless, fruitful, unforgettable city for five years or more. It was like they had all been told a secret no one else in the world was allowed to know. She sat there and made up distinct personalities for them, naming each one something she had never heard of.

Before her mother went to prison, Elena had proclaimed that someday she would live in that magical city and work at that very cafe, sketching every patron that came in. Her parents had shared a smile and chuckled a little. Her mom had leaned down grabbing the two sides of her face and said,

"Lannie, you can do anything, my brilliant girl. My perfect girl." Except now Elena understood that her mother, who had been an environmental engineer and her father, who had been a neurologist, had thought it naive and even sweet that their precocious daughter wanted to serve food on the streets of New York.

They had believed that she could swim to the moon and grab a hunk of it and dance her way back again. But she knew, even now, that they would have been bursting with pride and love and all those other things that turn stumbling children into confident somebodies even if she had decided to play her guitar on the sidewalk.

As the Waking started coming down the stairs, mostly by themselves, but sometimes in groups of two or three, Elena stood up from the old cushioned chair and decided not to think about the beautiful lunches that stayed trapped in her imagination. These people, these weary souls, were all that were left (although she liked to think there were hundreds of pockets of them across the country). They were the reason she hadn't thrown herself into the angry sea. It would have welcomed her with open arms and eaten away at her insides with its vagrant toxicity.

Elliot was last to show up, and she watched him limp a little as he walked down the stairs. She let the guilt wash over her, hungry blue gray waves, and then she released it. She felt at least partly responsible for the shakedown in the factory. But she'd also learned a long time ago that it was every person for themselves, and one had to control their eyes and their emotions if nothing else. Elliot had been at this for years, even longer than she, and he had taught her a lot of tricks since they'd first discovered each other in the courtyard.

After mealtime and when the city wasn't on an air quality alert, the guards would let the sleepers wander around in a haphazardly fenced-in area wedged between several of the housing units. Sleepers who got too close to the perimeter were treated with a sharp shock up their arm and an alert to the guards on duty that a naughty dog had tried to stray from its yard.

Elena had been stuck in a perpetual panic attack since she'd been assigned. Still nothing more than a child, surrounded by militia and sleepers, she hadn't spoken a single word out loud in eight months, and she wasn't sure she'd even remember how. Even more terrifying was that she had stopped seeing her visions. The stories that had always played in her mind had quieted completely.

When she saw Elliot for the first time, she'd written him off as another sleeper. But he had caught her eye for an almost indiscernible moment that day in the courtyard, and she knew. He had shuffled his way over to her so slowly that she was worried free time would end before he reached her. When he did, she marveled at how perfectly he mimicked the sleepers' movements.

"I'm Elliot," he whispered, mouth not moving at all.

"Elena," she said back.

"The power goes off every night when we're asleep," he told her.

"What," she hissed. She became angry at him for wasting their precious words on something so insignificant.

"Can't track us with the power off," he said and slowly shuffled toward the door as a buzzer signaled for them to all go inside.

She had stood there stunned and almost forgot to pretend to be a sleeper. Very slowly and like the faintest heartbeat, her inner voice woke up and started narrating again. Her visions, as if drawn with a mechanical pencil, softly appeared in the form of a roughly sketched starburst around the retreating Elliot.

Their meeting was one chance moment that led to a hushed conversation that tumbled into the very start of a barely-there revolution. There were fourteen of them now, and most of them were sitting in front of her tonight. They didn't hang together by any thread in any way; you could not categorize them, really, not by demographics. They were every age, came from every background. It was true that they had been grouped with the Resistance in some way or another when the country became divided, but the thing that had drawn them together in the netherworld was that they were immune to the mass drugging that had taken place across the nation to quiet the opposition. It did not affect them. Their bodies did not respond. And just like any other bird of a feather, they had somehow discovered one another, whether it was by chance at work in a factory or bumping into each other in the cobblestone courtyard. They were all caught in a tangled net together, in limbo between a waking world and a world that had been put into a deep dark sleep.

Elena stepped into the sliver of light cast from the moon through a window. The low chatter silenced immediately. So disciplined was this small army that it didn't take much for them to quiet their free-flowing thoughts and shut off their conversations.

"Hello. A lot has happened since our last meeting." Elena's voice always felt scratchy when she spoke out loud, like an instrument she hadn't used in a very long time. But it was low and steady, and commanded the room. She knew that somewhere, somehow, her mother was listening.

"Jones was discovered, as most of us know, although they don't know that he's immune—they just think there was a glitch with his dosage. He's been put into treatment, and we don't know if he's going to make it out." Everyone murmured, and Silver said in a whispered shout, "That's bullshit!"

Elena looked Silver in the eye. "Yes. It's bullshit. Everything is. But you can either play nice with the rules or you can go into treatment or you can get shot by a guard who thinks he's a cowboy." Silver cast her eyes down at the dirty floor. She was the youngest in the group, and Elena had first spotted her cowering behind the corner of a building, peering at them as they shuffled around in the courtyard. Later that night, after Elena heard the telltale hiss of the air filters silence in her room and the hum of the generator powering down, she had snuck out of her sleeping quarters to search for the girl in the shadows. She found her on the streets starving and scared. She was curled up in a corner, and Elena would have stumbled right over her if she had not been on the lookout. Silver had cried out in pain, and Elena immediately knelt down to put a hand on her back.

"Who are you?" she asked in a hushed whisper.

"Please don't hurt me," the lump whispered back.

"I won't. How did you get here?" Elena squinted in the dim light and saw that the young girl still had her hair, which was unheard of. Their sector was heavily patrolled, and Elena couldn't believe that someone had not been assigned and had gotten this deep into the city without being caught.

"I rode in one of the storage trains. I hid in between all their supplies," the girl said, looking up at her in a kind of awe that Elena had never felt before. Often shut up in her room while her mother rallied crowds by the thousands, Elena sometimes felt like she had grown up in her mother's shadow, never having the chance to step into her own light before everything was taken from her. For a minute, she was able to bask in the glow of this girl's admiration, and it felt good, like the sun that used to warm her skin when she was little.

"That was brave," Elena told her. She gently turned the girl's wrist over and pressed down hard.

"What are you doing? That hurts!" the girl said.

"You don't have a chip," Elena told her.

"What's a chip?" the girl asked.

"It's how they track you. They give you an assignment, and then the chip keeps track of you so they know where everyone is all the time. Well, most of the time. Do you know what's happened?"

The girl had nodded, but she looked confused.

"Do you know if you're immune to the drugs?" Elena asked. She was afraid to know the answer. If the girl wasn't sure, Elena would have had to test it and risk turning the girl into a sleeper.

"You mean the pills they forced everyone to take?" the girl asked with a laugh. "Yeah, I tried a bunch of my mom's. She made me because she didn't want me to be scared when they made me do it with a gun to my head." Her laugh had hung in the air as she realized what she had said out loud.

"And you were fine? They didn't work on you?" Elena realized she was holding onto the girl's wrist too hard and let go. The girl shook her head quickly.

"Listen," Elena continued. "It's pretty unbelievable that you went this long without getting assigned. But they're going to get you someday and assign you somewhere, and we don't want it to be at the testing plant."

"What's the testing plant?" the girl had asked, her eyes as wide as they could go.

"It's like animal testing, but on people. It's where they test all the stuff for the Republic. You can get burned or poisoned or worse. We have to get you the best assignment we can. I'll help you. OK? Do you trust me?"

"Yes. I trust only you," the girl told her.

Silver became Elena's shadow after that, and in many ways she was Elena's student—she taught the young girl how to steal and ration supplies from the militia. She showed her how to act like a sleeper, taught her all of her tricks so the guards would be completely convinced when she stumbled into the entrance of one of the newest factories. That's how Elena got her young friend accepted into Class II of the sleeper population so she could push buttons instead of being a lab rat. Elena wasn't much older than Silver, but she felt motherly toward her. That first night, and several nights after their initial meeting, the girl had crawled up in her lap and fallen asleep. But despite her love for this young woman who sat before her now, Elena knew she could not protect her from everything. She was hard on her; tried to make her tough; and ultimately put up a shaky wall built with love and discipline between them. She spoke sternly to her young charge now from the other side of it.

"Jones pushed a guard. He pushed her. So, not only did he break protocol and risk revealing that he was not, in fact, under the influence, he assaulted someone with a weapon used to gun down entire populations. We can fight this…" she waved her hand around above her, not knowing exactly what to call the state of the world. "This…mess. But we can't draw attention to ourselves. Stupid." Elena spit the last word at the ground and shook her head.

"I'm sorry," Silver whispered, and Elena knew how much this little speech had damaged her, but it was her only gift left to give.

Elena nodded and took a deep breath. "OK. Let's get a status from everyone." Elliot and Elena had managed to find representatives at most of the factories in the area by way of coincidence or intel from the Controller. Each person's duty was to report what had happened during the week, and Elena reported it back to the Command Center. She liked to imagine that this very scenario was happening thousands of times around the country, but for all she knew, it was them alone.

Each member of the group stood up one by one and gave their accounts as quietly as they could. Most of them told their story without emotion as if it had happened to someone else. Elena couldn't help but vividly visualize every detail of their stories and some of her visions were so painful, she begged them to go away.

One had their pants pulled to their ankles and had to stand naked from the waist down to a chorus of guards laughing and pointing and not considering for a moment that the thing they were doing this to was, in fact, a person.

One had been raped (Silver).

Two people (including Elliot) had been injured and of course they weren't supposed to feel a thing because of the amount of opiates coursing through their bodies. But what the guards didn't know as they kicked at the sleepers they were supposed to be patrolling was that for a select few, painkillers didn't work. Every single person in the basement that night knew they had to do everything in their power to keep that a secret.

All of them had worked countless hours doing tasks so far beneath their intelligence or talent or both, and it was all they could do to keep from screaming out in anguish from being forced to pretend they were a shell of who they could have been. Elena knew that for some of her soldiers, this was the biggest travesty. For them, enduring physical pain and assault were nothing compared to knowing what they could have amounted to if the world had gone in an entirely different direction.

But besides the torment, they had made progress. Someone had overheard the name of a high-ranking official who reported to the Secretary of the Dictator.

Silver, during her violent assault, which left her pushed against the filthy wall of a claustrophobic office, had seen a report that outlined plans for four more factories like hers within a ten-mile radius.

She had also overheard the minimum age for the workers: seven. It was the youngest age they could administer an effective dose of opiates and still have them function. She had heard that they were experimenting with the doses in the clinics that lined the city's perimeters. For the first time in a long time, Elena felt a sense of dread tickle the back of her neck as she thought about those children—most likely doped up already by their parents, or orphaned and wandering the halls of the holding centers until the age of seven, when they'd meet their fate.

When everyone had finished giving grueling details in oh-so-quiet voices, they all stood there for a moment in silence. They could hear each other's slow, steady breath. They were all so used to being reduced to their lowest common denominator, and they had worked hard to mimic the labored breathing of a sleeper. In every way, they were actors so committed to their craft that it was sometimes difficult to control when sleeper life ended and waking life began.

Finally, Elena got up and went to the front of the room again. The moonlight hit her in a way that made her short spiky hair seem almost purple. She had her head down, looking at her boots, the kind that they were all required to wear. They could not complain if their toe rubbed against the front or if the soles had worn too thin or had a hole that let in the stagnant rain water from the grooves of the cobblestone streets. She looked at the boots holding tired feet that had taken so many steps and traveled across so many states back when they had states. Those feet now stood for ten hours a day with callouses and too-long toenails and sweat in the hottest months because a sleeper's attire was the same no matter what the season. Even though most of the seasons were hotter than they ever remembered. Elena looked down for so long, wishing she still had endless black hair to cover her face as the tears fell in a clumsy rhythm down her cheeks and hit the concrete floor.

Then she looked up at them and mouthed, "Thanks, everyone." She was embarrassed. She thought she had run out of tears a million cries ago.

They all moved toward each other, the pretend-zombies that they really were, and found each other's limbs and pulled each other close and embraced. They were a mangled mess of conjoined parts that rarely enjoyed human contact, and they almost couldn't bear to be separated. But they had to go get tucked inside their living quarters before the power switched back on and the hiss of the air filters could sing them to sleep.

Elena opened the door and the cold, salty air hit their faces. The air quality was on a high alert that night, but she knew they were lucky to be near the coast. It was a tease of beach days and sailboats and shoulda-been lunches with mothers. They all breathed it in, dreaming, as they stumbled outside one by one. Back into the sleeping world, the silent world, for the next forty-eight hours. Praying that they could quiet their inner demons until then.

2018, ON THE WAY TO SOMEWHERE IN OHIO

The boy had been to four different foster homes in the short time since his mother decided not to get up from the dirty linoleum of the dollar store. He had migrated to a dark quiet place inside himself. He had become a tiny beast who threw heavy objects at the heads of foster parents and who had decided to only listen to the voices inside his head. He was called *menace* and *monster* and *white trash* and *filthy*, even though the homes where they placed him were always as bad if not worse than his superlatives.

He had come from little, from a small one-room apartment with a mom passed out on the bathroom floor, but at least he used to have a parent and a roof and sometimes food. That world seemed infinitely better than the one he resided in now.

Since when did a boy become an animal in a cattle car? There were too many times when he woke up and didn't recognize the ceiling. He was a vagrant, a gypsy, a tumbleweed that got kicked around from place to place.

He had ridden in too many sedans, nose pressed against vinyl, loving how it felt cool on his skin and smelled like sad stories, staring out of the window and watching the America his mother loved so much pass him by. He saw America's worst parts, her dirtiest. Her most desperate and disgusting. He saw kids begging and people who could barely walk because they had drowned all their sorrows with debilitating acts, and it had left them immobilized.

The last foster home had sent him back. His foster father had flung a lit cigarette at his head and had chased him down the driveway with a two-by-four after the boy had called him a racist shithead.

His social worker sat him down and gave him a disapproving stare. She was morbidly obese and had a permanent wheeze to her breathing patterns which alternated between heavy and desperate. She had too-long straggly hair that was balding on top and an overgrown mole held hostage between her neck folds. She wore a large grey skirt, grey blazer and magenta button down shirt with coffee stains and something else he couldn't quite decipher. Then he was sure: mustard.

"What happened?" She feigned concern, but the boy could tell that she was genuinely curious. She peered at her screen. "Says here that you called your foster daddy a Nazi?"

The boy scowled. "Not a Nazi, a racist. He was calling one of the little girls all kinds of awful names. He said he was gonna hurt her. My mama ain't teach me much, but she taught me that we're all children of god. We had a whole lotta racists where we lived."

"One of the little girls who lived there?" the social worker asked.

"Yeah."

She looked at her screen again. "Well, it looks like he sent her back, too. 'Pears like he decided she belonged somewhere else."

She leaned close to him, and he could smell her lunch. He decided she always smelled like old salami sandwiches no matter how hard she scrubbed, and he felt a little sorry for her.

"Listen. This is just some of the repercussions we gonna have to deal with."

The boy furrowed his eyebrows, confused.

"The President. He loose with some stuff, and those Nazis think they can come out of their hiding spots. But it's a small price to pay! He's gonna make this country what it was meant to be! I already got a notice about my new assignment. I'm getting placed in a couple weeks."

It didn't make sense to the boy. Not really. He still thought the President was a golden god who loved everyone and everything. Their leader was his mom's hero, and the boy still thought that he was made entirely out of good. He suddenly felt like everything he had ever believed was evaporating in his dirty hands.

"Son, you gonna be OK. I found you a family that's looking for kids. We're taking you to Ohio. You lucky. That's where my assignment is so I don't mind going there. Not one bit." She hoisted her body back on the chair as if she and it had different ideas about the simple act of sitting.

The other social workers had quit him. He knew he had red marks and bad discipline grades on his report, as described by the disgust on their faces whenever they scrolled through his history.

"OK," he said. He didn't even know or care where Ohio was. He knew it would all be the same sad story and part of him wanted to just get there so he could move on to the next earmarked page.

"I'm not totally sure why these people are willing to take you in. They know how...difficult you've been. But since the agency is gettin' shut down next month, I figured I'd take you there and give you a fighting chance."

"What? Why?"

"Because the government has a new plan. And like I said, I have a new assignment." She smiled, looking up at the ceiling as if she was sharing a secret. The boy wanted to tell her that nothing good ever happened to no one, and she was dumb to even think so.

He said nothing more as he followed her out of the office, finally noticing that people all around them were packing boxes and shredding papers. She opened the back door for him, and he climbed into yet another car.

They took the excruciatingly long trip to who-knew-where-Ohio. The boy lost himself in his thoughts that zigzagged between fantasy and reality. He invented a childhood in a big home with two parents and a pool and a shiny red bike. He imagined a future based on his zombie video games where he was the hero who saved everyone. He thought about when and where his mama would have died had it not been on that day at that time. He always had a feeling that she was one hit away from overdosing; he knew it from all the times she almost didn't wake up and from all the people they saw on the street who slumped motionless with a needle sticking out of their arms. The anticipation of it had been suffocating him, and he had started to believe that it didn't matter if it was on the floor of a dollar store or outside the local pub or in the bathtub with him screaming through the unlocked door. In his very worst moments, he admitted that he felt some relief when it all finally ended. The waiting had become unbearable.

His social worker, Jodiann was her name, chain-smoked cigarettes during the entire ride. He wanted to ask her a million questions about what was in his file, what was happening, why the agency was shut down, what would happen to the children without homes. He wanted the whole truth about the President from the very beginning, but his anger and stubborn solitude forced him to keep his mouth shut and not show that he cared about anything at all.

She turned on the radio, and the boy heard a voice he'd heard a million times before.

"Can you turn it up a little?" the boy asked.

Jodiann smiled and turned the knob. The President spoke with more authority than the boy had ever experienced in his life, and he wanted more than anything to believe his mama was right about him.

"And this month, we continue the war on drugs, the fight for quality healthcare and the distribution of jobs. We take to the streets and give people job assignments that will literally save their lives. People who had nothing and were forced to turn to narcotics will now be clean and will have a job they can be proud of! The people who need the most help and require medication will now have access to it in abundance. It is really an amazing time to be an American!"

The boy smiled a little as they passed a "Welcome to Ohio" sign. Jodiann pulled over to the side of the highway and put the car into park.

"Dammit. My phone's not getting service out here. Honey, I'm gonna pull up to that lot and try and get some directions. We ain't far now."

"OK," the boy said quietly. He felt a shiver of nerves at the thought of meeting another family and hoped at the very least they would just leave him alone.

The car crept over to a parking lot in front of what used to be a discount grocery store. The windows were shuttered and a makeshift wooden stand had been built in front of the doors. They crawled to a stop and the two of them stared out of the windows not speaking or breathing. Their mouths hung open, lower lips heavy with a multitude of sights and emotions.

There were men and women in military fatigues carrying the largest guns the boy had ever seen. He hadn't realized that such weaponry existed outside the confines of his fighter games, and he suddenly wished he could delete the assault rifles from the real world and put them back into his screen where they belonged. Two lines snaked from the store entrance, and the boy craned his neck to see what was happening at the front of them. He watched as the people on the right gave a staunch salute and gathered up a military uniform in their arms as if it was a new baby. Some of them looked so happy, they practically skipped back to wherever it was that they came from.

The other line was longer and moved slower. The boy studied the faces of the people—men, women and children—and realized they looked scared.

They were nudged along by the military people, and if they didn't move fast enough, guns were raised.

"Honey, sit tight. I'm gonna find out what's happening here. And try and get us sorted out." The boy could tell by her voice that his social worker was nervous and didn't like the looks of what was happening as much as he did. Jodiann heaved herself out of the driver seat and flashed her shiny new military badge at one of the guards.

The boy was wondering how to get into the line on the right and hoped he could someday get a shiny badge like Jodiann when she began to make her way back to the car. She stopped when she heard shouting, and the boy pressed his face so hard against the window that he wondered for a moment if he might break it. Jodiann's body was turned as if it couldn't decide which way to go.

"Take your medicine, ma'am!" a guard was yelling at a woman. Two children not much younger than the boy clung to her arms.

"You can go fuck yourself! I'm not taking anything and neither is my family!" she screamed at him. She was small and barely came up to the guard's chest, but she reminded the boy of a fierce mama bear protecting her cubs.

The guard looked nervously at his comrade who gave a short nod. The woman stood there breathing hard, not breaking her gaze for a second. The boy wanted to tell her how brave she was and that she was a good mama. He wanted to tell her that not everyone got a mama like her.

It happened so fast, the boy still isn't sure how. The guard pulled out a small pistol from a holster and pointed it at the woman's head and pulled the trigger, and she fell to the ground and every single person in her line started screaming. Jodiann turned back toward the car and ran, yanking at the door and shoving herself inside. The boy squeezed his eyes shut to stopper up the tears and nightmares as the car squealed out onto the road to the echoing of machine gun fire.

They passed three more stations like that one and saw lines of people who needed to get their "medicine." He watched as they were force fed their doses and transported to a neverland like his mama used to visit. He saw mothers and fathers give paper pill cups to their children and watched as they showed their own kin how to tilt their little heads back in front of an audience of assault rifles.

Jodiann finally pulled into a long driveway, almost completely hidden from the road by a tangle of bushes and weeds. The only reason she knew it was there, she told the boy, was that his new foster parents had told her about the giant lilac tree guarding the narrow entrance. It was the only one for miles.

The car made its way down the bumpy drive to a rundown home, greenish in color with long curls of paint coming down like disobedient tendrils. The house looked small at first glance, but the boy could see it expand into the far reaches of the unkempt backyard. The front lawn was littered with old toys and bikes, most of which were rusty or broken. Despite himself, he felt the child stir somewhere inside him, and he suddenly couldn't wait to get out of the car and run through the toy graveyard. No one had ever taught him how to ride a bike, and now he wanted more than anything to learn. He had not played with a toy in a very long time.

A woman and a man in their late thirties walked out of the house holding hands followed by four children of different ages. They stared unwaveringly at the boy like he was an odd-looking new puppy that had been dropped on their doorstep.

"This is him," Jodiann told the family. "Sign here."

The man quickly signed the screen she was holding and handed her a large wad of cash. She got in her car and raced down the dirt road. Large clouds of dust made them all cough, and the air felt heavy as they stood there awkwardly watching Jodiann tear down the driveway. The boy wondered if she wanted to get away from him or her life or the scene they had witnessed that they'd never, no matter how far they traveled across the country, be able to forget. He wondered, as she disappeared from his life forever, exactly how someone like Jodiann got to be in the line on the right and how a mother trying to protect her kids was forced to be in the line on the left.

The boy's new foster mother finally turned her attention to him. She knelt down on the grass in front of him, and he could see her sweet eyes that smiled even when she wasn't. He wanted to punch her and run away to live by himself in the woods that abutted the scrappy yard of half-dead toys. He wanted to scream at her, one inch from her face, tiny flecks of spit assaulting her freckled cheekbones, and then he wanted to wait, hungrily, for the slap that followed. He would feel the familiar burning sensation on his face and know that no one was going to get him a cute penguin-shaped ice pack for his stinging cheek.

But instead, he stared into those eyes. He knew that they had seen a whole world of things just like his had, and he wanted her to pull him into her lap and tell him her story. All of her stories. Despite his experience that everything in his short life went terribly wrong, he wanted this woman to love him, and in that moment he didn't even care if it was temporary.

She reached for his hand, and he didn't pull away. "Elliot."

He nodded.

"I'm Patti. This is Jonah," she said pointing to her husband. "These guys are Max, Edwin, Lucia and Sienna. They all came from somewhere else. Like you." The other kids gave small waves, and Elliot wondered how many cars they had driven in and if their mamas had died on the floor of a dollar store.

"We're really glad you're here." Patti pulled him close, and he let her, arms stiff by his side. As much as he wanted to, he could not make himself wrap those arms around her neck. Not yet.

After a moment, Jonah broke the spell. "Come on, Elliot." He took his wife by the elbow and pulled her up. He grabbed his new scrawny, abused, forgotten son by the hand. "We've got work to do."

* * *

Things had gotten worse somehow. It was an unpalatable hot breath of despair that stunk up the air all around them. The "forgotten ones" had not been saved like his mother had believed with all of her palpitating heart. At least not like she thought they would. They had erected so many stations handing out assignments, but despite the promise of a job and a badge and a worry-free life, some people chose to get in the line on the left so they could erase their pain. Pamphlets talked about "jobs for everyone." TV commercials on carefully monitored broadcasts boasted a beautiful future with a reunited nation. But since the day a man reached for his gun and shot a mother in front of her kids because she wouldn't take her medicine, Elliot's ideals of his mama's America had slowly begun to die.

Every day, he went on "runs" with Jonah and watched the lines grow.

"What happens to the people on the left?" Elliot asked one day. They had parked their car behind an abandoned building and snuck around the side to survey the scene.

"In the east, they made sure they were good and drugged and then they collected them in vans," Jonah told him. He was squinting into a set of binoculars and his voice was as steady as his gaze.

"Where do they take them?" Elliot grabbed onto the edge of Jonah's shirt without realizing it. It was a security blanket as he watched the heartbeat of the country slow to a stop.

"We're not totally sure. But we think they're putting them to work in his new factories."

"Oh," Elliot said. He wasn't sure who "we" or "his" meant, but he was afraid his voice would creak if he said another word.

They walked back to the car, and Jonah took his hand. It felt rough and strong, and Elliot would have held it forever. They got into the beat-up sedan and sat there for a minute.

Finally, Elliot found the strength to speak again. "What assignment will you and Patti get?"

Jonah chuckled for a second, and Elliot wondered what could possibly be funny. "In our old lives, we would have definitely been in the left line. We escaped New York right before they put it on lockdown." The laughter evaporated from Jonah's voice at the last word, and he looked lost for a second.

"This was Patti's family home. Her father was a pastor here. A huge conservative. He died about a year ago, and we gave a lot of money to his church. He always told everyone in his congregation that his daughter was a devout Christian girl. A conservative girl." Jonah laughed again. "We got assigned to the militia last week. They agreed to let us make sure the congregation is fully assigned and taken care of."

"But what will happen to us? To me?"

Jonah leaned over to him and took his chin in that giant hand. "Elliot, we're not going to work for the militia."

Elliot felt like he was going to cry. Nothing made sense and hadn't in a long time.

Jonah smiled at him. "We're leaving for Canada in two months. Or less. We're making the final preparations. You're coming with us! You all are."

Elliot fell asleep on the ride home and woke up in his dad's arms, carrying him to the house. He felt like he was in a hammock swinging between his very best dreams. He felt loved.

They walked into the kitchen together and Patti turned away from the stove, wiping her hands on her jeans. "It's time for dinner, Elliot," she said gently, putting one hand on his shoulder. He didn't flinch even though he expected to.

They joined the others at a large farmer's table stuffed in the tiny kitchen. Elliot had never had a family meal around a table; he and his mother had eaten in bed or on someone's stoop, splitting a Big Mac between the two of them. His other foster homes had often served a big pot of something grey and flavorless, and the kids were expected to serve themselves and find a corner to nibble their grub.

That first day, Elliot had watched as Patti spooned something from a small blue bottle on top of each kid's dinner, measuring out a precise dose. When Patti caught him watching her, she smiled.

"We don't know how far they'll take this nonsense," she told him, keeping her eyes on the spoon as she carefully poured. "Gotta protect my babies."

"What. What is that?" Elliot's small handfuls of trust for his two new parents started to fly out the window, and Patti sensed it. She put her spoon down and walked over to grab his hands and pull him close.

"Elliot, you know what happened to your mom?" Elliot gulped and nodded, wondering why everyone had to know what had happened to his mother. He wished his darkest secret hadn't been broadcast on the news or written in bold type in his file.

"And you know all those lines of people being forced to take bad medicine?" He nodded again.

"We can't let them contaminate us like they did everyone else." Patti dropped her voice lower, and it frightened Elliot a bit, but he still leaned forward to listen. "We're the Resistance. Soon every one of us will be put to sleep. If they find out who we really are, they could come after us. We can't let them. Understand?"

Elliot looked at her, feeling terrified and confused, then looked up at Jonah who gave one short nod. Patti continued.

"This is so they can't ever drug us. We have to take it every day." She leaned back and smiled as if it was the most normal thing to discuss with a child, and Elliot, trying to cobble all the pieces together, smiled back at her, settling on wanting her approval. He patted her awkwardly on the arm.

She put a plate laced with the blue-bottle potion in front of each foster kid, and Elliot watched as the others dug in, gobbling their food as if they hadn't eaten in years.

Patti studied his face for a moment as he looked down at his plate of food. The other kids abruptly stopped eating and stared at him.

He shrugged and picked up his fork even though his thoughts and memories were still crashing into each other, and he wasn't sure where they would land. He had tried his mom's pills when he was just four years old, locking the door of the bathroom (even though that lock had never worked) as she lay unconscious in the other room on their dirty sheets. He had wanted to visit the place where his mother's faraway stare took her, to swim in the sly smile that seemed to indicate she was having the best dream ever. It wasn't fair, he had told himself, that she got to feel happy all the time and he had to pretend to be. So one night, when he was huddled in the bathtub, he had decided to escape like she always did. The pills were left open on the counter, and one-two-three, he popped them into his mouth. It was a dose that would have sent a child on an irreversible trip to hell. But he felt nothing. He did not get to leave the bathtub on a rocket ship to a better life or even a more bearable one. Besides *that* day in the dollar store, it was the most tragic thing that had ever happened to him—the inability to escape. The realization that the thing that made his mom feel everything made him feel absolutely nothing.

For reasons he couldn't explain, he decided not to tell Jonah and Patti about that day with the pills. Instead, he mustered a hopeful smile and started to eat, shoveling the food into his mouth, laughing even, food spewing out onto the knotty table only to be scooped back up and shoved back in again. The other kids laughed and joined him, and his new motley family seemed almost normal. For a small cluster of moments that he revisited for many, many years after that, he felt safe.

2031, PORTLAND, MAINE

It was the night after the Cave meeting, and Elena sauntered around the courtyard lost in thought. Her visions were especially strong as she thought about her friends' stories, but while she tried to imagine each one exactly as it had happened, it always took on a fantastical version of itself even though she had lost the ability to imagine in vivid color. She slowly joined the masses of sleepers responding to one of the final buzzers of the evening telling them to come in from the air that threatened to choke them each day. They all instinctively moved toward their sleeping pods, and Elena's synapses crashed into each other like a pileup of cars on a foggy night. For reasons that never made complete sense to her, she was unable to visualize anything once those doors locked them in for the evening.

The guards were prodding people along, hoisting some up into their coffin-like beds with wooden poles or even assault rifles. The militia came from a long line of conservative government supporters and, while unwaveringly dedicated to their country (just like their parents and their grandparents, and so on since anyone could remember), they were decidedly not very forward-thinking. *Poor stupid sheep*, her mother used to call them. *They don't even know they're being lied to, or they do and choose to not believe it. They would rather die standing on their faulty ground than live with integrity!* They didn't fully realize that their place in the Waking World had decided their assignment in this dark one—many believed that they were lucky. Had they been considered a somebody, part of the Dictator's elite class, then they would have been living in the Republic instead of babysitting sleepers in windowless factories and housing towers. But Elena was sure, as she carefully watched them lug their big guns around and beat and rape the zombie-folk as casually as taking a cigarette break, that these officials considered themselves supremacists. She was forever grateful for just how dull-witted they were and that she was not now nor ever would be one of them.

She didn't wince as a guard pushed her up on her bed with the butt of his rifle or show that she understood how possible it was that the rifle could go off at any moment and tear her in two.

Another officer came over to her and said, "Open, bitch," pressing a thumb on the inside of her wrist. She hesitated for a fraction of a second, and the officer shoved his gun in her mouth to pry it open. *Steady*, she told her breath. *Stop it*, she told her heart.

The officer placed two "dream pills" in the back of her open mouth as another buzzer sounded. She automatically lay down in the tight quarters, her tongue acting as a dam. The dim light seeped into her dungeon as the officer closed the door and snapped it shut.

As soon as the flashlights moved away, Elena carefully removed the sleeping pills and mashed them into the crevice of her pod. She knew for certain that she was susceptible to them and didn't want to find out just how much on an important night like this. She lay there unbearably still for close to three hours, counting, becoming a human clock so precise it could almost control the minutes. She heard the slamming of doors, and she imagined the guards leaving for the night and retreating to their own quarters or finding their way to a bar with repulsive food (no doubt leftovers from the Republic) and cheap alcohol that impaired their intelligence level even more. Elena had seen firsthand what drunk, stupid, hopeless people were capable of.

Finally, there it was. The hiss let out a long, final exhale, and there was silence. It was as if the world had stopped spinning and looked at her expectantly: *Your turn, Elena.*

She contorted her body, making one arm as long as possible, telling it to be made out of rubber, and reached down into the side of her boot to find a very thin, sturdy piece of metal. She slowly flipped her body around, sucking back the pain from her screaming limbs, until she was facing the latch that held her coffin in its closed position. The metal put enough pressure on its jaws for her to undo its hold and slip out. She shimmied over to the emergency window that looked out onto the city and used her tool to slide it open. She pressed her forehead against the thick glass and took in gulps of polluted sea air. And, like prying open the most succulent oyster, she angled the makeshift key just right to release it.

The window was no bigger than a porthole, but she was able to squeeze her undernourished frame through it with just a bit of painful scraping on her hips. She clung to the side of the tower. She was a fly on a wall of an impossibly high building. It overlooked a sea that would have gobbled her up, killing her by way of freezing or toxicity or both, gleefully, all at once. A gust of wind hit her then, and she wanted to scream, *Take me! Take me now, you monster!* The small woman thought about jumping into the water's briny arms and letting it pull her down to its gritty bottom like an old shipwreck with a gaping hole. She had been fighting for almost fifteen years while the rest of the Resistance got to enjoy a forever slumber. God, she was so tired.

But the sea calmed as if to say, *Not yet, my dear,* and she climbed down slowly, carefully, to the bottom. As she landed, she took the form of a shadow. A dark Resistance fighter. A precious mouthpiece that had to fight stupidity and time and mother nature all on her own to get the precious information from her meeting to the Controller.

A creature of the night, she swiftly made her way toward the docks without making a sound, hugging the edges of a lost city.

When she'd been placed in her training center in Boston, she was just a child, but she had already known how to trick the militia into thinking she was a sleeper. It was at the training center where she'd met Cory. When the sleepers were forming a line at mealtime Cory managed to get behind her. He hissed at her back, barely audible, but she heard it.

"I know you're not asleep," he said.

There was the din of metal cups clanging together and guards barking orders at the sleepers.

"Excuse me?" she hissed back, careful to keep her mouth still, every bit an indignant eleven-year-old who had just been told she wasn't doing a good job at something.

"I can tell. I'm not asleep either. Obviously." He was a professional at being inconspicuous. She could barely hear him, yet she felt the meaning of every word.

"I have some instructions for you," he told her. "I'll find you later."

"OK," she whispered.

He found her in the yard where they were being trained in formation. As the guards tried to make sense of the mass of undisciplined sleepers in front of them, once again Cory managed to stand right next to her.

"I have a gateway radio for you. It's really small, real thin. You'll have to hide it on you. I'm not sure you'll understand how to work it, but you have to try."

"I know how to work a gateway radio," she replied. "My mom taught me how." She wanted to tell this know-it-all who her mom was, that he had probably been one of her followers, but she was careful to say as few words as possible. Besides, she was a Jane Doe—someone without an identity—

and her instincts told her it was best to keep it that way.

One of the sleepers had lost his footing and sent the group stumbling. Cory got as close as he could to her and slipped the radio up her sleeve. She quickly pinched the fabric to her wrist to keep it in place.

"When you get to your location, you need to hide it somewhere safe. Channel Two connects you to a command center for people like us. They'll expect you to report everything you find out. They'll help you."

She had done exactly what he'd said. She had been reporting every single thing she'd found out ever since. But the imaginary Controller living in his secret Command Center might as well have been god living in a fluffy white cloud. She could not see him. She barely got a response. He had never helped her directly or even, that she knew of, indirectly. She had started to believe that he didn't really exist at all.

She got to the edge of the dock and lay down on her belly, moving her body so her head and chest were hanging out above the water. Small waves lapped at the pillars, and she instinctively raised her torso up and down to avoid being hit by them. She imagined them as dragons licking something worse than fire at her. The oceans had not been able to sustain any life for quite some time and had reached the point of being dangerous to the touch.

Elena had seen guards toss sleepers into the liquid darkness in the rare occurrence that they didn't assimilate into their assigned place in the new world. Sometimes they did it just for fun. She had heard an unnatural sizzle when they hit the wake and hoped that they couldn't feel anything even though she knew, she had seen time and again, that they couldn't.

She had loved the water as a child. She used to graze it with her feet, swinging between two parents, or chase salty waves and blinding daydreams until the sun dipped into its surface. Now it terrified her, but she reached her gloved hands down the ragged pillar anyway and located the small radio wrapped in plastic.

She climbed down a metal ladder, tacked to the side of the decrepit dock, grateful for the low tide. Clinging to the ladder with her legs and thin arms laced through the rungs, she carefully removed the radio. It was a miracle that it still worked after all this time. She took a deep breath to steady her body and calm her mind. It was important to remember the codes and to get every signal right.

Elena almost chuckled as she sent the short but detailed messages in Morse code to the Center. It was a Russian spy movie, and she was on her latest mission. It was absurdity in its most ridiculous form: a woman dressed all in black clinging to a barely-there ladder and using what felt like an ancient form of communication in what was supposed to be the future. She remembered her mother's near-obsession with technology. *It's how we get things done, Lannie! It's the only way to stop this madness,* she would say as the government realized the Resistance was not backing down—after they had banned Muslims from entering the country and packed the Muslim citizens up in carriers to be shipped to their country of origin.

Even though Elena's father, Ben, had denounced his country of origin and his faith when he arrived in the U.S. at the age of fifteen, it was personal and it was scary. He wanted to lay low and stay under the radar. *No one can find out where I came from,* he always pleaded with her mother. It was usually late at night, Elena peeking around the corner of the kitchen, and his worries were often fueled by a brown liquid that sloshed around as he brought it to his lips.

I will not back down, her mother would always reply. *Not ever.* She was sure that he'd never be found out, not with his olive skin that could easily pass as Italian or South American and his flawless English accent. Not with his red-haired, freckled wife and his tenured job and his beautiful house in the suburbs of Pennsylvania.

Soon enough, they stripped away most people's rights like they were pulling off a stubborn Band-Aid. Then they took basic health care away (from everyone except for the elite class) and upped their discrimination game and perpetuated racial profiling and targeting and hate crimes and began systematically cutting off the rest of the world. The Resistance reached a fever pitch, and Sarah was their leader. They would not back down. Not ever.

But when the Internet and their mobile phones went dark, it was like their weapons of choice had been disarmed. It started happening shortly before Elena's mother went to prison. It began with social networks, which were being used to coordinate the movement. At that point, it was taking organized groups less than an hour to mobilize across the country in response to the latest executive order stripping them of their rights. The government quickly infiltrated their social feeds, posting fake petitions, trying to uncover signs of treason. If someone signed one, or posted something derogatory about the new President, their name was flagged and a tracking signal on their mobile devices came to life, recording their every word. The government hired football field-sized rooms of people listening and documenting anyone they considered a traitor. The most active members of the Resistance started having trouble making calls and sending texts. They became locked out of all their social networks. Internet searches for anything the government wanted to remain hidden came up empty.

The government bought huge conglomerates, all in the name of keeping tabs on those who opposed them: they took over all the phone companies and the service providers and the communication entities online and the search engines and the "intelligent personal assistants" that had become so popular and could be found in most homes. It happened so fast and without anyone knowing it, and U.S. citizens didn't realize for months on end that every single thing they said or did was being used against them. Their lives were cracked wide open and even a whispered conversation to a lover was recorded.

Elena had overheard her parents talking in the kitchen late at night after they had found out from a trusted source (in a secret meeting in the woods behind their house) that they were being watched. They had buried their devices in the backyard and bought as many gateway radios as they could find. They had purchased one burner phone in case of an emergency. Sarah had begun planning her revolt with the small army she had been building across the country. She hadn't known that it would be her last one as the leader of Purple Nation.

Elena finished her detailed message to the Center—a faceless group of people hiding out in what she could only imagine to be a gigantic submarine submerged beneath the Atlantic. She carefully put the radio back in its plastic wrap and secured it out of sight on the pillar. She had performed the same duty for most of her adult life. She always got a response—a quick thank you, a blip, a nod to her tireless and, frankly, life threatening hard work. Nevertheless, she found that staticky bit of noise so reassuring that it often brought tears to her eyes. Even if Cory had promised her that day at the training center that they would help her, she had given up waiting for a helicopter to swoop down and drop a rope ladder for her to climb up to safety. *They were supposed to save me!* she wanted to shout. *It has gone on too long,* she wanted to tell them. She wanted to jam her fingers into the buttons and yell at them and tell them to find a new broken mouthpiece. But she was too afraid that they would cut her off, and then there would be no hope at all.

She thought about her comrades who endured factory work and abuse and assault. At least they knew they weren't alone in the world—and all their struggles were for something bigger. That's what she told herself every night. Even if she didn't really believe it anymore.

* * *

The next day wasn't a meeting day, but Elena could feel Elliot's presence as she completed that week's task of pushing a button over and over and over again. She wondered if she could push the button so many times that her brain exploded, nasty bits of her skull sprinkled all over her sleepwalking co-workers. She imagined one of the guards coming by with a mop, business as usual, and without emotion cleaning up her giant mess so the assembly line could rage on. After all, the Republic had to receive their cans of synthetic smoked salmon on time.

Elena knew that the droids flanking her on either side were so doped up that they couldn't detect anything around them, much less her spy tactics. She had developed the most useful skill of looking at people through the smallest space between her sunken eyelids. It was something she had practiced endlessly so she could observe the sleepers (if only to occupy her mind) and keep watch on what was happening around her. But there was never a fraction of a second when she didn't appear completely high when in the presence of the militia. She knew what happened when one of them was discovered.

Elliot was careful not to move his eyes too much, and Elena could tell he was still smarting over his stupidity from two days before. She knew he was in pain. They both knew that absolutely nothing could help him.

She let her mind drift again to the past, a dangerous destination that filled her with such anguish, she often had to catch herself when she was freefalling so she didn't cry out loud.

She had gone with her father at least twenty more times to visit her mom in prison until Sarah was finally released. It came as a shock to both the young girl and her dad—they went from wondering if they'd be apart forever to suddenly getting the call that they could come retrieve Sarah that very same day.

Every time they had gone to visit, Sarah seemed worse, and Elena always thought, *This is not possible, she can't possibly be worse. If she goes any farther from her original self, she will disappear into thin air.* But with each meeting in the grim visitation room they found her mother slumped a little lower, and her inner light—the one that had once led people by the thousands—became even more permanently extinguished. It made Elena more terrified than she had ever been in her life, but it didn't take away from the joy she felt on the way to pick her mother up.

We will nurse her back to health, father and daughter both thought, probably in unison. *We will make things right again and everything will go back to normal.*

They slowly led Sarah out of the prison. Ben practically carried her, and Elena clung tightly to the small bag that held the protest shirt and purple armband that she had worn the day she was arrested. Both were still splattered with blood, but Elena knew her father wouldn't be able to throw them out. She was sure that when her mom woke up, Sarah would want to keep them to remember how hard her people fought.

Elena cuddled up to her mom in the backseat that day, nuzzling into the crook of her arm, but her mom just sat lifeless beside her. Elena had unbuckled her seatbelt and moved her mom's arm so it wrapped completely around her. She closed her eyes and pretended it was all OK. She imagined that they could go back to the day before the march and start over and that her mom was really her mom. They could chat about their big plans and their next move, and her mom would squeeze her tight and reassure her that this was just a blip in time, that they could not possibly let the world go into the darkest direction imaginable. But when she opened her eyes again, her mom was a form full of nothingness.

Ben was talking so fast, Elena could barely make out what he was saying. She realized he was giving her mother an unedited version of what the world was like since she was arrested three months before.

"They shut down all the public schools, well most of them, that stupid witch doesn't care about children, not even a little bit, Secretary of Education my ass, and the prisoners? The so-called Resistance? They're a bunch of dopers just like you back there, my beautiful smart wife, and now look at you! They did it to everyone who didn't want to go along with their little agenda! So, yeah, all doped up and they got you all hooked and now everyone's being released from prison. There are whole prisons standing empty! Being turned into factories, they say! Bringing all the jobs back, they say! Now it's our problem, huh? We get to take care of a bunch of fools…"

He quickly reached back to touch his wife's knee, "Oh honey, I'm sorry I…"

"Dad!" Elena screamed as they swerved into the other lane. Had she not still been a child, she would have insisted that she drive.

He turned back to face the road, but continued on, mumbling the rest. It was a self-inflicted diatribe, a rhetoric of madness. "And they've taken all of them away like they said they were going to, everyone warned us, and our insurance has been cut off and dammit Sarah, I don't know how to help you or if there's even someone out there who's awake and listening and willing to help."

Sarah did not understand a word of what her husband was saying—at least she didn't appear as if she did. Elena still didn't know if her mom heard or at least absorbed some of its meaning. Her mother and the rest of the prisoners, mostly Resistance (with a few hardcore criminals mixed in the bunch), had been the first guinea pigs for the President's antidote to opposition.

It made its recipients violently dependent on their dose. If they went for even a couple of hours without it, they became so sick they wished for a swift death. If they even had the capacity to wish for anything at all.

The prison didn't offer an explanation or send instructions, except to robotically read off her dosage and hand them seven giant bottles of pills. In so many ways they were still in the dark, fumbling around like fools with their trusty light of goodness. They still believed that things could get better.

The two of them brought Sarah into the house and sat her down in her favorite chair—the one she had curled up in a million times to read the newspaper or to put Elena's hair in a French braid, Elena screaming out that she was pulling too hard. Sarah groaned a little as they sat her down, but it wasn't in pain, not yet anyway. It was more of an exhalation of the past three months. Elena took it as a sigh of relief to be home.

The next day, Ben tried to wean her off the pills. But her episodes were so sickening, he started setting a timer to give her a hit every two hours. It was the only times her eyes looked alive, gleaming with a hunger Elena would never know. It was impossible for the immune to desire anything like the sleepers desired their drugs.

Two weeks later she found her father sitting on the porch with a glass of whiskey in his hand. It was 8:30am. It was a Saturday so beautiful, it choked Elena with memories of perfect picnics and competitive badminton games they had played together on days just like this one.

"Dad?" she called out gently. He seemed angry, an emotion she rarely saw him have, and she approached him nervously. She was afraid she would awaken the growing beast that now resided inside of him, just beneath the surface.

"What?" He turned to look at her, eyes rimmed with a purple-red.

"I. I just. We need some food." She looked down at her feet as if she had done something terrible, as if the entire world was her fault.

"Dammit!" Ben slammed his fist on the table and winced in pain. Then he stood up so fast, his chair toppled over. He picked up the glass of whiskey and threw it at the deck, looking surprised as it exploded into a million shards of glass. He stared at it as if it was not there and walked over to his daughter to gently place a hand on her head.

"I have to go out and get some stuff. Take care of your mother." Elena nodded, stone-faced, but as soon as he left, tears spilled out of her eyes and down her cheeks. She ran to get the broom and dust pan, careful to clean up every piece of glass. She knew that there wasn't a working hospital they could go to.

It seemed like there was more glass in that one vessel than all the glasses that were ever created.

She spent the afternoon brushing her mother's hair, talking to her as if everything was just fine, when Ben burst through the door with a half-full shopping bag. Elena stared at him with her mouth open, and he stared back, panting as if his load weighed more than he'd ever anticipated, and he'd determined he wasn't strong enough to carry it.

"Dad? What's wrong?" Elena whispered. She hadn't stopped brushing Sarah's hair, and Sarah continued to stare out the window at an imaginary moment only she could see.

She noticed the look on her dad's face then. He was scared. He had seen a ghost he couldn't unsee. He had come to a realization of the most terrifying variety, and his whole body was shaking uncontrollably.

"They are shutting down the grocery stores. I drove two towns over to get this." He gestured to his meager bag.

"What stores?" Elena's hand hung in the air.

"All of them."

He put the bag on the coffee table and pulled one of the pill bottles out of a high cabinet in the kitchen. The sound of the lid twisting off alerted Sarah's senses, and she cocked her head to the side. Elena thought she could see her mom sniff a little, and she wondered if the pills had a smell to an addict.

It was only four weeks later when her father decided to join his bride. Elena had just turned ten. On the morning of her birthday, she had walked downstairs sleepily in her pajamas to find her dad at the counter with a box of store-bought cupcake mix, a red mixing bowl and a giant mess.

"Daddy!" Elena cried, running over to put her arms around his waist.

"Hi, sweetheart. Happy Birthday." He gave her a small hug back.

"I can't believe you remembered!" It was the biggest present she had ever received in her decade of life. It was all that mattered.

"Of course I remembered." He forced his mouth up in a smile. He lifted up the box of cake mix. "I found this. Mom had it stashed in the back."

He sang to her that birthday, only him. She blew out her candle with a couple of ounces of little girl hope, wishing for her mother to go back to normal and for a do-over before that worst day in November.

Elena curled up on the couch after eating the stale cake and fell into a dreamless sleep. She was grateful for this day. She promised she would remember it forever.

But when Elena woke up, the house was too quiet, and she saw him sitting at the table, slumped over the black and white checked placemats, not asleep but not awake looking at something no one else would ever see. A small smile was still on his face. The bottle was open next to his scruffy beard, and his mouth was grotesquely ajar. She screamed, a sound that might have broken windows and sent neighbors running, hands clumsily punching 9-1-1. She screamed and wailed like a child being torn apart. But no one ever heard her.

* * *

Elena suddenly realized one of the guards was standing next to her, and she dragged her mind back to the present like a reluctant mule. The man was standing so close to her, she could smell his dirty breath, permanently infused with bottom shelf alcohol or the kind of rancid spirit that sticks to one's feet in a bar. Elena didn't dare change her breathing and continued to push her button. She focused on the padded part of her pointer finger pressing into the flat, worn round red button with the bits of brown rust and then she concentrated on how the nothingness felt as her finger hung in the air, waiting for the appropriate time to press, press, press again. She was a machine. She was a robot.

She moved her eyes to the side so subtly that even someone staring directly into her pupils would not have noticed it and saw that the guard was rubbing his crotch. She saw it grow. She carefully looked over at Elliot and sensed that he was trying not to lunge over the assembly line. She slowly pressed her lips together as a plea to him to control himself, and the hairs on the back of her neck leaned forward at attention as if they could stop him. They both knew Elliot would be killed, maybe thrown into the sea with a sizzle, the toxicity eating him alive. Then he would surely be replaced in the morning.

The guard started moving his pelvis around, a lonely dance. She told her eyes to slowly go back to the button, and to try not to think about it, but suddenly, Elena felt a hand grab her elbow hard.

Stay calm, stay aloof, stay comatose, stay asleep. I am asleep, I am not here. I am picnicking on a beautiful morning, peanut butter and blueberry jam, crusts cut off.

She felt herself being yanked off the line (*it is just my body, it is not me*). She imagined kicking that hardened crotch with her boots and punching him in the jaw and running away with a shrill cackle. But instead she told her fight that fists stay down. She told her flight that there was nowhere to go (*it is just my body, it is not me*).

Instead she was dragged to a windowless room with a door that locked.

Elena had only been raped twice—once right after she had left the training center, and once when she had just turned twenty (at least she thought that's how old she was) when a guard had helped himself into her sleeping pod. She lay there like a near-corpse trying not to scream.

She considered herself lucky. Silver, who was blonde with large breasts and a constantly shrinking waist, was pulled off the line several times a week. In the beginning, she would lay weeping in Elena's lap, telling her mentor that

48

she couldn't go on, that she was better off on the streets again, that at least she could hide there. But Elena would assure her she must go on. There were so few of them, and Silver was so important to the mission that they simply couldn't lose her. As the weeks and months and years passed them by, Silver eventually accepted her place in the dark world. But Elena absorbed each violation of her young friend, wearing every assault like a deep scar on her own body.

The guard propped Elena against a grimy wall in the small office. It was about ten feet by ten feet in size. A plain, metal desk sat in the center of it, and on the desk was a razor-thin clear screen seemingly suspended in the air. She could see streams of data racing across it, but they were going too fast for her to make sense of them. There was a large image of the first Dictator projected on the wall and a smaller image of Dictator Two. She knew their faces better than she knew her own—their portraits could be seen on every street corner and in every building and even in her sleeping pod. Propaganda videos ran twenty-four hours a day on every screen: in the factories, in their housing complexes, on the train, on the sides of buildings. The only intel she had into what she looked like as a twenty-four-year-old was a blurry face made out in a dusty window after dark.

He reached for a large pill bottle, pretending to examine it, turning it over in his hands. Then he slowly put it back on the shelf.

"I'm thinking we use the dirty stuff for such a dirty girl." He smiled as if they were two lovers about to try something they'd never done before. Three of his teeth were missing, but, impossibly, a piece of that day's slop hung onto the edge of one of the remaining ones.

The guard, whom she had identified from his nametag as Darren, pulled out a syringe and showed it to her as if he was presenting her with a great gift. He took a ball of black tar and put it in a special cooker, and *ding!* it was ready, and he sucked up the liquid, holding the needle above his head. Victorious.

Darren jammed the syringe into Elena's arm, and it ripped at her vein in pain. She welcomed it. She fled from feeling numb, even though it often left her cold and alone in the darkest night shadows. She knew the drugs were zip zapping around trying to figure out how to switch on her euphoria, but they couldn't. Darren smiled, like he'd given her a present, rubbing up against her.

He pulled down her thick black pants and grabbed at her hard with his dirty fingernails and his desperation. Then he stood above her, shadowing her like the towers they had built to contain people exactly like her, and unzipped his military pants, pulling them down to his ankles. He was more disgusting than she could have ever expected, with large puss-filled blemishes lining the insides of his legs near his testicles. His penis was small, but wide. His pubic hair, freakishly unruly.

He knelt down on either side of his comatose prize and plunged himself inside her, and it was infinitely more painful than the needle. She was transported back to the last moments she spent with her parents, mostly of her mom lying completely still in various positions in various rooms, and of her dad when he finally gave up for good.

Darren thrust at her again and again until he surrendered, a repulsive lump. When he let her go, she told her body to collapse on the floor, to leave all muscle memory behind, and he fell in a heap on top of her. A loud buzzer sounded, and he quickly stood up and scurried out of the room.

Elena noticed a small data stick sitting on the desk, a bit of it hanging off the edge. She had seen the guards use them before, plugging them into their devices, passing them around. She didn't know where he had gone or for how long, but her snakelike fingers shot up the side of the desk and carefully slid the stick off of it.

She heard a noise and slammed to the ground, going completely still, heart pounding *(stop it, heart)*. But he didn't come back, and she released a breath in a whoosh of relief.

She turned the stick around in her hands. It reminded her of the USB plugs her parents used to use, but this one was barely thicker than a piece of poster board and about the length of a deck of cards. Elena reached down, still watching the door, until she felt the edge of it hit the top of her high boot. She managed to hook it inside, and then push it all the way down. She quickly looked down to make sure it was hidden.

She was lying there staring at the ceiling, when a screen on the wall came to life. Dictator Two's face flashed on. He almost appeared to be staring down at her. A loud sniff exploded from her nose in disgust, and she quickly glanced at the door again.

Propaganda videos played on repeat for the sleepers when they were in their housing complexes, but this one was aimed at the militia: "As you know, my father-in-law has brought back jobs like never before in our country. And I continue to create them tenfold. We have built more factories than we could have ever imagined. And we won't stop, not ever." He stared into her eyes for a moment, and she was sure he could read her mind.

"Now, as the Republic gathers for our annual summit, we will decide how to make our country even better! Even greater! We don't need the rest of the world. We can make everything we could ever want right here, right now. This year, we're allowing ten lucky members of the militia to attend the gala. Submit your accomplishments as a member of our treasured army, and you could be one of the most fortunate people in the entire country!"

The Dictator raised his fist in the air as if to rally a crowd.

"We want for nothing! We answer to no one! We stand together! United."

The screen flashed off, a loud buzzer sounding at the end.

Darren burst through the door, almost angrily, and she barely had enough time to close her eyes again. He grabbed his prize by the lapel and dragged her up as she stumbled with what felt like useless legs. He pulled up her pants and smiled that toothless grin. This sick bastard was dressing his doll to present her to his comrades. She was his grand trophy of dystopia. He'd won without even really trying, and it didn't matter to him that he was the only one in the competition.

There were whistles and catcalls as he paraded her back out to her station and positioned her in the exact place where she had started. She could feel Elliot's rage, a sort of heat that radiated from him to her. But she didn't look at him. She did nothing more than push her round red button over and over again until feeding time.

2019, OHIO

Elliot had been living with his new family for a little less than two months when they started making final preparations. They had sat together at the table for every meal. They gobbled up every bite of their serum-laced food like it was their last, even though in the warm glow of Patti and Jonah's love, they always felt safe. Every night, they learned about the Resistance from Patti and Jonah and how they realized that it was their duty to save "all of the beautiful children" from the deep sleep. Patti told stories about escaping New York City as the government shut down the bodegas, grocery stores and restaurants, and how the militia loaded up whole neighborhoods into carriers to take them somewhere far away. People were angry and protested in the streets.

"It was incredible," Patti said, a faraway look in her eyes. "We all thought we could defeat them. Him. We had such hope!"

"Why didn't it work?" Lucia asked. Elliot already knew. He had been chosen to go on runs with Jonah each day, looking for more children to save before they left. It was an honor to ride in the beat-up car with his new dad, but he always came home a couple notches more traumatized every time. He had passed nameless microscopic towns from the front seat of that car and seen more stations forcing pills than grocery stores supplying food. He had seen one van so far. It screeched into a parking lot filled with addicts and had taken as many of them as it could fit.

Father and son had gone to countless abandoned stores to find provisions and saw people who had overdosed right there in the produce aisle, lying amongst the rotten fruit and vegetables. It always brought back his darkest memories like a sucker punch. He'd even retreated so far inward one time, Jonah found him hysterically pulling on a dead woman's hand, begging her to come back to life and lead him home.

"Does anyone know why it didn't work?" Patti was asking, snapping him back to the table. "Elliot?" Elliot shook his head quickly and focused on his food.

"It didn't work because they used their magic weapon!" Patti told them. All of the kids were silent, forks hanging above plates. "They put anyone who resisted them into jail. Even if they suspected that they resisted them a little. Even if they had only made one silly comment, they found out. They were always watching, all the time."

No one spoke. No one breathed. "Then they started feeding everyone their evil pills and the protests stopped. They drugged the Resistance, and they tricked the poor and desperate people who believed them. That's why we came here. It's only just starting to reach here. Back home..." Patti seemed to get stuck in a time and place that Elliot was afraid he'd never get to see. "We came here to escape. And to take our precious serum to Canada."

"That why we take our medicine, mama?" Max was six years old, but had been born addicted to opiates, and Patti and Jonah even suspected that his mother fed him pills for a couple of years after he was born. His speech still struggled, but Elliot knew he took in every word. Even in the six months Max had been taking the serum, his speaking and comprehension had improved.

"Yes, yes." Patti often said things twice: once to her audience and once as an affirmation to herself. "That's why we have to take our medicine every night."

She smiled at her family, and all the children smiled back, digging into their food with a reinvigorated energy, even stealing food off each other's plates and laughing.

Elliot saw Patti and Jonah sharing a worried look across the table, but as soon as Patti caught him staring, she broke into a face-splitting smile.

"Eat up, sweet Elliot! You'll need your strength for your run with Papa tomorrow." Elliot quickly gobbled up his food, stuffing worries of his own. He loved Patti and Jonah. If he looked deep inside and was really honest with himself (in quiet moments spent alone in his room), he loved them more than he had loved his own mother. But he hadn't told them his darkest secret, one even more incomprehensible than his mother's death. He wanted to tell Patti and Jonah every night at dinner or before bedtime when Patti tucked him in and kissed his worried forehead. But he was afraid that they would turn him away or kick him out because he was someone they couldn't save.

In the short time since Elliot had arrived in their driveway, Patti and Jonah had taken in four more children. The newest kids didn't come with a social worker like he had because, just like Jodiann had told him that day in her office, all the agencies had been shut down. Jonah found the abandoned children, and (*he couldn't just leave them there, so*) he picked them up in his strong arms and carried them to the car. It didn't matter that he didn't have a car seat to strap them into or that they were possibly damaged beyond repair or that it would take weeks or months to get them to stop screaming out in the middle of the night. They were infinitely safer in his rundown car than where he'd found them.

The runs happened every day at 2pm. Elliot would often sit in the front seat of the car, doors locked as Jonah casually walked around assignment stations, flashing his military badge adorned with a cross—one of the highest ranks in the militia. He would chat with some of the guards; he would lean against the side of empty buildings taking in every inch of what was happening around him.

Every time he returned to the car, Elliot would ask, "What happened, Papa?" and Jonah would put his hand on the boy's shoulder and say, "We couldn't save any this time." Elliot wondered what he really meant by "saving any" and what the point of all of it was until the day Jonah came running back with a toddler in his arms, yelling for Elliot to open the door.

"Strap him in! Hold him tight!" Jonah yelled, placing the screaming baby on Elliot's lap. He tried to wrap his skinny kid arms around the flailing ones so he didn't get punched in his face, but the small boy pushed him away, kicking with strong just-learned-to-walk legs and scratching with untrimmed fingernails.

Jonah jumped into the driver's seat, and the car squealed away, protesting the sharp acceleration in the ungodly sun.

"What happened? Was someone chasing us? Where did you get this little boy? Where's his mama?" Elliot felt so panicked, he wanted to take the wheel and drive the car back to look for the boy's mother. He imagined her running around the station, desperately searching for her missing child who she'd seen *just over there*. He pictured a guard taking out his gun and ending her search with a swift finale to the forehead, and he held the little boy even tighter.

"His mama overdosed by the abandoned garage, and he was screaming. I was afraid they were going to hear him and get him." Jonah's eyes were wild, his voice desperate.

Elliot's heart slowed down in a sort of morbid relief, and he nodded as if grabbing a child from an OD'd mother and running away with him in an old Toyota was normal. He began to sing softly into the boy's ear. It was a song his mother used to sing to him, but he had selectively forgotten all the words and only had the melody to offer. His voice was still young and childlike, and it almost seemed to put the entire car under a spell. The baby quieted after a minute, stuck a thumb in his mouth and fell asleep against Elliot's chest.

He went on these rides with Jonah each day during his short time in Ohio. Some felt like a sightseeing tour and some felt like a spy mission. They would observe the pill heads, what Jonah had been calling "sleepers," and Jonah wrote notes down with blunt pencils on scraps of paper. Sometimes, they found a child lying next to a mom or dad, screaming, crying, and it would take Elliot back to the exact time and place when he was the hysterical child pulling at his mother's dying body. Jonah lifted these lost children up, and their family grew. One day Elliot, holding onto Jonah's sleeve as he carried a small, curly-haired girl to the car, asked him, "Papa, how many will we bring home?" Jonah stopped and knelt down to look him in the eye. The girl was whimpering, half immersed in the sleeping world and half awake.

"All of them, if necessarily. There's no limit. We leave in two days after the latest batch of serum arrives, and we can pick up children on the way to Canada. When I see a child hurting, I hurt. I have to do something. I have to do everything I can. Do you understand?"

Elliot did. Despite years of trying to build up a thick shell that silly emotions couldn't pass through. They stared at each other like that for a second, and Elliot considered this man both a god and an unrealistic dreamer at the same time. He knew all about believing that the world could change; he had watched his mother think it, and then it had been yanked so hard out from under her that she would never get up again. As he witnessed what was happening all around him, right there in that moment—babies left for dead as parents choked down an irreversible poison—he realized that the world had changed after all, just as his mama had told him it would. It was different now. It had disintegrated into nothing.

2017, NEW YORK CITY

Benton Cohen had been working in the same lab since he finished his Master's degree five years prior. He loved the feeling of his routine each morning, like an old coat with worn elbows and renegade threads escaping from the seams. The walk from his apartment in Chelsea to his lab in TriBeCa was a series of mini-dramas that were always the same and always different. He took comfort in the man with the raisin fingertips who handed him his coffee and two bagels each morning, both of which were terrible, but he couldn't bear to take his money from a man with kind eyes and give it to the Starbucks across the street. Or the man who always asked him if he could spare some money and the nod he gave to Benson when he handed over his second bagel instead. The man never seemed to recognize him even though they had been having the same interaction nearly every day for two years, yet Benton knew that the man liked poppy seed toasted with butter and jam because he had asked him once.

He would always arrive first at the lab and spend some time admiring it, breathing it in, arranging his work, rearranging it. He lined his chemicals up like little soldiers who were ready to perform their very important mission for the day. He wiped down the already clean workspace that he had previously scoured the night before with organic cleanser and a soft rag that he then took home and disinfected himself. It was all part of his process as he mentally prepared himself for the nine to twelve-hour stretch that lay ahead. Head down, mixing, matching, testing, starting over from scratch. Throwing hands up in frustration or triumph, which varied from moment to moment. Finally looking up and realizing the day had evaporated into dusk.

As an undergrad, he was given the choice to study either the chemistry of cleaning products and their effects on the environment or the chemistry of addiction. There were loud whisperings of just how much we were truly pillaging the Earth, and Benny was passionate about protecting it. But at the time, he felt like they were on a trajectory that placed the planet on the up and up. He figured he could better serve an area of study in which he was already an expert.

His father had been a profound alcoholic and had expired in a pool of his own vomit. Benny was only eleven years old at the time, but already looked like a grown man. He had found his father lying on the floor, and had screamed out to a mother who had already left them three years prior. A neighbor heard him—kind old Ms. Margaret from down the hall—and came running on wobbly ankles to kneel and pray to Jesus that he might help the boy. Save the boy. She held his hand while they waited for the ambulance to arrive, patting it once or twice and singing him gospel songs that she had memorized better than her own grandchildren's names. He knew that despite her kindness that day, she was relieved that she'd no longer hear glass shattering against their shared wall or father/son wrestling matches (not the good ole fun kind, but the kind where dad, through his blind drunkenness, tries to break son's arm, and son does everything he can to knock dad out so he can run away to safety).

Ms. Margaret had turned to him that day and said, "I think you'll be safe now, son." If going to live with an auntie who was also an alcoholic, but the quiet kind who barely spoke to him, was safe, then he supposed she was right. It was a baby step in a better direction.

When he chose to study the chemistry of addiction, it was because he already had a leg up on the rest of his classmates. He had lived addiction. It was his home, his family, his caretaker. He knew it. He breathed it in each day with ragged, heavy breaths.

He fell in love with his studies. They became his only lover for quite some time, and they were attentive to his every need. He swam in the research like it was the most delicious ocean. He drowned in people's stories of being held captive by their own vices. For some, it was a prison they could not now, not ever, escape. Not with love or support or "hitting bottom" or trying to claw their way out. Only death could set them free.

Benson wanted to know why. He had to know why. It was the only way to cure them.

He listened to every single person, sometimes for hours upon hours, as if they were telling him a story he had to hear to be whole, and if he did not hear the end, he would explode. He was enthralled by them. They were beautiful specimens of suffering. But he was not mocking their pain. Not ever. To him, their misery was eloquent. An uninhibited dance. Man tangled in desire. It was Benny's life's work, his raison d'etre, to release them from what held them against their will.

The opiate epidemic had spread across the country like a veiny monster. It didn't discriminate between moms or teens or rich people or people who hadn't even known what an opiate was before their doctor prescribed it to them for their toothache. They didn't realize its strongman grasp until they had become someone else entirely, and even then they said, *I can stop at any time.* It didn't matter that everyone who had ever known them was sure it wasn't true. It made them lie and steal and hurt any person who came into contact with them, not caring if it was the person they loved most in the world, not minding if that person bore them or they bore it. They abandoned, turned away from, gave up on. The drug became their only friend. And like any friend who knew your most intimate demons, it was impossible to free oneself from its grasp for fear of your insides being spilled out onto the sidewalk.

Benny watched as the drug companies (his nemesis) doled out bottle after bottle of poison. It claimed to release people from their pain as it led them into a nuclear cloud of despair. He admired Big Pharma as only a hero can admire his opposition—he had never seen such a blatant act of evil performed in broad daylight. They cackled in the faces of innocent families as they took everything away. *How free,* Benny thought, *to exist without a conscience.*

Sometimes the pills weren't enough or they ran out, and the cartel moved into the smallest towns, delivering black tar heroin as if it were a pepperoni pizza, and every single addict hit the streets to get a piece. It was an epidemic. It was beyond that; it stretched the word into unfamiliar territory making it uncomfortable when it rolled around in one's mouth. Benny truly believed it was a genocide, and its victims were simply trying to make a better life for themselves. They just wanted to dull some of their pain. The hurting was too much, the high was too good, the cycle was too hard to break. It didn't matter the reason, yet it all became the same reason: they all just needed more.

It was exactly twenty-three days after the election when Benny received his first visit from the government. They were visiting every lab like his, they said. They had heard so much about his work. They were just checking things out. They just wanted to make sure there were no conflicts between his work and the government's agenda. The new healthcare reform had a very specific perspective when it came to dealing with addiction, and they wanted to make sure he was falling in line.

Benny wasn't stupid, and he had been studying human nature for years. He understood what their thinly-veiled questions meant and what they expected him to say in response. He knew they thought he was a threat to the profiteering of the big guns. They were right. He was. But contradictory to all his instincts, he had to make them believe that he wasn't going to stand in the way of their precious healthcare reform or else he knew his work would be for naught. It would be like it never existed.

He minimized his staff and stopped publishing his findings. He was a black scientist who had been fighting Big Pharma's agenda, digging away at their piles of gold with a kid-sized shovel. To them, he would be easy to squash, and it would be joyous to make him go away. To him, the only thing that mattered at all was finishing his work.

He was so close. He was *this* close.

It was a hot summer night when Benny rushed over to his friends' apartment in the West Village, bottle of wine in hand. The usual bustle of a Friday night seemed eerily still, but he shrugged it off blaming the heat. He walked into their Perry Street building and pressed a finger on the worn elevator button. The door opened into a vestibule with a pile of shoes and a single ornate door. They owned the whole floor, which in New York real estate terms, meant they were unbelievably wealthy or lucky or both. In this case, it was definitely all of the above.

"Benny!" His former classmate came over and hugged him, putting her hands on his shoulders as if to take him all in. "You look skinny. And worried."

Benny laughed. "Shouldn't I be worried? Also, your neighborhood is like a ghost town."

His friend laughed back. "Nah. This will all blow over, right? Come in. What can I get you to drink?" Her optimism was one of the things he loved most about her, but he had started to feel disenchanted with her sunshiny spin. He felt like the world was ending, and he wanted to be working through the night, pounding the streets, holding people who still believed in this regime by the shoulders and shaking them hard enough to reassemble their sensibilities.

"Anything. Thanks, Patti." She nodded and returned almost instantly with a perfectly blended cocktail, garnished with fruit so fresh, it belied the shocking decrease in edible produce he had noticed at the grocery store.

Benny walked over to the floor-to-ceiling windows, but didn't get too close. Perched in what felt was the highest point in the sky, he could see the Hudson River smacking against the side of Manhattan. It had gotten angrier somehow. He was on the edge of the Earth, and it could, at any moment, pluck him from his precious island and engulf him in its rage.

Music played in the background—foot tapping songs from the eighties sang by artists who hadn't lived long enough to see the worst of it. People chatted in small pockets, laughing at what had to be an ironic joke because in Benny's mind there was nothing to laugh about. A fireplace, a real one, crackled in the background, and it was comforting even on a hot summer night. Although he never had a fireplace as a child, it made him feel nostalgic, and the glow filled him with a faux hopefulness. It all felt so normal, and Benny wanted to curl up in the corner and cry. Things had gotten so hopeless so quickly, and reminders—two friends weeping and embracing in the corner, the deep groove of perpetual worry in Patti's brow, the lack of partygoers on the streets of one of the hippest neighborhoods in the world—kept him more than a couple of ticks from truly relaxing and letting go. He glanced at his phone to check the time because he knew curfew would arrive too soon, and he was already dreading it.

A curfew in the city that never sleeps. It almost made him chuckle as he thought about his wildest nights out in New York when he would still be dancing at 4am. He remembered the times when day or night didn't matter as long as there was more city to drink in. Now, only six months since the new regime had put the country in its chokehold, checking the time had become a nervous twitch that he wouldn't be able to break until everyone's phones stopped working entirely.

His friend Jonah walked up to him and caught him looking at his phone again, checking it for the fourth time since he arrived. "You'll stay here if it gets too late. We have the room." Benny nodded, grateful. There were so few cabs that he would probably have to walk. He knew if they turned the lights out early, the beasts of the city would creep out of their corners and come out to play.

Patti walked out of the kitchen and clapped her hands. "Let's eat, everyone!"

The guests found their way to the table and servers appeared all around them, bringing out oysters, roast, salmon, braised greens. They filled each person's wine glass to the very brim, and after all of the food was perfectly placed and all of the drinks were poured, everyone sat in silence. They stared at the food. Benny thought that Jonah should run and get his brushes and paints, so perfectly still were they as subjects. He breathed the meal in. The grocery shelves in his neighborhood were becoming scarce, and most nights he struggled to cobble together a proper dinner. So many of his favorite restaurants had shut down, the owners leaving town because they were scared or they had been deported or worse. Although he didn't know what "worse" really meant.

Patti finally spoke. "I know it has been a very difficult six months. We didn't know it would be this difficult, did we?" She mustered a small smile, and her guests smiled back, some of them grateful. A couple of people took big slugs of their wine.

"But we are lucky. We have each other. We have our intelligence, our talents, our will. The people will not stand for this."

Patti had been saying a similar speech for so many months and with each rendition, her voice lost a little bit of its luster. They had started out with such great chutzpah, and now, as the curfew reigned and the city became quickly divided into those who were with the government and those who resisted, her words had lost some of their meaning. So many of the Resistance had been arrested and some of their close friends had vanished into thin air. There were rumors of "drugging" people who were associated with the Resistance, but they were only hushed conversations had on cobblestone streets, and Benny almost didn't want to believe them. It was too impossible to believe.

"I know things will get better," Patti continued with her almost unwavering go get 'em attitude. "I know it." She took a sip of wine herself. "We just have to hang in there and stay connected." She paused and looked at each one of her friends, her gaze finally resting on Jonah's face. Benny watched as he reached over and touched her fingertips, just barely. It made him long for someone to end the world with, sitting on the floor of his apartment eating ramen from the container and reminiscing about all the good times they'd had. He suddenly felt extremely alone.

"Let's eat!" Patti picked up her fork as if to show just how normal it was to sit around her table together on a Friday night. Had it been just a year ago, they'd be talking about the upcoming election and what a circus the whole thing was. Now they were still waiting for the shock to wear off.

People dug into their meal as if it was their last great one. It might have been for some of them. In the moment of silence, Benny cleared his throat and everyone turned to stare at him. Another cocktail appeared magically in front of him, and he took a long drink.

"Excuse me. I have some news." Forks hung in mid-air, and he felt nervous. He was an adjunct professor at NYU and had given dozens of lectures across the country, but there was something about having his friends' eyes on him and the weight of what he was about to say that made him feel self-conscious. He was never very good at boasting.

"As you know, I have been working on an antidote to the opiate epidemic for, well, for a long time." His friends nodded encouragement, but a couple people went back to eating.

"Well…" Benny looked at Patti. "I've discovered it."

They stopped again. Everyone was frozen. Benny was sure that if he blew hard enough, they would have fallen over.

Patti whispered, "How does it work?"

"It's simple. It's a serum. You put just an eye dropper's worth of it on your food or in a drink once a day. Then you are immune to addiction. It works for many types of addiction. Even alcohol." His voice caught in his throat in an unexpected burst of emotion, but he quickly regained his composure. "It works best for opiates."

He paused for a minute, and they all waited. He silently thanked them. "I'm also working on a cure. It's a cure for addiction. If it goes the way I want it to, it will be instantaneous with none of the effects an addict might experience when they're detoxing. I'm *this* close." *This close.*

"Benny." Patti looked at him like she would burst with pride. "This is such amazing news." Even though they were only a month apart in age, Benny gladly accepted her motherly admiration. He thought it was a shame that Patti and Jonah had decided not to have children. They would have made incredible parents.

She raised her glass. She suddenly looked quite drunk, but for the first time in a long time, she looked—at least to Benny—powerful again. "To resisting!" she shouted.

Everyone else grabbed their glasses. "To resisting!" Then they all shoved back their drinks and slammed them on the table. They grabbed each other's hands, some people crying and some laughing, some wiping away tears and sweat with a friend's knuckles. They didn't know if Benny's discovery could change things or what it meant in that moment or what it meant for the future or if it even mattered. To them, it was something. It was a win. In a series of devastating losses, a tangible victory coming out of the mouth of a friend helped them to pick their resolve up off the floor.

In a different time and space, it could have been everything.

2019, OHIO

It was an unusually hot day when Patti and Jonah loaded their belongings into their new RV. Jonah had arrived with it two days prior and the kids had squealed with joy as they ran in circles around it. Patti and Jonah put only their absolute necessities in the minimal storage spaces, and the kids soaked up the very last moments of their home. Some were using chalk on the driveway, drawing pink castles with green menacing dragons, and some were splashing around with soapy water and pots and pans. Almost every run Elliot went on with Jonah produced more toys—some new and some that needed a lot of fixing, but they took them all anyway. The kids liked to joke that the broken down toys were like the bunch of them and just needed a little love to be right as rain. Their parents didn't care that their lawn looked like a salvage yard or that toys grew in piles along its perimeter—they were leaving it anyway. Each child was permitted to take a toy they could carry in their hands and store in their bed.

Patti had taken in the neighbors' chickens after Susie Jo and Bob had both disappeared in the assignment lines and made eggs every way imaginable. No one ever complained about eating too many eggs or that they didn't like sunny-side up or that they didn't have hot sauce or ketchup. She had been hard boiling eggs for days and was now carefully transporting her loot to the fridge in the camper.

Elliot paused for a moment to count his brothers and sisters. It had become a nervous habit—when he felt like something bad was going to happen again or when things were too good to be true. His eyes held for a minute on Eleanor, and she looked over and smiled.

Jonah had found her on one of their runs only a week ago. Her father had died two weeks earlier, and she had been sitting in the corner of the grocery store four towns over near where the bread was supposed to reside.

When they arrived at the abandoned grocery, Elliot had helped his dad pry the automatic doors open, and he stood outside for a minute, in the dusty, thick air, congratulating himself. Even though Jonah wasn't his biological father, he wished and prayed to look and be just like him when he grew up.

It felt like no one had gone in this particular grocery store in months, maybe even years, and it hadn't been renovated since its heyday in the fifties. The linoleum creaked and cracked under Elliot's growing feet.

The store smelled like rotting meat, and father and son had to pull their shirts up over their noses to mute the stench. They scurried throughout the aisles, bags in hands, gathering whatever canned goods they could. *The nonperishables, Elliot! Always go for the nonperishables!* Jonah always said, even though he had told him so many times before.

Elliot had reached the end of the bread aisle and was examining some high-fructose wraps to see if they could be salvaged when he saw her. She was curled up under a shelf, whimpering. Breathing slowly. Her breath was ragged, and if it wasn't for her wheezing, Elliot wouldn't have noticed her at all. He heard a noise, like the hiss out of a helium balloon, and knelt down on the dusty grocery floor.

"Hello?" He touched the girl's back. She flinched as if he had burned her.

"Hello?" He said again. He knew Jonah would never leave a child alone and afraid. He just had to get her to turn around and take his hand, and he would lead her out of the store and to the rundown car and they would drive, drive, drive to meet the kids, and she would soon be sitting with his unconventional family eating their serum-laced dinners as they packed up the only love they'd ever known in a camper bound for Canada.

But it had not been that easy with Eleanor.

Elliot tried to pull her away from her shelf space, but she clung to some unknown entity between the moldy rye and pumpernickel. He called out for Jonah, but his dad was somewhere else and did not hear him. So he pulled. And she clung. He grabbed her beneath the armpits and yanked as hard as he could, and then she screamed. Jonah came running.

"Dad, she won't come. I think she's stuck. Papa, help me." Elliot looked at this man, his father, and truly believed that he could fix anything.

Jonah knelt down on the dirty floor, crawling up close to the girl. He touched her back gently. She didn't flinch.

"Hello. I'm Jonah. This is Elliot. We just want to help you. We can give you food. Water."

"I have food," she mumbled, pushing her arm out from her hiding place as if to reference the entire store.

"Yes, yes. I see that," Jonah looked at Elliot and shrugged. It was true. She had picked the best place to hide out in the most desperate of all the places in the country.

"But. See. We have a family just a couple towns away. There are lots of kids just like you. Elliot was like you. At least I think he was. Do you want to come out and just talk to us?"

They sat there for a full eighteen minutes. It was an aisle that, in its busiest, had seen the foot traffic of many a housewife who needed to make sandwiches for their too-many kids and toast for their Sunday morning eggs and bacon. Elliot tried to imagine his own mother coming to a store just like this one. He had gone grocery shopping with his mom once or twice, and he felt like he had traveled to a different world altogether. It was one where he could have anything and everything he'd ever wanted and, with his Blow Pop in hand, he had felt like a king.

Finally, slowly, Eleanor came out of her cave. She sat looking at them with a sunken, filthy face. Despite all the resources she had surrounding her, it seemed like she was starving. He wanted Jonah to scoop her up like he had done with the little kids, but she looked tough, like she might scratch him if he did, and Elliot was afraid she'd hurt him.

"What do you want?" She spat at them.

"Hey there. Hey. So, what's your name?" Jonah's voice calmed Elliot's nerves, and he hoped it settled the girl's.

She waited another six minutes. Then, with an exasperated sigh, "It's Eleanor."

"OK. Hello there, Eleanor. As I said, I'm Jonah, and this here is Elliot. We want to help you. We've helped a bunch of children just like you. Will you come with us?"

Elliot thought for sure she would say no, *no way*, because in a normal world a girl her age would never, not ever, go with some strange man and boy. But her current situation was equivalent to a modern-day apocalypse and against all sense and reason she took Jonah's hand. He hoisted her up in his arms, and Elliot lugged their stash from the store.

Just like the rest of them, she fell asleep on the car ride home. It was as if they were lost puppies knowing they had finally found a home. Every bit of fight in her was released, and she just let go.

Elliot watched her as they drove. Her face was pressed against the window, framed with a backdrop of assignment stations and drugged people being loaded up into more vans. He tried to imagine who her family was. He felt he could easily slip on her same-sized shoes and know exactly what she had come from. He wanted to say that he understood, and that he was so so sorry and that she could tell him all about it someday, and that she would learn to love Patti and Jonah and the other kids. He wanted to hold her hand and give it a squeeze like his mother used to do to tell him that everything was going to be OK. But he knew that kids like them didn't believe in reassuring squeezes. Not really.

When they took her home, she didn't speak to anyone for two days. Patti brought her a bowl of dinner each night and sat with her in the corner of her room, hand on her back as she ate up every single bite.

After four days, she laughed a little when one of the little kids did a new dance he had made up. After only five days and what Elliot believed to be the millionth time he asked, she said "yes" in a quiet voice when he asked her if she wanted to play. As he pulled her by the hand to join the other kids, he felt like he had won the biggest trophy in the entire world.

Since that day, Elliot counted seventeen "yeses," each one getting louder and more filled with joy. In that nether land between the Waking World and the Dark Ages, things seemed to happen at a time-lapse speed, and Elliot soon felt like they'd been friends forever.

But on that afternoon two days before they were supposed to leave, he couldn't focus on playing tag. He kept stopping to count and recount. He couldn't help but feel unsettled, like the Earth was spinning in the wrong direction. He was sure the very bad things that had erupted since that momentous day in November were about to find them.

Patti walked down the long dirt road to the mailbox, and Elliot marveled how the sun seemed to follow her stride and make her glow. But as she made her way back to the house, Elliot stopped short and Eleanor crashed into him. Patti had nothing in her arms. She looked like she had lost a child, like she had lost everything. Elliot felt the Earth start spinning a notch faster, and he suddenly felt very dizzy.

Jonah ran over to her as she dropped down to her knees. The children were all frozen in the yard. Tiny statues.

"What? Where is it?" Jonah gathered his wife in his arms.

"It's not here, Jonah. It's really late." She was grabbing at his shirt, looking up at the sky as if to ask a god she did not believe in to help her just this once.

Elliot knew it was the serum. He had heard her whispering to Jonah yesterday, *He would never be late. We can't leave without it. Something's wrong.* To them, it was their lifeblood, the only thing that could save them and the world and keep the Resistance going.

That night, Patti was inconsolable. The large family sat stuffed around the dining table, trying to joke and tell stories or share something that they had learned at Patti's makeshift homeschool. No one mentioned the fact that their dinners were not laced with the potion. But Patti kept looking at each plate as if she could magically make the serum appear.

After dinner, Elliot could hear his parents talking on the porch. He crouched down on the ground and pushed his ear against the screen door.

"What are you doing?" Eleanor asked loudly.

"Shhhhhh!" he hissed at her, violently waving his hand for her to go away.

"Fine, little spy!" she said, giggling and skipping away. Elliot scowled at her, but couldn't help but smile. He pressed his ear against the screen again.

"It's out of our systems by now," Jonah said, staring up at the clouds drifting by. The sun had started to dip behind the horizon. It looked like a dull version of itself, like it had grown tired of watching over this mixed-up world. Patti sat slumped against Jonah's shoulder, her own tired sun. Elliot could see her head give the slightest nod.

"We'll be OK, Patti. Even if we don't get the shipment, we have a sample of each left. It might not be the latest, but it's something."

"We don't even know if someone can help us duplicate it or if it's enough! We should go back east to see if he's alright," Patti said, her voice so high-pitched, it sounded like the animals Elliot sometimes heard late at night.

"You know that's not an option. We don't even know if he's there or if there's a city left to go back to. And you know they'd catch us. It's so much worse there—it's just hitting here! Imagine what they'd do to the kids…"

Jonah's voice faded away as they heard a crunch on the driveway and saw a black town car drive toward them slowly. They stood up quickly, and Elliot could see Patti straighten out her dress.

The car stopped and sat parked near the tree with the old tire swing for what seemed like hours. Patti and Jonah were completely still until, almost in slow motion, Jonah reached over and touched her fingertips.

Elliot wanted to run to them and crawl into Patti's lap, but something told him he shouldn't dare go outside. He moved to the window, allowing only the top half of his eyes to peek over the sill. He couldn't stop shivering on this unusually warm day, and he didn't know why. Finally, two men and a woman got out of the car and began walking slowly toward the house. The boy had felt a great number of things in his short time on Earth including the deepest pain and loss and disgust and anger at the world and fear of what might come next and finally joy with his new family. But never, not ever, had he experienced what he was feeling now. It was a crippling panic that began at the ends of his toes and ended somewhere at the back of his throat. He felt like he could choke on it.

"Yes?" Jonah shouted to the group, and Elliot thought his voice sounded funny. The three people, dressed all in black, looked at each other and laughed a little.

"What do you want?" Patti ventured. But they didn't answer and just kept walking closer.

The visitors stood at the bottom of the step. They seemed to stare down at Elliot's parents even though they were actually gazing up at them.

The woman finally spoke: "Are you Patricia Matthews? And Jonah Matthews?"

Patti looked at Jonah for a long time before she said, "Yes. What do you want?"

The woman smiled. She had shoulder length thick blonde hair, green eyes and red lips. Elliot thought she looked like the villain in the comic book Jonah had found for him on one of their runs. He kept it stashed under his mattress and had read it so many times the ink was worn away, and he could barely make out the words.

"We just want to talk to you. See your lovely home." The woman swept an arm across the house. "Meet your beautiful family. We've heard it's grown."

Jonah put his arm around Patti protectively. For a moment, there was a standoff.

"Well then!" The woman clapped her hands. "Won't you invite us in?" She had a hint of an accent, but Elliot had met very few people from other countries and had no idea where it was from. The two men took a step forward, and when Patti and Jonah didn't move, the group clomped up the stairs and pushed past them.

Elliot bolted up from the ground and ran to the room the boys all shared. His brothers and sisters were crowded in there playing board games that Jonah had found from a shutdown toy store in town. The boy stood in the doorway for half a minute, allowing himself only this short amount of time to take them all in. He loved how they wanted to be together all the time, no matter what, and how they always played games by the rules, and how they somehow never fought. When he was little, he had told himself that he never wanted brothers and sisters because they would steal his stuff and pull his hair. Now he couldn't imagine life as an only child—they were everything to him.

Eleanor noticed him standing there. Sweat was dripping in an unsteady rain down his forehead and temples. It felt cold against his skin. "What's wrong?" she asked.

Elliot squeezed into the room and closed the door behind him. "There are people here. Bad people, I think." He couldn't stop shaking.

The bigger kids instinctively put the little ones behind them, forming a human wall. Then they crawled toward the door and pressed their ears against it. The woman was talking again.

"Mmmm. Dinner smells good. Shall we call the children for suppertime?" Elliot could hear the woman's boots clicking on the old wood floors as she paced around the kitchen.

"Russian," Eleanor said.

"What?" Elliot whispered back.

"That woman is Russian. My Grandma was Russian."

70

Patti was trying to stall the inevitable. "Let's just give them a couple more minutes to play."

The woman's tone changed sharply. "Call them. Now."

"Kids! Can you please come out here?" Jonah's voice was muffled through the bedroom door. Even though they were terrified, the kids got in line as they'd been taught to do and filed out to the kitchen.

Now that Elliot could see the woman up close, he noted that her skin was flawless, almost eerily so. She had no expression in her eyes, and if he had to guess just by looking at them, he would have said she was a robot. Or an evil witch who had come back from the afterlife. He waded in his fantasies as they all found their places at the table, if only to escape even a little bit of what was about to happen. His throat grew so tight, it felt like someone was stitching it together.

The woman clapped her hands, and the children all jumped.

"Now, children. Please sit down at the table." And they all did.

"It has come to my attention that your pretend mommy and daddy have been breaking the law. Did you know that?" She pointed at Sammy, who was only four and a half, and he shook his head quickly, sticking a set of chubby fingers in his mouth. Patti had just broken him of the habit a week earlier, but obviously none of that mattered now.

"It's true. It's true," the woman continued. "But we don't let traitors break the law. We don't let traitors do whatever they want. Your parents have been doing whatever they want. They are part of the Resistance, and the Resistance must be punished. Because otherwise there would be no order! There would be chaos!" She started to laugh hysterically, and Elliot's shaking resumed. Two of the little children began crying quietly. Lucia started pulling her hair out in long black strands. Eleanor was sitting across the table from Elliot stone faced, without even a hint of an expression. He believed that this woman could have said anything, and Eleanor wouldn't have flinched. He was proud of her, and it was his biggest regret that he didn't tell her exactly that.

"These criminals," the woman pointed to Patti and Jonah, "Tricked our government forces. They somehow escaped the big city before the lockdown. Imagine that?" She patted Max's head, but he didn't move.

71

"Running through the city like rats and getting out just as the tunnels shut down. Now they've been running from the law and coming here pretending they were as virtuous as the Reverend," she waved her hand up to the sky as if to refer to Patti's late father. "They even scored themselves military badges! Well, this disgusting family may have gotten away with the worst case of treason I've seen. But today that changes. Otto!"

One of the men, who Elliot now realized was standing perfectly still at attention, quickly saluted his boss and then reached into a leather bag to pull out a large bottle of pills. Elliot had seen pills like these hundreds of times when he and Jonah had visited the neighboring towns and on the way to the foster homes he wanted to forget and on the countertop of the bathroom of the apartment where he lived with his mother in the slums of West Virginia. They were his mom's breakfast in the morning, her snack, her lunch. They were what sent her to the other world that didn't include him, and they were what kept her from tipping back the other way for fear of the violent detox that would rip her into two bloodied halves. "The comedown," she had said to him once, as if it was a place, "I can't go to the comedown. I can't go near that shit. Not ever."

But Elliot knew that the pills in Otto's hands were even worse. If such a thing was possible.

"Two each," the woman commanded Otto, and he carefully placed, with gloved fingers, two pills in front of each child. He filled ten glasses halfway with water from the faucet, and no one told him that the water had been compromised by a local processing plant and that it had to be filtered before drinking and that even then it was probably not safe. It seemed to take an eternity for Otto to fill the glasses with toxic water and hand one to each child and finally to their parents. When all of the pieces of this cruel game were in place, the woman called out to the other man.

"Abraham!" The woman clapped her hands and with that one gesture, the other man reached into a holster and pulled out his gun, aiming it at Jonah's head. Some of the children began screaming.

"Now, now. There is no reason to be hysterical," the woman said to a group of children who didn't deserve to see even one more horrible thing. "Quiet or he's dead!"

The screaming was reduced to whimpering.

"Here is the deal. You eat the pills, and we don't shoot your daddy. You don't eat the pills, we shoot him. Then we'll probably shoot mommy, too. Understand?"

Some of the kids started gobbling the pills up before she even finished her sentence, and Patti shouted, "No!" which was met with a gun to the head from Otto.

Elliot looked from the table to Jonah to Patti and back to the pills. He ate them quickly, gulping them down with water.

"Now you two," the woman handed Patti and Jonah three pills each and, looking into each other's eyes, they swallowed them quickly.

The children slumped over almost instantly or stared out at an imaginary sky. Patti and Jonah slid down onto the floor. Patti tried to grab for Jonah's hand on the way down, but it slipped out of her grasp. Everything they had ever believed in melted away in a matter of moments with a handful of pills, and Elliot felt almost happy for them because now they were free. They didn't have to keep running or saving lost children like him. They didn't have to load any more supplies into the RV or worry that the serum hadn't arrived. The salvation of the country did not rest on their shoulders; they did not have to race the cure to Canada before it was too late. They could join the rest of them who had abandoned all their worries.

Eleanor was staring at something just past Elliot's right ear, her head tilted to the side. He wondered what she could see now. A smile that he had never noticed before danced on her lips, and he sighed. She looked content. One of the youngest kids started convulsing, and Otto quickly put something in her nose, which made her body quiet down. Soon she was snoring.

Elliot looked around at the only real family he had ever known. He wanted to run to his parents and shake Jonah awake or crawl into Patti's lap and tell her to stroke his hair. He wanted to tap Eleanor's shoulder and shout "You're it!" and run away giggling as she toppled over a chair to chase him out of the house and into the joyful graveyard of adopted toys. He wanted to scoop the little ones into his arms as he had seen Jonah do so many times and run with them down the dirt road to the place where the grey sun hid behind the rotting Earth. But instead, he shouted.

"Why are you doing this?"

The woman turned to look at him, her flawless face attempting an

73

expression of surprise. She knelt down so she could look directly into his eyes. She spoke softly.

"You don't feel anything?" She asked it almost maternally, as if she was a concerned mama, and he considered reaching out to touch her face to see if it was real.

He looked at her for a long time, not knowing what to say and not wanting to tell his darkest secret to someone so evil. He wished he could run over to Patti and wake her up to tell her first, but he knew that once someone took a dose of those pills, there was no returning. Finally, he just shook his head.

She threw her head back and laughed; he could see her chest heaving with glee and menace and all the things in between. The two men were standing back at attention and did not crack a smile. When she had gotten her fill, gathering all of his pain and gobbling it up like it was her favorite meal at a fancy restaurant, she reached over and grabbed his hand.

"We are doing this because people decided to resist our great leader. Millions of people. Do you think it's easy to control millions of people who are sad and angry and want to hurt our noble and honorable Dictator?"

Elliot shook his head again. Her hair was the color of butter. Her face looked like it was made out of marble.

"You're right. It wasn't at first. We had to put people like your mommy and daddy into jail just to get them to stop shouting and stomping their feet in the streets and saying their crazy talk all over the Internet. We had to pack up all the people who decided they could just come here and cross over our borders and take our jobs and hurt our people. We had to send them back to their own filthy countries or put them in a special prison of their own. None of the stupid crybaby Resistance believed how good it could really be if they just let go. So we had to show them in our own way. Just look." She gestured around the table at the children who were sleeping with their eyes open, finally stopping to point at Patti and Jonah. "They don't have a worry left inside of them."

"Wouldn't that be divine, little...Elliot is it? Elliot with the junkie mom who left him in a poor person store all alone. The one that had to travel across so many states just to find some stupid souls who would love you? Tell me, Elliot. Why is it that you are still awake when all your brothers and sisters are drifting along in dreamland?"

"I don't know," Elliot told her. He didn't.

She stood up slowly and tousled his head.

"Otto!" she shouted, and her soldier turned to face her, saluting her with his right arm outstretched.

"The boy is coming with us. Let us go. The Dictator will be very interested to meet him."

Strong arms plucked Elliot from his chair as he kicked and screamed and tried to bite at their heavily cloaked limbs. They muzzled and restrained him, walking with him down the long drive and shoving him in the back of the town car.

He watched as they drove away from the only real home he had ever known, from the only parents who had ever really cared about what happened to him tomorrow and the day after that. The RV became smaller and smaller, as did his fleeting chances of escaping across the border to a better life. Once again, he was staring out of a car window, watching the sleeping world pass him by. But this time, he was sitting next to the devil's helper. Driving into the depths of hell.

RIGHT HERE. RIGHT NOW.

Hi. This is the author. If you're terrified and feel like the world is close to ending every single day and scared that what you've always believed to be your human rights are being taken away and that the Earth is being robbed of its oxygen and that our children's futures are being sacrificed, take a deep breath. We are still here. We are still fighting. We are still awake.

2031, PORTLAND, MAINE

Elena rode home on the super speed rail as it wove through the streets that had once been alive with commerce and fishermen pulling in that day's catch and people spilling into the streets waiting for a table at one of the city's renowned restaurants. She found comfort in the ragdoll-like quality of her body as the train pushed its way to the edge of the city without so much as a bump or a wobble. It was like gliding through grey matter.

She was still raw from the rape, but enjoyed a brief escape on the train, something that she now found familiar and expected. Even though it was barely so, she was grateful that she was still alive. Sunken into the bucket-like seats, she let herself be engulfed in the only part of her day that gave her access to modernity. She drank it in and fantasized about what could have been had they not taken everything away. She thought about what it was like in the Republic and what kind of modern conveniences they enjoyed. She wondered if they were all robots. If they ate real food or rode on unicorns over diamond-crusted bridges. For her six-minute ride every day, she allowed herself to indulge in the what-ifs of her damaged world. That day's focus was on the waste of talent, the engineers, scientists, musicians, artists, teachers, technicians, craftspeople. The great minds, the minds that could have had one unbelievable thought that changed the trajectory of medicine or space travel or life as they all knew it. She thought about their brains now, an army of walking mush. The government had taken what could have been and turned it into a pile of oatmeal, all in the name of making sure everyone stood on the same side of an imaginary line. She wondered if the second Dictator and his cabinet had any inkling that people like her still existed. It was one more thing to fantasize about, but it would have to wait until tomorrow because the ride was always too short.

They pulled up to her housing complex and a buzzer sounded, signaling them to get off the train. A group of sleepers stumbled down the stairs together and made their way to the entrance. Some of the sleepers got confused for a minute and turned around to climb back onto the train, but the guards moved them along with their assault rifles. Elena cringed inside as she remembered *that one time* when four of the sleepers had been sprayed with bullets because one of the guards unknowingly had his finger in the wrong place at the very wrong time.

They were all herded through a long corridor and sent to a counter to get the last of their three meals of the day. The guards called the food "gravel," mocking it. It was nothing more than a thick protein shake that was nearly impossible to choke down because of its chalky, gritty texture. Elena had seen the guards dare each other to drink it and come up choking after only a couple of slips.

"You sleepers stupid or something?" one guard shouted at a man who was quickly sucking down his gravel shake. "Them things taste like shit!" The guards laughed, pushing the man over and sending him flying into a pile of dirty cups.

Gravel was one of the thousand reasons Elena wished she wasn't immune to the pills. How blissful it would be to sleep through the gravelly sludge that made her feel like she wanted to gag and threatened to give her away every single time she had to eat.

When Elena drank the shakes, she always thought about her mother and the mission to defeat the regime, to destroy it and make everyone associated with it pay dearly for what they had done to the people they had promised to protect. She loosened the muscles in the back of her throat in the name of the Resistance and slugged it down. She knew it was all she would get until morning; she knew she needed it to stay alive; she knew she owed it to her mother—what she had started and was never able to finish.

They slowly moved in a jagged line toward the cleaning room, a human car wash. They were sanitized from head to toe through their clothes, wiping away any trace of sweat or factory dirt or polluted air that tried desperately to climb into their pores each day.

After cleaning, the sleepers were encouraged to watch a screen in the common room for a couple of hours or go out into the courtyard until bedtime. Most of them sat slumped in hard plastic chairs, but a couple of sleepers stared at the screen, possibly absorbing some of what was being said. Sometimes, one or two people started coming down before their nighttime dose, and the guards rushed to them with a paper cup of pills, which they grabbed at more hungrily than any meal. Elena cringed as she carefully watched them gnash their medicine down with their tongues, their throats, their everything. The opiates had been intensified in such a way that the comedown was like free falling through a thornbush. It was like dying again and again. Violently. One cell at a time. The only solution was to take more. It was always available, always at the ready, and it seemed to be in such abundance, Elena was sure that when the human race finally ended, they would all be buried in a surplus of white pills.

It was this day in particular that she sat in a green plastic chair, the color of puke, the color of her mother's puke when she was coming down from the drugs they had given her in prison. It was the color of the bile her father had cleaned up off their hand-woven area rug, until he finally decided that he wouldn't let her reach that point again. He made sure she had every single pill exactly when she needed them so she would never feel the dreaded sickness ever again. The chairs were the same color as the ones they had sat in on those twenty-two visits, twenty-one of which were not visits to her mom at all, but rather visits to a shell of her mom. Elena despised the color, but she sat in the chair anyway because her feet burned from standing all day, and her dignity was roughed up from her forced meeting with Darren.

One of Dictator Two's latest propaganda videos was on the screen. How he was helping the poor and the sick and the needy just as his father-in-law had done for twelve years. How he had taken everyone's pain and anger away. The video cut to the floor of a pill manufacturer where the Dictator stood with a hard hat on. Millions of pills just like the ones Elena had been forced to eat for so many years made their way down the assembly line as high-functioning sleepers pressed buttons and pulled levers.

The Dictator plucked a pill from off camera and held it up, looking her right in the eye and saying, "This country was full of pain and anger. Some people wanted to fight the great progress we were making across the nation. But we've changed all that. We've given our citizens a reason to smile again." He grinned as his beautiful blonde wife and children joined him on screen. The stream froze, but Elena knew it would start up again in a couple of minutes. She stared at the Dictator's flawless wife. Tall, thin and wearing all red, she was smiling, but her eyes gave her away—she was looking out into the universe as if she wanted to escape.

Elena almost felt bad for her, but then caught herself. This woman had been an advisor to the Republic when her father was in office, and now that her husband was Dictator, she was even more of an accomplice. She was as evil as the rest of them, if only by proxy.

The video started up and repeated over and over again for almost an hour until the buzzer sounded. The sleepers all stood up in unison and sauntered toward their sleeping quarters. They had been reduced to Pavlov's dogs, and Elena was careful to appear just like them.

A guard pushed Elena into her pod, and she almost winced. Her hip was bruised from Darren banging her into the floor, but it was the least critical of her wounds. As she crawled into the bed, she remembered her beautiful childhood bedroom with its flannel sheets and whimsical wallpaper. She could close her eyes and feel her favorite stuffed animal nuzzled up against her face and her mother's strong arms around her as she sang her daughter to sleep, the beautiful sights inspired by sound dancing around them.

Once Elena was tucked in her pod like a salty canned fish, she began the task of reaching down to retrieve the data stick. It took an excruciating forty-three minutes until her fingertips made contact with the edge of it. She slowly pulled it up to her face, holding it two inches away from her nose. She begged her eyes to adjust and like trained puppies, they finally listened.

It had the emblem of the Republic on it, but it didn't give her much more information without plugging it into something. She turned it around and around, looking for a clue, but there was nothing. Sighing, she began the slow and arduous task of sliding it back into the lip of her boot.

She knew that data stick held secrets that could help them, but she had no idea what they could be. Her fantasies tumbled on top of each other as she tried to guess what it would tell her until she finally fell into a deep, dark, dreamless sleep.

2030, THE REPUBLIC
(FORMERLY WASHINGTON D.C. AND ITS SURROUNDING AREAS)

Savannah sat in a cream colored chair in the gold plated office, watching her husband scream into the phone, then throw it against the wall. It hit a small glass bird that she had presented to her father when he had taken office, and she watched as it fell to the ground and shattered. She remembered handing it to her father after his inauguration speech, kissing him lightly on the cheek and almost fumbling as she gave it to him. How devastated she would have been if she had dropped it that day! But today she didn't flinch as it exploded into tiny pieces. She sat perfectly still as her secret service agent, David, spoke into his sleeve and a housekeeper instantly appeared to clean up the mess. Savannah had experienced fourteen years of fumbles and screaming and throwing and unruly behavior from two Dictators: her father and her husband. Thousands of things she thought she cared about had been shattered.

When it all began, she was given a seat at the table and a loud, clear voice and a purpose. She took the power in her manicured fingers and tried it on, holding it high above her head like a deserved trophy, letting it wrap around her slim neck like a medal of honor. She dressed the part and played her designated role of President's daughter. With every closed door meeting, she grew hungry for more.

But that was in the beginning. In the Waking Years, she really believed that her father was going to make a difference and save the country. She had been to almost all of his rallies and had watched his spirit overtake his followers. They blindly believed every word he was saying even though she knew in her heart that most of it wasn't true or even possible. Their daily existence had become so difficult and hopeless; she didn't blame them when they abandoned all reason simply because they needed something to believe in.

She was quite possibly one of the most privileged women in the country, and even she had needed something.

With each passing year, her conscience grew. It went to war with her inflated ego, which had become puffy from overuse like an overstuffed chair. Soon it became more powerful than herself; it haunted her as she watched in horror what was happening to people across the country and even people she knew and loved. She tried to talk to her father, catching him late at night in the Oval Office, trying to get him alone, but his Chief

Strategist rarely left his side. She tried every angle she could think of to get him to see reason or even just look her in the eye and tell her the truth about his plans for the country. But he couldn't. The person she'd known as her father had disappeared. Slowly, she started shutting down, keeping her mouth shut, staying out of it, retreating to her room. She knew the Dictator didn't care if she was kin. Not really. If she was seen as part of the Resistance, she would be drugged and ostracized like the rest of the drones she had seen in the factories. She couldn't imagine herself there, yet she had nightmares about it all the time.

She spent nearly every day for the past fourteen years sitting in her fancy rooms, eating her fancy meals made out of synthetic materials that had been formulated to mimic steak dinners or kale salads. Nothing was real anymore because nothing could grow. Most of the animals were extinct except for a small lot of pets they grew in petri dishes, customized to the customer's liking. Pink curly haired micropoodles. Black and white sloths so small they could ride on your thumb. They had tried to grow livestock, but the process was slow and the meat tasted like cleaning fluid. So they crafted all of the food out of chemical compounds that were artificially flavored and preserved to last until the end of time. Despite her early protests during her father's first term, he and his party had plunged ahead and destroyed the dirt and the water and the crops and the weather and the air and the earth. Her world was grey smog. Barren trees. Sandy, gritty grounds. Desperate wastelands. Gold plated rooms.

Lifeless skyscrapers, as far as the eye could see.

Since that day with the Japanese dignitaries, she had swiftly become nothing more than a trophy wife—a pretty thing to sit in straight-backed chairs—and she had to make sure she didn't look a day over thirty-five, even though she was now forty-nine. It didn't matter that her husband never even glanced in her direction anyway. Or that her now grown children never even bothered to talk to her or visit her or show her affection or love. They lived in the Republic in their own penthouses not far from their parents, and she was lucky if she saw them once a month. When she did, it was usually because they had a ridiculous request, like needing to hire another servant to file their toenails, and she wanted to scream at them, "Do you even know how the rest of the country is living? Do you understand what spoiled helpless brats you've become?" But instead she smiled and nodded as their father granted every wish and whim. She winced at her children's behavior as she compared their lives to that of the factory workers. Then she spent hours sitting in her room, guilty that she was sickened by her own kids and sometimes even jealous of her two sons because she realized a long time ago that they had more power than she did. They were the successors. They were in line to be the next Dictator.

Her husband had been planning the nation's annual event: a conference where the elite from across the Republic could plan the upcoming year. She had been to twelve of these events over the years and each was more grotesque than the last. There was so much food piled high on banquet-style tables, and it mocked the people who had been put to sleep long ago. It even taunted the militia who made up most of the lower middle class, and who were forced to work an ungodly amount of hours. They ate the leftovers that trickled down from the Republic, food Savannah would not even feed her synthetic pets, but they didn't know any better. When her father was elected president, they had been the working class. The forgotten people. They had believed with their rusty hearts that her father, their new fearless leader who said and did anything he wanted, was going to change everything and fill their pockets full of hope. But his followers were wrong: he was using them to build an army of loyalists, and the most unfathomable part was that they still, to this very day, didn't know they had been duped. They saw what happened to the Resistance or anyone who chose to speak even a whispered word in opposition, and they decided to believe that their new life under the Dictator was infinitely better than the life of a sleeper. They were content to drink their rancid ale and eat the scraps the elite turned away.

Her father had made sure every member of the Resistance, anyone who stood their ground on the Senate floor were taken care of. He made sure to target the press and most of the Democratic Party and celebrities, and soon any opposition who hadn't been "put to sleep" went into hiding or started pretending they were on his side after all. But he found them anyway. He found them all. He found their children and put them to sleep too.

Savannah and her family had moved to California a year after her father had taken office in an effort to overtake the screaming liberals. When they first arrived, it seemed like an impossible task. Most of the state was "infected" as her father called it, but in the end they succeeded. To Savannah, it was the only fond moment she had looking back on her life in politics. When they lived on the west coast, they were free from her father and his tantrums. Her husband's love and affection returned, and together they basked in the warm California sunshine and the sweet thrill of a job well done. But even that was a charade, and the moments of joy she had working side-by-side with her husband as her children played on the beach with their nannies were plagued with the fact that she had helped overtake an entire coast. She had put people like her, with partners and families and jobs and daily routines, to sleep. She was reminded of it every time the west coast headquarters gave reports to the east. The two government hubs existed as bookends for the web of factories that dotted the middle of the country like an ever-growing cancer.

On year three, they had shuttered all communication with the outside world. Savannah didn't know for sure if it was a purposeful pursuit to put their country in isolation or if all of her father's outbursts had simply disconnected them. *They don't want to hear the truth!* He once yelled at his cabinet, and no one knew what to say. Then his Chief Strategist had leaned down to whisper in his ear, and his face grew into the most detestable smile.

She still remembered that smile; it haunted her nightmares, making her sweat through the sheets and call out for her mother. In the beginning, her husband would place a calming hand on her shoulder or gather her in his arms, but as her father and Chief slowly ripped J.J. away from her, he stopped reaching over to comfort her and soon slept in a different room altogether.

Savannah missed traveling. From her perch in her iron castle she longed for other pockets of the world. For all she knew, there were still green pastures rolling through the hills of Ireland or grand piazzas connecting the streets of Rome. She had not left the country in twelve years and woke up each day wondering if this was the day they would be attacked. Every night she went to bed both relieved and disappointed that they had been spared, only to get up the next morning to start over again.

She knew that if a bomb or something worse didn't end it all, she would be on this decaying Earth for forty or fifty or even sixty more years because people like her were granted youth and life and permanence for what seemed like forever.

It was exhausting. It was terrifying. For all she knew, there was no one else beyond their borders at all.

She had gone on the factory tours in the outskirts of the Republic and had even visited some throughout the country when her father was still in power, wearing a hard hat atop her long blonde hair, careful not to snag her heel on a wire or an uneven board.

A scream sat at the very back of her throat as she'd watched the workers, laughingly called sleepers by the militia, push buttons and pull levers. She thought about what their lives could have been like, and it brought back painful memories of her best friend. Deanna opposed Savannah's father taking office, but over lunch one winter day in New York City, they had held hands across a three-hundred-dollar meal and vowed to remain friends no matter what happened.

Savannah knew her friend had joined the protests that were erupting across the country, and had heard of her arrest. She pleaded with her father to help with Deanna's release, but at that point, he had become too resolved to accept anyone or anything that opposed him. He refused her again and again. It was one of the first of many unreasonable refusals that slowly tore her apart.

The moment she heard that Deanna had been released from prison, she called her right away.

"Yes? What the fuck do you want?" It was Deanna's husband.

"Christopher. Hey. It's me, Savannah." She knew her voice sounded shaky, and she felt a hand of despair grab hold of her throat, making her croak out the words.

"Oh, I know who it is. How dare you call my wife, you bitch."

"What? Chris, it's me." Savannah had been a bridesmaid in their wedding and was one of the first people to hold their daughter when she was born. She had stayed at their home more times than she cared to remember after late nights of too much wine and had vacationed with them every summer in the Hamptons. She considered them family. They were her family...

"You knew what he was doing. You and your evil father want to rule the world, huh? Oh, and your squirrely husband. What a joke you are, Savannah. What a stupid, lying joke." Chris was screaming into the phone, and she recoiled as if she had been hit with his spit.

"My father? J.J.? I have nothing to do with..."

"You knew it! You did this!" Chris yelled and hung up.

She ran to her car, tears spilling down her cheeks, her hands shaking as she pulled her keys out of her purse. David and another secret service agent sprinted behind her as she hopped into the driver's seat and sped away. They dared to keep up with her through downtown Manhattan traffic and over the bridge. She swiped angrily at her tears, only caring a little if mascara had run down her cheeks. Her car screeched to a stop on the most picturesque street in Cobble Hill as she parked illegally in front of Deanna's brownstone. She threw her keys to David who had pulled up right behind her. Then she ran up the twenty-three concrete stairs in four-inch bright red heels, breathing heavily as she reached the top. Despite her panic, she knocked gently on the door. It opened almost instantly.

"Oh. Hello, Ms. Savannah." It was the housekeeper whom Savannah had met hundreds of times but only bothered to notice in that very moment. She felt a horrible guilt creep up her long legs because she knew this woman would not stay in the country long under her father's latest executive order. The guilt and shame and panic grew as the housekeeper, whose name escaped her, led her into her friend's most perfectly decorated home.

Deanna, the Ivy League graduate, the always beautifully manicured mother of two was sitting slumped in a chair, a small river of foam drifting out of the corner of her mouth. Savannah had always seen her friend in complete control, never a hair out of place. Three days after she gave birth, Savannah saw her in spin class, putting the rest of the riders to shame. She was never without flawless makeup, and her hair and style were always four steps ahead of the rest of the world. It was so alarming to see her like this, Savannah was left speechless.

She knelt down next to Deanna and put her friend's hand against her cheek.

"D? It's me, Van. I'm here now. Are you there?" She knew she was squeezing the limp hand too hard, but she didn't care. Deanna didn't respond except for gurgling.

The housekeeper walked in with a glass of water and two white pills in her hand.

"Excuse me, it's time for Ms. Deanna's dose," the housekeeper announced. She said it almost in a singsong voice as if it was perfectly normal that her boss was lying there like one of the beautiful decorative pillows.

"Dose?" Savannah asked the question quietly, but she knew exactly what had happened to her friend. She had heard rumblings during her last visit to Washington, and Chief had been walking around with a perpetual evil glint in his eye.

"Yes, the dose they give her in prison, Ms. Savannah," the housekeeper said. She handed Deanna her pills, and she greedily gobbled them up, foregoing the water. The housekeeper turned to look Savannah in the eye.

"You know exactly what happening here, Ms. Savannah. You not a stupid girl." The singsong was gone, and her voice had lowered an octave.

"Just remember when you go back to that fancy life of yours. Your family did this to Ms. Deanna. You did." The housekeeper pulled the blanket up to Deanna's shoulders.

Rose. That was the housekeeper's name. Rose.

"Rose!" Savannah called out. She stopped in the doorway.

"Yes, Ms. Savannah?"

"Can anything be done to help her? What can I do?"

Rose chuckled a little, and it made Savannah feel five years old. "Do something? You ask your powerful papa what to do. If they find cure to the worst addiction I ever seen so these poor people don't feel like dying without their pills, then that's something."

Savannah stood up, looking at her perfect friend and the perfect Cobble Hill home. She shakily kissed Deanna on the hand and ran out to the street to the waiting secret service car, dialing her father's line with clumsy fingers. She didn't notice that her car was still parked sideways or that the other agent had jumped behind the wheel to follow them.

"Deanna has been taken!" she screamed into the phone as soon as her father answered. It was a special phone line shared between just the two of them. In her entire life, he had never not picked up.

"Taken?" he laughed a bit. "What do you mean, darling?" She could hear someone in the background asking who was on the phone. She knew it was Chief. He was never more than three feet from her father.

"She went to prison and now she's a zombie," Savannah spat. "Tell Chief it's none of his business who it is! Why is he always in our lives?"

He laughed again. "I'm quite sure she just had too much to drink. And you know Chief just wants to make this country great. Just like we do. And it's already better. It's just fantastic what we're doing. Just fantastic. This is what we've always wanted. Everyone wanted this. All the people. Everyone. I have to run to a meeting, my dear. Please come back to Washington. I think your little holiday has gone on long enough. That Deanna was just a spoiled brat anyway. Always has been. What?" Savannah could hear him talking to someone. "OK, then. I really have to go. We'll talk." The phone went silent.

"Dad!" she screamed. David didn't flinch or turn around and scold her for distracting him. She sounded and felt like a tantruming child, and she suddenly wished he would veer off the bridge so they could meet their watery destiny.

She never went to see Deanna again and three weeks later, she heard from a post online that her friend had overdosed. On the day of the funeral, J.J. found Savannah curled up under their organic cotton sheets. He sat down next to her and put a hand on her hip.

"Don't you want to go to say goodbye? It would be a gesture to her family. Maybe Christopher would talk to you. Maybe you could reconnect with your friends. You haven't talked to anyone in ages." She was grateful that her husband cared about how she felt, but she wasn't sure he believed her story about the visit. He had brushed it off, laughing a little, saying how Deanna always "overdid it." He didn't agree that her father was some evil man behind a curtain slowly drugging anyone who got in his way.

"Van, Deanna did this to herself. I never thought she was happy with Chris. That guy was always kind of an asshole."

She turned to look at her husband angrily. "Deanna would never do this to herself!"

"OK, OK. I just think it's ridiculous to think this is some kind of government conspiracy. I still think you should go." He put a finger under her chin and forced her to look up at him.

"I can't," She said, burying her face again in the down pillows. "You don't know how he talked to me. Not to mention all our friends will probably never speak to me again because they know it was Dad who did this to her."

"Like I said, no one forced the pills down her throat, Van." He took her hand and placed it on his knee.

"He might as well have. He gave the order. Or Chief did. It doesn't matter anymore, I can't go. I just want to get to Washington as soon as possible and start over."

J.J. got up and walked out of the room shaking his head.

She had sat in bed for the rest of the day and held a scarf that Deanna had given her for her thirtieth birthday, running it through her hands and trying to remember her friend's smile and her other housekeeper's name.

That day seemed like ages ago, and it felt like it had happened to someone else entirely. After watching the world get torn down to nothing and losing everyone she loved (either by way of mind or body or both), it was like someone had tipped her over, and out from her beautiful blonde head, every bit of substance had been emptied.

She felt someone touch her arm, and she leapt out of her daydream. It was her aide.

"Sorry, Sarah. I was deep in thought." Savannah placed one hand on her heart as if to steady its beat.

"So sorry to disturb you, Ms. Savannah. I thought you might like your dinner now." Sarah lowered her eyes so that they were poised on the tips of Savannah's shoes.

"Oh. Right. Yes, I will eat now, I suppose." Savannah let her aide lead her down a long hallway to a glass elevator, David just a couple of steps behind. Sarah pushed a button with a thin finger, and it rocketed them up to the ninety-seventh floor. The doors opened to a grand dining room with a twenty-person table. At one end, a beautiful meal and a giant glass of wine had been placed. Savannah sat down, just her alone, and turned to look at Sarah and David who were standing next to her like statues.

"Sarah. If you don't mind, I'd like to be alone tonight." She felt terrible saying this to her aide who had become her friend—her only friend—in this new world. "David, you too."

Sarah opened her eyes wide and looked up at David. They shared a brief look of concern. Savannah knew that she was not supposed to be left alone under any circumstance, except when sleeping or showering, but even then David stood guard outside her door, and Sarah sat on a small stool outside the bathroom in case Ms. Savannah needed anything. She also knew that the two of them were more loyal to her than anyone in the world. Savannah had saved Sarah's life, and David had helped show Savannah the path to righteousness. It was the one redemption in the sea of havoc her father and now her husband had created. She watched now as her trusted servants bowed deeply, then walked quickly through the heavy doors, shutting them with barely a sound.

The Dictator's beautiful wife bowed her lovely head and started to cry. From deep inside her abdomen, she felt a sob rise up, and she stifled it with her perfect red lips. She cried for Deanna, for the factory workers, for her children who had been turned against her and thought her a stupid, helpless woman and whose world had been stolen from them. For what could have been in the country she had embraced with gloved hands during her younger years. She cried for all that she could have become—she was smart and focused and more than a trophy, so much more, and yet she meant nothing to anyone except for when someone required a glued-on smile and robotic wave. She had been humiliated beyond repair in front of people who mattered to her; she had become a pageant queen, a disgrace. She represented one of the most hateful regimes the world had ever known, and she could do absolutely nothing to control it. She was ashamed.

She pressed her forehead against the edge of the wood table. "Reclaimed" wood, it would have been called before everything started to become serious and horrible and desperate for all but a large handful of the Dictator's elite followers. But just as she felt the sharp pain of wood cut into her flesh, she felt the smallest buzz in the recesses of her breasts.

Then Savannah, daughter of Dictator One, wife of Dictator Two, tears frozen on high cheekbones, reached down slowly for the slim device tucked deep between her cleavage. She pulled it out and looked at the tiny screen. It was rapidly translating the Morse code into words, stumbling across in slow dribbles, then bursts of news that sent a glorious shiver down her spine.

For the first time in what felt like decades, Savannah smiled. Finally, she started to feel just the slightest bit alive. She hoped and believed in her still-shallow heart that maybe, possibly, slowly, things could change.

2019, THE NEW REPUBLIC

The black town car sped along potholed roads for about an hour until it reached a small abandoned airport. Large rusted planes were scattered across the tarmac as if they were standing in line for the scrapyard. A private jet waited at the start of the runway, a silver tube of possibility against a dull blue-green sky. They wove in between the stand-still planes, and if it hadn't been so frightening and depressing, it would have felt like one of Elliot's video games.

Elliot had never been in an airplane, and the thought thrilled him. It was at odds with the agony he'd felt watching the agents harm his family, but he couldn't help himself. He had just revealed his secret to the only people he needed to keep it from, and he was going on a plane most likely to be put in a prison or even tortured to death. It made him feel free. He had nothing to hide anymore. He could finally stop running.

They boarded the plane and sat him down in the softest seat imaginable. A man in a tuxedo placed a meal that had only existed in his most absurd dreams in front of him, and he could have survived for weeks on the smell of it alone. He stared at it in shock and thought about Patti and Jonah and his brothers and sisters whom he had grown to love more than anyone despite only knowing them for a schmear in time and despite all his distrust in the world. He thought about them sitting around the table staring at a sun that did not exist, and how by now they would have started to come down, but maybe one of them would have noticed the enormous bottle of pills left on the table (one of ten bottles left behind) and hungrily grabbed for it, not able to unscrew it fast enough and someone else might have become frustrated and shoved a sibling aside. Because they could not wait to get the pills in their mouths because they were already beginning to feel the alternative, the dreaded comedown, the repercussion for being free-thinking or associated with the opposition or weak or inhabited by the devil like his mama.

"Eat," the woman said, startling him. "A child like you doesn't know when his next meal might be placed before him. Does he?"

He shook his head and looked at her divine hair and skin and nails and clothing, and then, like a rabid animal, he began to eat. It was the best dish he had ever eaten in his life. The flavors exploded in his mouth, and he almost didn't know what to do or how to act because it was so incredible. He ate it as fast as he could because he had never been taught how to savor something.

After cleaning his plate, he looked up in surprise as another identical plate was placed in front of him. He ate that one faster than the first, not caring that sauce was splattering all over him or that he might experience a stomachache from eating so much after years of eating so little. It didn't matter. When he closed his eyes at night as an adult in his cramped sleeping pod with its metal walls, he could still taste that meal. He never ate anything like it since, and he was positive that he never would again.

With the rich taste still skipping around on his lips, the plane took off, and his guts jumped for joy. He sat glued to the window watching the Earth pass by beneath him. He was flying. *Flying*. Humans could fly in a giant metal bird in the sky. There weren't pill stations in the clouds or suffering in the atmosphere. He was humbled and shattered by the magnitude of it all. He could not turn away from that small window for fear that the whole experience would evaporate into a cruel mirage, and he sat as still as he could with his nose pressed hard against the glass.

When he looked back at that collection of moments, he sometimes wished he had died right then and there. Having known a family who loved him, having flown miles above everything he'd wanted to forget and leave behind. How grateful he would have been to crash down down down and explode into a burst of happiness before things got so much worse.

The plane touched the ground gently, and his new reality set in. A strong-armed man grabbed him by the back of the neck and led him to another waiting town car with his captors in tow. They traveled toward what had now been established as the Republic, and Elliot took it all in with a tired breath and a wide-eyed stare. He was in awe of it. Glittering scrapers hugged the sky with the kind of confidence that made everything beneath them feel inferior. The Dictator's name clung to each brand new sparkling tower in a golden shout. The man from the news was their leader for the foreseeable future, and he made sure that every building was a salute to him.

Elliot had never seen anything like it in his life. It was like ripping off a bandage and exposing a raw wound to an unforgiving world.

They pulled up to the tallest building that stood like a general leading its soldiers to victory or death or somewhere smack in the middle. The large men dragged Elliot out of the car and ushered him through a lobby lined with what seemed like gold armor. They all crowded into an elevator made of glittering glass. He ticked off on his fingers all the things he was experiencing for the first time, and he felt like a ping pong ball being batted around by two grand opponents: awe and fear.

They reached the top. And the doors slid open. And there he was. There *he* was.

The man he had stared at and cheered for every night for over a year. Feet tucked between bony knees wrapped up in filthy sheets. Mama leaving intermittently to chase her high, to crush her demons. The nagging fear of being left alone in the world and the hope that this man, *this* man standing in front of him would save him somehow like he had promised. Elliot knew that he had been wrong, that his mother had been wrong about the Dictator. But he couldn't help feeling like he was seeing a god he had blindly prayed to every night. It was the most incredible, sobering sight he had ever encountered.

"It's you," Elliot whispered. The rush of emotions knocked him over—an aching for his mother and an admiration for what power really felt like when it was towering over you. But he also felt something else: a painful loathing that clung to the bottom of his lungs and made it hard to breathe. He now had every reason to believe that the Dictator was responsible for what had happened to his foster family and the world glistening or crumbling around them, depending on which side of the fence one stood.

The Dictator knelt down on one knee so he could look the still-young boy in the eye. Elliot could smell his expensive cologne. It was intoxicating, and Elliot coughed a little to keep it at bay, worried that it contained a spellbinding quality that would leave him unable to control his own thoughts. He drank in the tightly-knit fabric of the Dictator's tailored gray suit and the sheen of his red silk tie. He tried to memorize every line in the man's face; he named the color of his eyes. Frost. He wanted to remember every detail of this man and this moment for the rest of his life.

Finally, the Dictator spoke, and it was the same voice he had heard echoing through his sad life night after night. Feet tucked in knees. Mommy pushing him away. Mom lying on floor. Not getting up. Never getting up. Riding in cars. Watching, watching, watching. Falling.

"So, you're the boy who doesn't like our pills," the Dictator said. It was not an accusation. Elliot was surprised. The man was genuinely curious.

Elliot was even more surprised when he found his voice. It sounded strong.

93

"No. That's not it, Sir."

"No?" The Dictator turned to the blonde woman and laughed. "Then what? Tell me, boy."

"I mean. It's not that I don't like them. They don't work on me." Elliot had no idea that he should have kept his mouth shut. He got a thrill from telling this man that he had no power over a young boy who had come from the gutter and that some people in his country still had a mind of their own. Elliot's ego offered him a stepstool, and he gladly climbed on top of it. He didn't care if he toppled over in the process.

"I have never heard of such a thing, boy. I really haven't. Our beautiful pills work on everyone. Everyone. They're beautiful, these pills. They take away our problems; they take away the people's problems. I think you just need a stronger dose!" The Dictator slapped Elliot on the side of the arm, and the boy stumbled a bit.

Elliot nodded, looking down at his hand-me-down shoes that were already too small.

"Fantastic. Great. This is great. We're all agreed. Alice, take him to testing." The Dictator stood up and gave Elliot one more hard slap on the back. The blonde woman grabbed the crook of Elliot's arm and dragged him out of the room. He turned and took one final look at the Dictator's face as it stared at him in wonder and, Elliot thought, even a little bit of fear.

He didn't know it then, but that moment before he was dragged down a hall was one of the last interactions with the real world as he knew it. From that point on, he would never again have a conversation that wasn't screamed or hushed. He would never play tag in the yard on a warmish day or read his comic books under his worn blankets with a flickering flashlight. All of his lights were about to be turned off and, without his consent, he was being thrust into the dark years. Little did he know at the time, he was actually quite late to the party. The east and west had been assigned, drugged, taken, put to work. The middle of the country had been last, but he was sure his family had already been packed up in a van before his plane touched down.

Alice and the men piled into the elevator, surrounding him on all sides and then took him out to a waiting car. He didn't resist them, partly out of intelligence and partly out of the kind of understanding a dog has when it's being taken to the pound. They sped toward a facility not too far away, and he was escorted to a simple room with a bed and a bin for his belongings, of which he had little. On the bed was a hospital gown with ironic white fluffy clouds set against a faded blue sky.

"Get dressed," Alice commanded. The adults in the room didn't move. The two men stood at attention again, and Alice stood with her hand on her hip, staring at him. Elliot shrugged off his shame as he undressed. He pulled the gown around his bony shoulders and became an instant patient. There was a sudden chill in the air, and he desperately wanted to crawl under the hospital sheets and pretend he was somewhere else.

"Elliot," Alice said, her sharp voice cutting through the padded room. He turned to look at her, bare legs glued together.

"We will get to the bottom of this. One way or another. You are a stupid boy who crossed the wrong line. Trust me. You will pay for it." She turned on her heel, and the people who had taken him from his family filed out, pulling the heavy door behind them. They silenced the room with a lock sliding into place.

Exhaustion crept up into Elliot's toes and infiltrated all of his body parts, and he made his way toward his bed, curling up under a surprisingly soft blanket. He soon fell into the deepest sleep, not knowing or caring what his dreams were. Anything, he figured, was better than this.

* * *

The new patient woke to the feeling of being restrained, and he realized heavy straps were pinning him down to the bed. He tried to pull his arms up, but he couldn't move them at all. A crippling panic set in.

Technicians in hospital gowns and masks stood over him. One held a dripping needle that looked so large, it almost seemed like a cartoon version of a syringe.

"Ready for dosage?" she called out to the team.

"Standing by," someone shouted back, and the needle plunged into a vein in his arm. He could feel a flesh-ripping burning sensation, like his body had detected poison and was trying to push it away. But then it dissipated, and he felt nothing.

The woman came over to him and blinded him with her light, standing over him for over a minute. He blinked rapidly, tears streaming down the sides of his face.

"Patient appears to be unaffected by treatment!" Bodies began moving all around him, and he was quickly whisked out of the room. His gurney chugged down a long hallway with grey-green walls and buzzing fluorescent lights, and he counted to twenty-five before he got back to his padded cell. It made him wonder how many rooms and patients they had here and if other people were unaffected by the drugs like him. Then he wondered if he was the only one. The nurses rolled him onto his bed, almost angrily, and shut the heavy door behind them.

It wasn't long before Alice came in to chat. One of her servants was carrying a heavy chair, and he placed it next to Elliot's bed for her to sit down. She was wearing a preposterous outfit: a red silk suit with the largest buttons Elliot had ever seen.

"It seems as if you were right, Mr. Elliot," she said. The more she talked, the more he picked up on her accent, noticing gentle variations in her carefully practiced English. "You showed no response to the treatment we gave you. And we gave you a very high dose. For a child, that is." She looked annoyed, like he was a stain on the front of her silk suit that she couldn't get rid of.

"That garbage doesn't work on me," he told her, balling up his little kid fists.

"Oh, it will. It has to. We will just have to keep increasing the dose until your brain is mush, and you become a worthless sleeper working in our factories and eating dog shit. Just like your mama. We didn't even have to give her anything—she found the pills all on her own!" She laughed, and her buttons shook against her chest. Then she got up, snapping her fingers for her servant to grab the chair. Just as quickly as they had appeared, they were gone.

Later that night was the first of his shock treatments. He was woken up out of a nightmare, and someone shadowy forced a mouthguard into his mouth. He tried to scream and couldn't, and he felt an eerie sense of Deja vu, as if he was living his dream exactly. The plastic guard felt funny pressing against his lips and tongue, and he couldn't swallow properly. It was like he had been forced underwater and was stuck just beneath the surface. No matter how hard he struggled, he couldn't get a full gasp of air.

The same person fit an apparatus around his head, a type of metal crown, and she shoved cotton into his ears. Someone else gently placed a cold wet cloth over his eyes and the world went dark. He was left alone with his own maddening thoughts. He wondered if his thoughts alone could kill him.

The electricity jolted him into the moment, and pain and torment and anguish and disbelief ripped through his small body. He was supposed to be playing soccer or building with Legos or learning something new in school. But instead he was in an insane asylum being treated like a crazy person because his brain did not cooperate with the Dictator's plan.

When it was over, they removed the torture device and left him alone with two tears suspended in the corners of his eyes.

They thought it would work. But even after one more shock treatment and a dose that should have sent him into an oblivion, he defiantly scowled at them and was dragged back to his room, his screams of resistance bouncing off the walls.

Before the next shock treatment, they blasted music into his cell and projected heinous images of torture that would make even a sleeper go insane. They found photographs of his mother, smiling before she got really sick, before she had him, then later after she had lost several teeth from a bar fight. They showed the news and security camera footage of his dead mama lying on the floor, and the seven-year-old version of him crying and begging for help.

After four more days of torture, Elliot was reduced to a small ball curled up under his soft blanket. Even after the death of his mom and the countless foster homes and the poisoning of his foster family, he had held onto some of his childlike stubbornness and maybe even a little bit of hope. But it was all gone now. They had made sure of it.

If things went according to schedule, he had two days until they gave him another dose. So this son of an addict decided to inhabit every nuance he had ever learned from his mother. He became her.

Like clockwork on the second day, one of the nurses came to his room with a wheelchair. He climbed in without protest.

"Finally," the nurse said. "You know the reason you even here is because you's a fighter. They don't like them fighter types."

Elliot didn't respond as she chattered away. He had already slipped into his new persona, and it fit like the baseball glove he'd never had. He felt comfortable. He felt free. He pushed the fight deep down inside him and slipped on a suit of valiant armor that would trick them all.

"You either wit 'em or against 'em. And if you against 'em, they punch you right out." She laughed loudly, but Elliot thought it sounded hollow. Her life wasn't so great with its grey-green walls and twenty-five buzzing lights and sinister tasks of transporting child patients to torture chambers. He imagined her trying to fall asleep at night and found comfort in the thought that she probably couldn't.

The medical team was even bigger this time, and he thought it was ridiculous that they needed so many people to stick a needle into the arm of a kid. Technicians stood in front of thin screens. They were poised to input important data about how they could make this one resistant child go to sleep forever. They sat him in a chair this time. He was no longer a boy, but a shell who felt nothing, not now, not ever again. He detected the needle prick on his soft skin and felt the glorious plunge of syringe into flesh. The delicious burn of dope entered his bloodstream (he could almost picture it), and he told his body *go go go!* like his cells were little fighters in the most important war of their lives.

His body fell in line. It knew what was at stake. His eyes glazed over. His mouth went slack. His muscles fell into the deepest slumber and welcomed the impending atrophy as they prepared to operate at five to ten percent from this day forward. He slumped over and allowed some saliva to dribble out. He told his heartbeat to slow down and made it so by raking his breath back and forth across his throat.

"We got him!" The team was cheering and slapping each other on the back, and Elliot thought how absurd and disgusting it was to celebrate drugging a young boy.

The nurse wheeled him back to his cell, whistling along the way.

"They got you good! Oh yah, they did take all the awake outta you. That's right." He could hear her sneakers squeaking on the floor, and he wondered if she was dancing. "We gonna celebrate tonight, don't you tell me we ain't. I'm gonna drink so many of them ales."

She got to Elliot's room and heaved him up onto the bed, breathing hard despite his light weight.

"I'm gonna leave these right here," She said, placing a paper cup full of four pills on the table next to his bed. "I never tried the stuff, we ain't allowed, but I seen the comedown. Prolly feels like Jesus gone come down straight for you to hand you o'er to the devil. You gonna want these. They extra special for little tough kids like you."

Elliot knew they were watching his every move—he had seen the security camera in the corner right after he'd arrived in his room. He waited for what he thought was about two hours, then he told his body to shake just a bit (like he'd seen his mama do so many times) and then a bit more, and then he desperately reached for the paper cup of pills, gobbling them up, mashing them with the back of his throat as if it was a matter of life or death. In almost every way, it was.

One week later this young boy-turned-sleeper was put on a carrier to Maine to get his assignment and begin training. They poked and prodded him into his seat, and he was careful to stare blankly into a great abyss.

"That him?" the guard sitting across from him asked Otto, who was Elliot's escort to what used to be New England.

Otto nodded, not wanting to engage, but the guard pressed on.

"Man, y'all really got him. Messed him up good, didn't ya?" The guard nodded toward Elliot, then grabbed his charge's elbow before she slipped down too far. She was so doped up, she could barely sit in her seat without sliding down to the floor in a giant puddle.

Otto looked at the guard with disdain. Elliot could tell the man was much lower in rank than he. "You got her dose wrong," he told the guard. "She's like a vegetable. We need them to work, not be corpses."

The guard's smile disappeared, and he quickly typed something on a screen. "Yes, sir. I'll take care of it right away. Sorry sir."

Elliot found the exchange amusing, and he suddenly felt content being a sleeper. He was sick of running and fighting and caring about people who were going to be taken away from him anyway. He found some comfort in his slumber, his newly adopted zombie-like state. He was happy to be shut down, silenced, disengaged. But he was still awake.

2031, PORTLAND, MAINE

The buzzer sounded loudly at the factory. Elliot had heard the same buzzer hundreds of thousands of times since he went through training the first day he arrived in Portland. Each shrill buzz had a slightly different intonation that caused the sleepers to stop, go, sit, move, engage, stand still. Some meant to pause their work and some meant that it was time to leave and board the train. Some meant meal time and some signaled that it was time to saunter to their sleeping pods. This particular one meant it was time for their pills. All of the sleepers stopped what they were doing and stood there, waiting. Elliot could sense the hunger all around him, and it always reminded him that he would never desire anything like that, not ever. The sleeper next to him was smacking her lips like a starving dog. They could not exist without their dope. They had been turned into animals.

The guards came down the line to hand out the pills to each sleeper. It was the fastest they ever moved, grabbing for the cup and gobbling up their goodies as quickly as possible. The timing was so precise: they all began to feel the slightest twinge of a comedown right before pill time. It was a foolproof way to ensure they ate their medicine in its entirety and that they were cognitive enough to do so. Sometimes right before the pills were devoured, Elliot thought he detected a glimpse of awareness from some of his coworkers. Once, he even thought he saw a real sign of life from one across from him in the line. He had reported it during his meeting, but had never witnessed anything like it since. Years later, he wondered if he'd just imagined it.

A guard he had never seen before marched up to him, and he grabbed at the pills clumsily, desperately as he had observed the rest of them doing so many times. As he had trained himself to do.

"Wait!" he heard another guard yell. The woman in front of him stopped what she was doing looking terrified. Elliot guessed she was about eighteen years old.

"I'm sorry. Did I do something wrong?" she asked. Elliot actually felt badly for her. She was just a kid. It wasn't her fault that she had been born on the other side, probably from parents who had voted for Dictator One that day and believed he was going to make the country *better than it's ever been*! If Elliot's mom had lived, he might have been wearing the exact same uniform doling out pills to the former Resistance. This young, terrified woman was most likely cut from exactly the same cloth as him.

"This there sleeper gets a special dose. Read the report!" The guard was now standing as close as he could get to her, and Elliot could see that she was shaking. She looked like she was going to cry.

"Yes, sir. So sorry, sir."

"I thought you were one of them brainy chicks? Aren't you some sorta technician scienteest-type? Doncha even know how to read the dose?"

"You're right, sir. I should have paid closer attention. I'm so sorry."

She scrambled back to wherever they got their endless supply of pills so she could give him his super dose. He wanted to tell her to stop, that it was a waste of time, and that she didn't need to be reprimanded by this bully because it didn't matter how many pills they gave him or how strong the dose was because he wouldn't feel a thing. Even after shock treatments and mental torture, and "upping" the dose so high it might kill someone, Elliot felt nothing. He wanted to help her, to save her.

She returned a minute later with tears brimming in her lower lids, and as she handed him the small metal cup, she caught his gaze for a moment. He tried to tell his eyes to look away, to glaze over, to see something in the horizon that only a sleeper could see, but he couldn't pull them away. He watched as she opened her mouth to call out, then reconsidered and shut it. Instead, she gave a small nod, so subtle he could have imagined it. Before he dragged his pupils down to safety, he caught a glimpse of her nametag: Maggie.

The *get to work!* buzzer screamed out across the factory, and he went back to his task like the rest of the workers. He could feel her eyes on him as she walked away. He couldn't get her look out of his mind as he performed his duty over and over. She had caught him, tuning into what could have been a giveaway that resulted in more treatment and more torture or even a deadly toss into a toxic sea. She recognized his consciousness, but hadn't given him away. She also spoke intelligently, and not with the hillbilly dialect that was prominent among the guards. He wondered if he'd been completely wrong about her. Maybe she hadn't come from a place of crawling desperation. Maybe she'd come from somewhere else entirely.

She was different. But were any of them different? Don't trust anyone, no one can be trusted. Can't they? What's to lose now? Maybe this is the way out? No. Fuck them. They're the enemies. Are they? What if she can help? Never, you idiot. Never. Elliot had an argument with his own brain for the rest of the day, grateful to have something to occupy his thoughts. His logical side knew that this woman helping them was just a fantasy. She was one young person and a weak one at that. There was no way she could set them free. The last person he had encountered from the other side who had tried to help him had disappeared.

The meeting that night was at a different restaurant basement—there had been so many incredible eateries in the city (or so they had heard), and he wished he could have seen it in it's prime. *What did lobster taste like?* he wondered. From how it was described on dusty menus, it sounded like the most delectable thing in the world. He thought about the meal he had devoured on the private plane on the way to the Republic, his last real meal, and his mouth salivated. Except for that one moment, he had forgotten what real food tasted like.

Now, only a couple of mess hall-type places remained for the militia to enjoy some booze and slop. But even that would have been luxurious to someone like him.

When he arrived at the meeting, Elena was the only one there. It was the first time he had caught her alone since she had been taken to the back room and brought back visibly changed. He saw bruises on the tip of her collarbone that peeked out from her black shirt and could only imagine where else she'd been hurt. If he allowed himself to think about it for too long, it made him want to tear the guard apart into a thousand bloody pieces.

"Hey." He startled her. She had been staring off into a different time and place. He hoped she'd been able to enjoy a moment of peace sitting there alone in that basement, and he was sorry to interrupt it.

"Oh, hi." She was quieter than usual, with less fight to her. He was sorry to see that too. He realized how much he counted on her to lead them—how much all of them counted on her.

"I...I saw what happened." He tried to be there for her, but he was so out of practice when it came to a regular conversation, let alone an intimate one. "I saw what happened the other day. If there's anything..." Elliot felt awkward. He scrambled for his words, but they had disappeared into the cracks of the old basement.

"It's nothing," she cut him off. "It's all part of my day job." And she laughed a little, but it was muted with a heavy sorrow.

Elliot kicked his boot on the dusty ground. "Fuck those assholes," he started.

"Elliot. Stop. Male bravado won't help. Use it for the mission. I feel like the Controller is close to cracking...something. I don't know what it is, but I think it's something." He could tell she was reaching for some fantasy that existed in her daydreams alone. But he worried that it was just reaching, and she would fall down, hard, in the process.

"Elena, I'll do the radio tomorrow. If you want."

She looked at him for so long, he wasn't sure if she had heard him. But finally she said, "Let's go together? I could use the company."

"Definitely."

"You sure? It's a risk." Elena mustered a small smile. He was honored. He knew it took all of her strength to stretch her mouth into such a foreign expression, and she did it all for him.

"What do we have to lose?" he asked, laughing a little.

"Absolutely nothing."

The others started coming down the stairs, and the two friends became serious again when they saw a large cut across Roger's cheek. Dried blood powdered his face, and the swelling made one eye look smaller than the other.

"I'm fine, I'm fine," he said when he saw their expressions. "I had a run-in with an assault rifle. Good thing I ran into the right end of it." He chuckled.

When the group was seated, Elena once again stood at the front of the room.

"Hello, everyone," she said, her eyes shining. "Tonight I have a special treat." She reached down below an old table and pulled up a bottle of wine. It had already been opened with a corkscrew she had found in the corner of the basement.

Everyone gave a silent cheer, waving their hands in the air. Even if nothing else good happened that week, Roger and Silver's smiles were enough to keep her going.

"Also..." she paused for a moment, trying to find the words that were deeply intertwined with her encounter with Darren. She carefully extracted them, shards of glass from an open wound. "Well, I found something out this week. It's pretty big. Or it seems that way. I was able to...I got a chance to see the guards' propaganda video, and I found out that they're having their annual gala in the Republic, and they're inviting ten members of the militia—kind of like a contest. We know the gala happens every year, but this is...interesting. I'm going to tell the Controller tonight." She held up her bottled treasure. "I think that's more than enough reason to celebrate."

She took a big swig and passed the wine to Elliot. Roger stood up to talk about how a guard had slammed him in the cheek with his rifle because he slipped on a wet step.

Elliot took a long sip of the wine, relishing the sour hit of blissful aged grapes in his mouth. It tasted better than anything, better than the meal on the plane or Patti's cooking or the burger he had shared with his mom on the stoop of their dungeon. Maybe, he thought, putting the bottle to his lips one more time, things could change someday. Or maybe this was the best day he was meant to have. He decided to savor it, looking up and seeing Elena's eyes staring into his. And his heart creaked open just a little bit more.

* * *

Elliot crept up to the dock the next night, nothing more than a shadow. He breathed in the stagnant salt air and let himself pretend for a moment that he was about to go fishing on a boat with Jonah. Father and son would chat about this or that, maybe about something funny one of the other kids did that day, and then suddenly, he'd feel a tug on his line and together they'd pull in a fish so big, it could feed their entire family for two whole meals. He shook his fist at the stupid ocean because he was never given a chance to travel to the sea with his newfound dad. He had been allowed exactly two months and four days with the only father figure he had ever known, and when he really thought about it, he felt like screaming up at the choking sky until it collapsed on top of him to shut him up.

Elena was already sitting against a building near the dock watching the waves. She didn't look over at him as he sat down beside her.

"You know, when I was little, we used to go to the Jersey Shore. We had this little cottage near the beach. It was tiny, but for us it was just perfect. We'd spend every weekend there, and one year, we spent the whole summer."

Elliot didn't dare breathe. It was the first time she had really opened up. Even though everyone from their group had shared at least some select details about their past, he knew nothing about her life before the darkness.

"It was just us three. Me. Mom. Dad. We had our own choreographed dance in that tiny little house. We'd make dinner together: burgers or pork chops and a salad we'd picked from our garden. Then we'd laugh and talk about the silliest stuff. It didn't matter what we talked about. Not really. Sometimes we'd spend a whole dinner talking about what kind of sand castle we were going to build the next day. And then we'd clear the table and do the dishes together. I would always put too much soap in the sink, and we'd flick the suds in each other's faces and mom would laugh so hard. We never got in each other's way, and we always worked together no matter what. As a team. It was fun." Her voice caught, and she paused. Elliot could feel her gulping in the briny air and a painful stab of the past.

"We would sometimes spend all day at the beach eating lunches covered in grains of sand. We would stay there until the sun went down. And then we'd go back home again and cook food on the grill. Corn on the cob. Sand in the sheets. At night we'd count my mom's freckles. I'd draw our adventures and write stories that I'd read to my parents before bed. I wonder if the house is still there or if the ocean carried it away. If I ever found it again, I'd crawl in between the sheets and never come out."

She almost seemed to forget he was there. She was caught between this world and another. He wondered if she was trying to claw her way back in time like he had wanted to do since the day they had ripped him away from Patti and Jonah.

"My mom and I would play the piano together on rainy days. She taught me everything. She was so smart." Elena bowed her head to her chest.

"What happened to her?" Elliot's curiosity got the better of him, and the question flew out of his mouth before he could stuff it deep inside with all the other things he had decided not to say. He was terrified that he had pushed her too far, but Elena turned to look at him and smiled.

"She was a rebel. Part of the Resistance. She pounded the streets and

105

shouted her cries of injustice." Elena pumped her fist in the air, and Elliot laughed.

"She was in their faces about everything: staging sit-ins in their offices, going to their town halls. She led this big Resistance group. She wanted to change the world." Elena's face was beaming with pride. "So they arrested her, and then they made her a sleeper in jail. Isn't that what happened to most of them?"

Elliot shrugged. He was suddenly embarrassed. It was something he thought about a lot—how most of his comrades' families had been forced into addiction, and his mom had found her way there on her own. It never eluded him that he would have been considered an ally of the government had his mom not overdosed and had he not found Patti and Jonah. He would have been in the right line, not the left line, collecting his uniform and badge.

Elena ducked her face under his so he was forced to look at her impossibly dark eyes and spiky hair. She put a hand on his shoulder. "Were your parents drugged too? I remember you telling us about them. You lived in Ohio, right?"

He shook his head, feeling something unfamiliar at the back of his throat. When he realized what it was, he desperately tried to swallow it away. Tears. He had not felt such a thing since the day he had transitioned from boy to sleeper in the clinic. He thought he'd left all his irrational little kid emotions behind in his padded cell.

When he finally found his voice: "Those were my foster parents. My real mom died two weeks after the election. I never knew my biological dad. My mom said he might have lived somewhere in Florida, but I never met him. Patti and Jonah took me in after my mom died."

Her eyes were wide, and her brow was furrowed with concern. "How did your mom die?"

He swallowed hard. "An overdose. Heroin."

"I'm sorry," she said. Then Elliot started chuckling.

"What?" she asked.

"It's really funny that my mom was a sleeper before everyone became sleepers."

"Funny?" She reached for his hand, and it felt unfamiliar, and it felt perfect. A burst of tiny tingles exploded from her touch as if his limb had fallen asleep and was in the process of waking up again.

He laughed again. "Hilarious in a way that you have to laugh or else you'll kill yourself by jumping off that pier over there."

She smiled and squeezed his hand. They sat like that for a very long time. The tingles turned into the warmest sensation, and his heart fluttered uncontrollably. He wasn't sure he'd be able to slow it down again.

Finally, she stood up and pulled him up with her. "Ready?" He nodded. He wasn't. But they had to let go.

They crawled down toward the edge of the dock together, and Elena reached down for the radio. She lay on her back, the small device pulled close to her face, and sent the update. When she got her confirmation, she looked at Elliot, and they both smiled. This one was not just business as usual. This one felt good.

As they walked back together, they made sure to stick close to the buildings and stay out of sight. Elliot knew that Elena was so used to clinging to brick facades, and he watched in awe at her almost catlike movements. He was clumsier, but allowed himself to be pulled along as an elastic extension of her arm. As they approached the street where Elena's housing complex stood, they heard a group of guards' laughs echo against the cobblestones. She grabbed his arm and pulled him into an alley so tight, it scraped at his shoulder blades. They could hear the guards. They were ten, five, two feet away, but finally clomped by them with their heavy boots and stopped half a building away. Elliot could smell the booze on them as they passed and thought about his slug of wine. Even though the militia was horrible and cruel, Elliot thought about how amazing it would be to take Elena on a date to one of those stupid mess halls where they ate slop and drank ale until dawn.

"What we have here?" one of the guards asked.

They could hear the beep of a scanning device. "Alfred Bernard," someone said quietly. "He must have gotten out of the courtyard." Elliot recognized the voice. Even though he had only heard her one other time the day before, he knew it was Maggie. "Alfred, how did you get out?"

"Newbie, he ain't gonna answer you. He don't even know his own name! But it look like he got a Purple Nation tattoo. We treat them Purple Nation sleepers real special, don't we Karl?" Karl howled to a moon sheathed in pollution. He seemed to think it was the funniest thing in the world.

"What we do to him, boss?"

Elliot pictured Karl as a large baboon with a perpetually confused look on his face, jumping up and slapping his long arms together at the delightful thought of torturing a sleeper. He imagined him to have a crew cut, as most of the militia did, and to have several teeth missing. He was sure Karl looked and acted like all the rest of them—he was a deplorable who came from a long line of deplorables. His family had not been part of the Resistance. His daddy had probably disappeared before young Karl could talk. His mama had most likely voted for Dictator One and surely for Dictator Two. He believed in a nation where they deported his mama's neighbors to their countries of origin even though they had never lived there, and he still saluted the flag even after the government bankrupted his family. He shouted, "America!" out the window of his Jeep even after his mama was forced to join the militia and stand for hours on end despite her diabetes and her bum knee. He followed and praised and hooted and hollered at how great this goddam country was even though they sent his three brothers and his mom to completely different regions to work for twelve hours a day for no money, for only room and board and food and ale. He believed in this failed fantasy because he didn't know any better. He was born into this world and, as he gazed at the falling down sleeper in front of him, Elliot knew that Karl felt a hatred that had been conditioned for decades. If asked, he would not be able to answer why he despised this man stumbling before him.

Elliot and Elena could hear scuffling boots, and Elliot resisted the urge to peer out to see what was happening. He could feel Elena's nails digging into his arm, and the pain almost felt good. It made him feel alive and grateful and responsible for saving whatever sleeper had collapsed in the street. Except he couldn't, at least not until the guards were gone.

"Karl, pull his pants down!" the boss was shouting. They could hear Karl struggling with the task, his labored breath echoing down the narrow street. It sounded like he slipped a little on the wet cobblestones, and he laughed at himself and his clumsy incompetence. Elliot wanted to taunt him: *you can barely even torture a sleeper.*

"Now kick him, Karl! Kick him in the nuts!" The boss sounded like he was at a rodeo. Elliot remembered his mother watching rodeos on TV. Even at his young age, he thought it was a stupid sport and cruel to the animals. He remembered one of the riders getting trampled, and he had thought, *Good.* The horse didn't want him bouncing around on his back anyway.

They heard the breath exit out of the Resistance sleeper in one giant whoosh, like a full balloon had been released and was zip zapping around the atmosphere. The man was someone who could have easily been Elena's father, and Elliot knew that Elena felt the painful thud in her own bones as his knees hit the cobblestones. They could hear the sickening sound of boots slamming into his stomach and the guards' laughter flying down the winding streets, taking flight as it reached the open sea. Finally, a voice rose up.

"That's enough!" It was Maggie.

"What, you like sleepers or somethin', newbie?" The other guards howled as if someone trying to save a dying man, a man being beaten to death on the street, was the funniest thing in the world.

"You wanna fuck this sleeper?" the boss asked, and a new round of hollering skittered down the cobblestones.

Maggie murmured a quiet, "No." It was obvious that she had reassessed her situation and decided it was not one she would easily win. Elliot could hear the concern in her voice; he had not imagined it. It was something he had not heard from a member of the other side in a very long time. It felt melodious on his ears like an old song he had forgotten he loved.

He huddled with Elena in the alley for another twenty minutes until they were absolutely sure the guards had gone in for the night, and then they silently crept out of their hiding place and knelt down next to the very still sleeper.

Elena put two fingers on his pulse and waited longer than was necessary before whispering, "He's dead." Elliot nodded. They bowed their heads in respect, but in reality, this man had died a long time ago—possibly in a prison like Elena's mother. He still wore a wedding band, a hopeful symbol that he had loved someone once and someone had loved him back. Maybe he had experienced the joy of having children; hopefully he had not experienced the pain of losing them. It was safe to assume that this man's freedom had been robbed from him not too long after the election while he was marching in the streets.

"Elena, we should go. The power goes back on soon." He looked down at the sleeper one last time. "And they'll be coming to get him." Elliot tugged on her sleeve, and she was finally able to tear her eyes away. She put her hand in his, and as Elliot pulled her through the shadows, he was determined to remember the warmth of her calloused palm and promised silently to protect her no matter what.

2018, NEW YORK CITY

It was after midnight, and Benton was in his lab in Greenwich Village. Everything had been shut down in his city: his beloved restaurants and coffee shops, the bookstore where he found his treasures, the place where he used to buy a cupcake at 10pm and eat it safely on the bench outside. Now he rarely dared to venture out of his lab. He was not white, and he was not a fighter, at least not in the traditional sense. He was a man of science, albeit a mad one, and he had become obsessed with the only thing he had left in his life: his work. His hair had grown to an epic length. Long locks had started to twist and curl in a protest of their very own. His beard was unkempt and had grown up the sides of his cheeks and down his neck as if the two ends wanted to escape from each other.

After the lockdown, Benny had moved his lab to a more discreet, underground location. He had forfeited his small-yet-beautiful rent controlled apartment and now slept on a cot in the back room of the lab. He was in hiding. His phone had been cut off. He had been a nomadic loner much of his life, but for the first time, he truly understood what it was like to be completely on his own.

Back in 2012, right after Hurricane Sandy, he had ordered a large supply of survival goods. He remembered how his girlfriend at the time had teased him, calling him a "true New Yorker" who hadn't been able to handle life without electricity or his mobile device for four days. She complained every day that the stuff was taking up too much room in their storage unit. She tormented him with it. She called him a fatalist. She had said that his buying twenty-five years' worth of survival food was insane. He often imagined calling her up now (if he was able to call anyone at all) and saying, "I told you so. I TOLD YOU SO!" but they had broken up long before the world started ending, and he would have no way of reaching her. For a moment he wondered where she was right now. Then he wondered where everyone was.

They had started locking down Manhattan and the outer boroughs five months ago, so slowly at first that no one really knew what was happening. The protests had grown to a fever pitch after the inauguration, and most of the people who resisted the new leader had been jailed or had watched their loved ones go to prison or had decided to flee to more conservative parts of the country to hide. Illegal immigrants had been ripped from their families and deported by way of sleek white vans. Now there stood a government-controlled headquarters in the ominous Midtown towers, and the militia marched the streets trying to weed out any leftover Resistance fighters or people who didn't fit into the Dictator's grand scheme of things.

Benny laughed a little as he thought about a brunch he'd attended six months before the election. Two of his friends had announced that they were moving out of the city, that they were utterly "over it." He had teased them endlessly, telling them they had given up and were soon to be victims of the suburbs and a boring life. "I will never leave this island!" he had announced, raising his wine glass in the air, sloshing a bit over the edge and onto his hosts' expensive tablecloth. The rest of his friends had all laughed and agreed, *Yes, yes, yes, this was the only place to live in the world*. The greatest city ever created. Except now he was sure that they were all gone in one form or another, and he had become the last standing eternal New Yorker. Through fire and brimstone and an administration that insisted on ending everything good about their country, he would remain in the city he loved. Even if it meant he had to retreat into a cavernous hideout.

Back when the election first happened, he believed that the term would last four years at the most and in 2020 someone else would be taking office, desperately trying to fix the irreparable damage all around them. But all that remained were people who either continued to believe in what the Dictator was doing or were too terrified to cross him. The new election would be unanimous. The Dictator would reign on.

Despite everyone he'd ever cared about leaving the city, there was one person left whom Benny still trusted. Of all the people he had ever known in the world, Clara was not his first choice of confidants, but one did not have the luxury to choose such things in such circumstances. She had been his student when he taught for a brief stint at NYU, and he had both enjoyed and despised an affair between them. She was so young when they first met, barely twenty years old, and she had looked at him like a god back then.

When he thought about her breasts pushed against him in the dark classroom after everyone had gone home for the night, he felt a distant surge of electricity and shame. There were days when he had ducked out the back of the school lab so he could avoid her waiting for him, leaning against the brick wall and batting her eyelashes like a bad movie about a teacher and his seductive student.

But there had been other days he couldn't wait to see her, mostly when he felt frustrated with his work or with the city or like he would never amount to anything after all or when he had been having reoccurring nightmares about his dad drowning in his own vomit. Those were the moments when he rushed out through the front entrance and (without saying a single word to her), grabbed Clara's hand (just for a moment) and pulled her in the direction of the subway. Sometimes he didn't stop her if she put her hand on his knee and slid it toward his crotch. He didn't care if one of his colleagues saw what was happening, that he was most likely taking advantage of this girl's age or her admiration of him or of their miles-apart positions in the world. He was so full of himself back then that when he looked at her, at her perfect body and her unfathomable naivety, he always looked down on her.

Clara's parents were evangelical Christians from the rolling pastures of Iowa and had the sort of views that Benny scoffed at over expensive meals in Brooklyn Heights. They believed in their almighty god, and anything that opposed that belief was a sin to them. Their only daughter bore the brunt of their convictions: she was so sheltered that everything, absolutely every experience she had as a young adult on her own for the first time was like that of a four-year-old. Sometimes Benny felt his face flush with embarrassment when she clapped her hands gleefully for a subway performer, or he pretended he was somewhere else entirely when she mispronounced "quinoa" or "hors d'oeuvres." It was shocking that she was able to navigate the city on her own and that her parents had let her go to college at all. When Benny had asked her about it once, she told him, "I said I'd run away to a Muslim country and marry a Muslim man if they didn't let me." She had been proud of her silly trick, and Benny cringed at the thought of her using such a thing as a threat. He found himself wincing from things she said as if she was continually slapping him with her stupidity and her crass views of the world.

She didn't belong in New York City. Not really. Yet, it was what saved her from becoming a close-minded bumpkin, rolling along shamelessly in the never-ending pastures of Iowa.

On the day of the first mass arrest, she'd tried following him home even though he wanted to be alone. He turned to her and shouted every twenty feet to *Go home, Clara!* until he heard her whimper, like a stray dog, and finally stopped to wait for her to catch up.

"I'm scared," she said to him, and he chuckled. She was a white Christian woman who came from a conservative family. The only thing that would have made her a better candidate when the assignments were handed out was if she was a wealthy man.

"Clara, listen." He turned to face her. Over her shoulder, he could see that the bodega where he had gone to for countless late night snacks, the one with the three-legged cat who always hung out behind the register and the "sushi grade" salmon on a stick, had been boarded up. Clara looked up into his eyes, waiting. She could not understand for a single moment what it was like to be a black man, let alone one whose views didn't fit into the current sweeping government agenda. He believed in science and civility and kindness when the people who ran his world wanted none of the above to thrive. He almost felt bad for her in her stupid plastic bubble, but he felt worse for himself. In two weeks, the government would be handing out the first assignments. People who had been heavily associated with the Resistance had already been incarcerated and drugged. People like Clara who came from a conservative background, whose parents and aunts and uncles and cousins and grammas and grandpas had all voted for the Dictator the first time around would be invited to be part of the militia. Most of the Dictator's inner circle had already been asked to live in the glittering new city he was building, officially called *The Republic of the Elitist Nation*. But people like Benny who had not spoken out per se, but who also hadn't supported the regime, had to run away or hide. He knew he could never let them find out that he was continuing his work.

That day on the street, the city already started going grey, fading into darkness as businesses went under and streetlights went out. It was as if a mist had settled over the buildings and sidewalks, putting everything in a chokehold. Benny had experienced an awakening three months ago when Patti and Jonah packed up everything they owned in an old car they had bought from a guy off the street. The three of them had embraced in front of his friends' beautiful West Village residence, their home that had watched over the changing tide. He watched them stuff some clothes and duffel bags full of cash in the backseat. They carefully put a large supply of his immunity serum into a compartment in the trunk with the promise he would send them the cure when he finished so they could bring it across the border. He waved as they drove away toward the tunnel, and he knew he had to disappear so he could finish his work. He also knew he needed Clara's help.

"Clara," he began again. "I need to...go into hiding for a while." He was speaking slowly so she could understand. She nodded, but he knew she didn't really grasp what was going on.

"I have food to last me for a long time, and I moved all my work to a secret place. But I need your help. OK?" She nodded again, this time looking pleased with herself. He knew she was in love with him, and it was clear she would do anything he asked. Benny waited as the familiar guilt washed over him. He had a sinking feeling he would be putting her in danger, but in the end, his work trumped his worry.

That same day, he had carefully given her the instructions. In one month, they would meet just inside the 14th Street subway station. He'd give her a package to send to an address.

"Show me where your hiding place is," she begged him.

He thought for a minute, and her large doe eyes almost won him over. But he quickly shook off the impulse to indulge her and considered the fate of the country instead. The only people who knew the location of his underground lab were Patti and Jonah, and a handful of trusted confidants he had met online. He had told them about it almost in jest, something like, *"If the world ends, you'll know where to find me,"* but in his quest to prepare for a disaster (natural or man-made or a little bit of both), he felt a need to tell someone about his escape strategy, and he simply chose the people he felt he could trust the most.

When the gravity of what was happening hit home, he worked for months to move everything he owned into his hideout—an old control center he had found through his obsession with the New York underground—and with each trip he made to his new dark, dank home, he grew more confident that he had done the right thing by staying. His city needed him. His future patients needed him, wherever they were. Who knew what would happen if this beautiful city and the humanity that made it go 'round each day were wiped away completely? He had to remain even if to someday tell the story of what had happened.

Clara got her assignment three days later, and it was exactly as Benny had predicted: *Militia, 5th Rank, Overtake New York City*

It was their last meeting before he would give her the package. He had convinced himself that his work was for the greater good of the country— no, the world—and she was the only means by which to distribute his precious cure to Patti and Jonah. But at night, in the darkness of his underground lair and his own conscience, he was faced with the truth: he was essentially using her as a drug mule. It was on that day he gave her the address on a scrap of paper, warning her to memorize it, to get rid of it, to never let anyone find it under any circumstances. She had looked scared.

"But I have a hard time remembering stuff. You know that," she told him.

"I know you can do it," he'd said. "I should go before they patrol the area." They had met in the kitchen of an old restaurant, and when he said he had to go, her eyes turned hungry and she moved closer to him. He had let her pull down his pants, and he pushed her against a wall. They went at each other almost violently, as if it was the end of the world. As if it was their last chance at a handful of what could have resembled love.

On the morning of their meeting day one month later, he carefully packed up his precious bottles in bubble wrap he had taken from a packing supply store. He placed the instructions on how to duplicate the cure to addiction in a plastic sleeve and slid them in the side of the small box. Then he taped the package shut, using almost a whole roll of packing tape.

He waited until dusk, feeling like he was going to go mad with anticipation. His heart ricocheted around the lab, rattling bottles and nerves.

The shadow version of him crept out of the underground lab, clutching his cargo tight to his chest, and made its way up the subway stairs, his back glued to the wall. The city had become thick with smog, small particles dancing around and tickling the insides of his nose, but he wore the heavy air like a cloak as he made his way to their meeting place.

Clinging to the sides of buildings, he stopped right before Union Square. There was a stench in the air different from the air pollution, and he demanded his eyes and nose adjust. Something was wrong.

Benny crept down a set of subway stairs and swiftly made his way toward the exit that opened up directly into the square. It was a place he'd spent countless sunny days doing absolutely nothing, soaking in the intricacies of the city right through his pores. But as he crouched toward the subway opening, the smell almost made him gag.

He crawled up the stairs on his belly, making no sound at all and trying not to think about how each step probably had a layer of human excrement. It was unbearably dark except for a faint orange glow from an emergency light off in the distance.

His hand reached for the next step, and it hit something softer. Ignoring their better judgment, his fingers reached around what felt like an arm. He allowed his eyes to look up and demanded they adjust to the light. Reddish hair escaped from under a military cap. Eyelids were stuck open, but the blue eyes did not see. Not anymore.

"Clara," he tried to whisper, but no sound came out. Blood had pooled around her, an outpouring of final moments exploding from a gaping wound in her neck. He felt an ache in his throat, and his guilt mountain started toppling on top of him, threatening to smother him to death.

"Clara," he mouthed again, agony bubbling up out of his mouth and pooling over his filthy beard. He felt disgust and shame and the grossest type of painful confusion. He reached down for her hand and felt the crumpled piece of paper balled up in between slender fingers.

"No. Oh god, no." He pulled it ever so gently from her grasp and stuffed it in his pocket. Then, clutching the package as if it contained the only friend he had left, he slipped back into the underground and deep into the darkness.

2017, WASHINGTON, D.C.

They had decided to go to the march together as a family, but Elena was forbidden from actually marching. Had it been up to her mother, they would have walked hand in hand, shouting their protests, waving their signs. Her mother had been planning for months and had mobilized such a powerful group of women, Elena believed they could have ruled the world. But her father was worried, always a mother hen, always clucking around his daughter's every move to make sure she was safe. Elena had heard them up late one night yelling at each other (which rarely happened), and it was about her.

"Well, why can't she go and see the work I've been doing for the past six months? She needs to be surrounded by these powerful women! She's our goddamn future, Ben!"

"I will not, *will not*, put her in danger. You got lucky with the other marches. Nothing happened. But this one has a lot of aggressive groups, and things have gotten even crazier with the supremacists. The answer is no, Sarah. I can't do it."

Ben supported everything Sarah stood for and everything she had ever done. Elena sometimes caught him staring at her mother's determined face as if she was a god, but Elena knew he believed in lying low and conducting more, in his words, "behind the scenes forms of protest."

As they argued, she could picture her father growing red and balling up his fists at his sides, flames coming out from the top of his head. She felt torn in half, a clean split. She adored both of them so fiercely and part of her was honored that they loved her with such a force that they would have pulled her apart to simultaneously keep her safe and save her future.

They finally settled on a compromise and rented a hotel suite a couple of miles from the heart of the march. Elena could order a sundae and watch her mother change the world on TV, her father told her smiling. But she was old enough to understand that it was a silly little kid concession. She would have done anything to march in the center of Purple Nation—anything except upset her father or make him worry.

Elena spent the morning helping her mother put finishing touches on her signs, looking up as her mom patted her shoulder proudly. She knew it didn't matter what she added to the signs—her mother loved her no matter what and was thrilled just to have her daughter's mark on her work. She helped tie a purple bandana around her mother's head, trying to swallow the tears that burned the back of her throat.

When she was ready, Sarah stood in the doorway, and Elena felt her heart exploding with pride. "Dad, can't I please go? Please." She begged him one last time, and Sarah looked up at her husband hopefully.

"Not this time, sweetie. Maybe the next time after things settle down a bit." His mouth was drawn in a tight line of concern. That morning, Elena had heard him plead with Sarah to stay home, but everyone knew it was a waste of time. He couldn't make his wife do anything, and if he didn't support what she believed, Elena knew it would break up their tiny family circle.

"OK, then. I'm off." Sarah opened her arms wide and embraced them both. Elena didn't want to let go, and Sarah finally had to gently push her away. She pumped her fist in the air and walked down the hall, only looking back once at her family who urged her along with their love.

Elena and her father sat down on the couch and turned on the TV as she dipped her spoon into her bribe: piles of chocolate and vanilla and peanut butter and whipped cream. People were gathering in the streets by the thousands to show their resistance to the president's fascist regime. They cheered when they saw her mother's group, all dressed in purple. And while their wrists were too small to be seen from so far away, Elena knew they all donned the same tattoo: a solid purple star.

The march began, and the shouts echoed in the streets. The energy was so palpable, Elena and Ben could feel it through the television. They watched the millions of people who had shown up carrying their strength and their stories and their uncompromising requests of fairness and equality. There had been many, many marches before, but this one had an electricity that Elena truly believed could ignite a firestorm.

They watched, holding hands so tightly, and her father finally told her to "let up or you'll break my fingers!" and they both laughed. It felt glorious to let out even a small chuckle because while an excitement pinged between them and around the room, they couldn't shake their fear that something terrible could happen.

Suddenly, Sarah appeared on the screen. They looked at each other and held their breath.

"You're the leader of Purple Nation," a reporter asked. "Tell us how you created such a substantial group."

Elena and her father shrieked, and Elena's ice cream spoon went flying, landing on the white carpet. Neither of them noticed as they held each other tight, watching their hero on TV. On TV!

Sarah took a deep breath. "Well, I couldn't have done it..." and then she stopped. She turned to look behind her. Then they heard the screaming. Then they saw the running. Gas, tear gas everywhere. Running, screaming. Sarah pushing past the camera to start running herself.

The screaming, the running, her mother was out there and they were not there to protect her, and the ice cream melted as Elena rocked back and forth on the couch imagining colorful confetti floating around the room and turning grey as it hit the ground. Her father called everyone he knew to find out anything he could.

They wouldn't learn what had happened to her for four days. No one understood it at the time, but it was the end of a presidency and the very beginning of a dictatorship and an army and an irreversible divide and a massive effort to put people just like her mom into a deep dark sleep.

2018, BETHLEHEM, PA

It was two weeks after Elena's father had popped the pills, one, two, three, four, and joined her mother in her vapid state of escape. Elena wanted to point out, in her precocious way, that her mother had not chosen to be this way, that she would have wanted Ben to fight for all of them and find a way out of this. She wanted to tell her father that he was weak and stupid for taking the easy road and leaving her all alone to fend for not only herself but her parents as well. She had taken on foraging for food, carefully avoiding the assignment stations whose lines grew daily. She cleaned the house, mopping up her once smart, reliable, perfect parents' vomit from their beautiful hardwood floors.

She was doing the dishes when she could feel someone standing behind her. She slowly turned around and her father was standing three feet away, shifting back and forth on his feet as if trying to propel himself out of his body. He was a zombie. It was a horror movie.

"Yes?" The ten-year-old was angry. She couldn't stand to be in the same room as his weakness and wanted to grab his shirt and scream at him in repulsion. *He was supposed to protect her!* She wanted to shout. *She couldn't do it on her own!* But she could, and she was, and he was someone else now entirely. He wouldn't have heard anything she'd shouted anyway, not really, so she didn't bother.

"Elena. Lannie." His speech was jumbled. She wanted to tell him that he had no right to use her nickname and that he wasn't even her father anymore. But she kept her mouth shut in a tight line and remained quiet as she watched him struggle with the words.

"Need ma pills," He attempted.

"I know," she told him and started to turn back to the sink.

"Need ma pills, Lannie." His voice sounded like a whine, and she remembered all the times when she was little and she wasn't allowed to whine. *My ears don't hear whining!* her mother would say, her father nodding in solidarity. *Use your words!* Elena wanted to throw it all back in his face because she was the parent now in this twisted world where evil reigned and people who fought for the good of the country were turned into vegetables.

"Oh? You need your precious pills, huh?" She had her hands on her hips now.

"Yah. Ma pills, Lannie."

"Fuck you," she said. She had never cursed before and certainly not to her parents. It felt delicious coming out of her lips, like she had snuck out of the house and took a sip of alcohol in the creaky woods that sat at the back of her yard. She felt powerful, and it felt good.

"What diddya say to me, young lady?" Her father tried to act authoritative, but he was slurring his words, and it looked like he needed to sit down soon. He stumbled a bit on his own feet, his slippers making a repulsive sound on their tile floor.

"I said, fuck you, Bahadur!" she shouted.

Her father stumbled back at the sound of his given name. It was his Iranian name. After he took the pills for the first time, abandoning her forever, she decided she needed to know everything about him. Late at night, and sometimes in the afternoon when her parents were passed out in this room or that, she'd dig through their drawers and their files.

Her mom had always been an open book: she was Irish Catholic and had seven siblings (she was the youngest). She was brought up in a strict household and had gone to Catholic school where she was tormented by the nuns. In fifth grade, or so the story went whenever she told it to Elena, she learned about sin and that everything was, in fact, a sin. People who didn't think like her or believe in the same things as her family were sinners. To Sarah, even at such a young age, it had felt wrong. So wrong so deep in her bones that she decided (stomping her saddle shoe in protest) that anyone who told her Jesus loved everyone in one breath and denounced people who were different than her in the other had to re-examine what the hell they were doing.

Elena had always laughed at that part. *Re-examine what the hell they were doing!*

Her father was different. In some ways, Elena believed that he was her mother's one grand rebellion to her parents who never really acknowledged his existence let alone their marriage. His past was a dark hole, and Elena had always felt like she existed with a half-empty family tree. She knew nothing about his fifteen years in Iran or what his mom looked like or his dad or if he had any brothers and sisters. Elena could find no photographs in her search, only a United States passport marked with Iran as his country of origin. His accent had no hint of his past; he never talked about how or why he had come to the United States; he never spoke of the religion he'd embraced day in and day out during the early years of his life. It was like it never existed. It was like his former life never happened.

His Iranian name hung in the air. He grappled with it, wrestling it with his too-slow reflexes. Elena could tell it didn't sit well with him at all.

"Done call me that, Lannie," her father slurred. She stomped her foot on the tile floor in anger, imagining it was being hugged by a giant saddle shoe, and then the defiant little girl pushed past her dad and ran up to her parents' room.

Her mom was passed out in the bed, completely still except for a little shudder from time to time. The bright blue sheets with the poppies on them were twisted in her mother's legs, and Elena reminded herself that she had to wash them—that they hadn't been washed in weeks because her mom rarely left the bed anymore. Elena had curled up next to her one day and lay there for hours, pretending that it was just a lazy Sunday morning and that Sarah had been up late the night before plotting to overtake the country with people who cared about its survival.

She was so angry at her father that she rushed to her mom's closet, her safe space to get lost. She shut the door and pulled a large wooden chest into the center of the floor, sitting down in front of it. It creaked when it opened and smelled like cedar. She breathed it in. It was her mother, her childhood, the memories she held onto between small hands and tight fists.

She took out old photographs and articles her mom had written, now crumpled and smudged. The most prestigious articles and awards had been framed and hung in the study, and Elena and Ben had made her mother read them aloud while they sat in front of the fireplace, all wrapped in brightly colored blankets and sipping hot cocoa. Their family had piled everything that mattered to them in a leaning tower of accomplishment and happiness, and Elena realized that everything she loved could be knocked over in an instant.

At the very bottom of the chest, Elena's fingers brushed against a leather envelope. She had to dig her fingernails around the edge of it before she was able to pull it out.

It seemed to be ancient, and a watermark stained the front. When she opened it and saw her mom's handwriting on the weathered pieces of paper, she felt like she was being hugged. They were reminders of scribbled notes on Post-its in her lunch bag or perfectly chosen cards on her birthday. It was the exact same script "Santa" had used on her presents even though she had defiantly told her parents that she didn't believe in such things when she was only four.

With angry tears in her eyes, she studied the papers for a minute before folding them and tucking them away in her back pocket. Then she curled her body around the chest and fell fast asleep.

* * *

Elena awoke to a loud banging downstairs and sunlight creeping through the bottom of the closet door. She opened it a crack and could hear what sounded like glass shattering. Her father was shouting with his slow speech. She heard him cry out in a sleeper's version of anger.

Without hesitation, she instinctively climbed into her parents' dirty laundry basket. The clothes hadn't been done in over four weeks, and she gagged on the smell but burrowed down as far as she could. She held her breath and waited.

There was murmuring outside the closet, and then she heard the closet door creak open. She didn't dare move at all, and finally it closed again.

She sat there for another thirteen hours. She was starving and thirsty and had to go to the bathroom, which she eventually did all over the laundry and herself (careful to take the folded up paper out of her back pocket). Still she waited, shaking and shivering in the chill of her own urine and fear.

When she was sure it was safe, she carefully climbed out of the basket and opened the door a quarter of an inch at a time. Her mother was no longer in the bed; the sheets twisted around her absence. Elena wandered downstairs and into every room of her beautiful childhood home. Her parents were gone. She ventured a quiet, "Hello?" but no one answered. She said it loudly, braver this time, because she knew, as much as she knew everything she had ever loved had disappeared, that she was completely alone.

She found her way back upstairs and took off all her clothes. She turned the shower on and let it get as hot as possible, grateful that they had not turned off the hot water yet. She stepped in the pelting water and let it burn her skin. She stayed in there so long, she stopped wondering where the droplets began and her tears ended. Then she dried herself with the fluffiest towel she could find. Somehow she knew this would be a luxury she might not have for a long time.

The go-bag had always been packed. Her mother had insisted that they all have survival bags ready (*for when it all goes down*), and she had always made Elena try on her clothes each month to make sure they all still fit. Everything was folded to its smallest possible size. There were iodine tablets and food packs. A small gateway radio and some cleansing cloths and some first aid supplies. She carefully tucked the piece of paper into the hidden side pocket and zipped it up, patting it for safe measure.

The young girl got to work layering her clothes, as her mom had taught her to do. She put on every pair of underwear she had, three pairs of pants, and four shirts. She turned to stare at herself in the mirror.

With a cry in her throat, she grabbed the pair of scissors that her mother had used to trim her long hair. *Just a little! I don't want it too short!* she always said, believing that hair above her shoulders was the worst thing that could ever happen to her. Holding tightly near the root, she cut as closely to the scalp as she could, long wavy locks falling onto her white rug. She didn't stop until nearly all of her hair was gone, awkward little bits sticking out from her small head. Her eyes looked gigantic and her cheeks hollow. But she choked back the horror of her appearance and the current state of her life and, with resolution, pulled the pack on her shoulders.

She allowed herself a full thirty seconds to look lovingly around her childhood home, her only home. She drank it in, she swallowed it down. She stored it in a place where she would never forget it, but where she could turn off all bits of her past life with a single command. Then she slipped out of the door and found her way to the edge of the woods.

2020, THE REPUBLIC

The Dictator called his daughter for the first time in months, and she answered nervously on the first ring. The man who had read to her at night (sometimes) when she was a kid and had given her everything she had ever wanted (always) and had (mostly) been there for her and had defended her and supported his daughter her whole life now felt distant and unreachable and even sometimes cruel (like that one unforgettable time). If she talked to him when Chief was in the room, she felt like she didn't even know who her dad was. Chief might as well have had her father sitting on his knee—her father had become a ventriloquist dummy.

Savannah had started to feel like everything had been robbed from her. Her best friend was dead, her husband too involved with her father's executive orders to notice her. Her children were taken care of by highly paid nannies, and Savannah was positive that they thought she was stupid and a terrible mother. She knew everyone thought that. Her businesses, including her clothing line, which she had put everything into, had been dissolved years ago. *"There's a new focus now!"* her father had said, and she nodded like a bumbling fool even though she hadn't asked for any of this. No one had expected him to win the presidency, and now she and the country and the world were facing the consequences.

Spoiled brat, she scolded herself as she thought about the people she'd seen in the factories. They didn't even know or care where their families were. At least she knew she could walk down the hall and be face-to-face with her own father despite him feeling like an increasingly deranged stranger.

She heard him breathing on the other end of the phone.

"Dad?" She could tell he was excited about something. His breath was always five pounds heavier when he was "onto something." She had lived through so many of his schemes, and they had become more distressing over the years. Some of them left her with her mouth open in the kind of shock a little girl feels when she realizes her parents are not superheroes.

Hers was a monster.

"Dad? What is it? I'm traveling to the edge of the Republic today to make an appearance for the new factory opening." She hated the factories and everything they stood for. She was embarrassed how she was being used as the Vanna White of factory openings. They loved to have a pretty face and body to match to cut the ribbon and open the doors to the drones. Sometimes she couldn't bear to go and sent J.J. instead, but it was always followed by a phone call from her dad saying something like, "J.J. doesn't look good in a tight red dress, Savannah." She forced herself to smile and wave for the camera if only to avoid one of those phone calls.

"Forget that," her father told her, and she could hear the breathing getting one and a half pounds heavier. "I have something delightful to show you."

The way he said delightful put such dread in the center of her chest that she felt like her air had been closed off. She wondered if someone could die from anticipation.

"Someone will come to your room at exactly eleven o'clock. Then, we can get lunch." He sounded as excited as the day he had won the election. Despite herself, she was cautiously thrilled to have a special lunch with her father.

At exactly eleven o'clock there was a sharp knock on her door. She opened it as if a bomb was waiting outside. It was Chief.

"Hello," she said. Seeing him always brought on an avalanche of emotion— since that day when they went to dinner with the Prime Minister of Japan and some of his associates, she knew Chief was the devil himself. The dinner had been held in the wine cellar of a Michelin-starred restaurant, and she was the only woman at the table. She'd waited patiently for her turn to speak and by the time she found the courage to interject with one of her questions, Chief was quite drunk. As she opened her mouth to let the words out, Chief looked her in the eye from across the table and cut her off. Then he did the unthinkable.

"And just look at our beautiful Savannah. Savannah, did you have something to say?" Savannah struggled to find her words, but her mind was racing.

"No?" Chief asked, a laugh at the edge of his voice. "Well then let's admire her beautiful dress. Savannah, stand up! Let us see you!"

She had looked over at her father, and he had stared down at his drink. She longed for J.J., but then she wondered if he would have done a thing.

"Dad?" she had whispered. He pretended not to hear her.

She looked at Chief who was smiling and slowly stood up.

"Isn't she lovely?" Chief asked the room. Most of the people in it refused to meet her eyes except for her father's squirrelly advisor, Phillip. He looked at her like he was watching his favorite show. Some of the Japanese associates tried to get back to their conversations as if to spare her.

"Now turn around, Savannah," Chief commanded, and she realized who was leading the free world. It felt anything but free.

She slowly turned around, and Chief released a loud clap that made her jump.

"Just lovely," he said again. "OK, you can go now."

She had wanted to drop to her knees and scream at her father, but women like her did not make scenes like that. She stared at him for another full minute, begging him with her eyes to at least look back. When he didn't, she picked up her notebook filled with her carefully thought out questions and walked out of the room with her head held as high as she could.

"Your father wanted me to get you myself." Chief was thoughtfully gazing at her now, almost through her. She was worried he could read her mind and would use every thought against her. She was terrified that he would suddenly reach out and tear her heart from her chest in an absurd real-life Tarantino movie. But instead of pushing him and running away from him, she obediently followed him down the hall. She was ever the good child. The golden child. Her agent David followed closely behind, and she could feel his protective shield warm her back. She knew that he would do anything to serve her. She knew he would die for her, easily stretching his body in front of hers to catch a bullet. She also knew that he was in love with her; she could see it from his gestures, hear it in his voice. She could tangibly touch it when he stood a couple feet away from her.

She didn't know what love was, or if she was even capable of feeling it again, but she was sure that David knew something that she didn't, like he was in some secret club she hadn't yet been invited to. And it left her feeling empty, and it left her in awe of him.

The three of them walked in a single file line, passing paintings of past presidents, some of which had been taken down and burned because their "ideals were misaligned" with her father's. She looked at the portraits that remained, pausing at the one of her dad, larger than the rest, feeling David pause behind her. Her father stared down at her as if questioning if she was still with them, and she was grateful that she had never been asked outright. She didn't know what would happen to her if she told the truth.

She followed Chief out to a waiting car, and the driver opened the door for them. She slid into the back seat, and he sat down next to her. David sat in the front seat, head cocked in her direction. She was sure he could feel her panic as if it was his own.

They drove through the new Republic. Skyscrapers covered every square inch: shiny new, sparkling in the dull sun, emblazoned with her last name in a brilliant gold. If she didn't have a driver to take her everywhere, she might have forgotten which building was hers. It was easy to get lost in a sea of blinding sameness.

One of the towers stood out from the rest, and Savannah was sure she had never been there before. It looked like an old brick castle with a skyscraper stuck on the top of it. It was as if a bratty child had glued an ugly toy to his parent's family heirloom. Without meaning to, she felt herself speaking to Chief.

"What was that building?" She felt stupid, like a little girl who knew nothing about the world around her, but she hadn't traveled outside her very small circle since she had arrived in the Republic three and a half years ago.

As expected, Chief scoffed at her, and she regretted asking the question.

"Never mind," she began, but he stopped her.

"No, no. It's fine. You wouldn't know, you sheltered girl. It's the Smithsonian."

"The Smithsonian? I went with my mother when I was a kid. It didn't look like this." She swept her hand in the direction of the castle-skyscraper, its once beautiful gardens littered with statues of her father and other Dictators whom he respected.

Chief laughed a little, and it made her stomach turn in protest. "We made it better," he said, staring out of the window. Proud. "We made everything better."

They pulled up to the building, and David hurried to open the car door for them. He held Savannah's gloved hand, perhaps for a moment too long, as she stepped onto the gold sidewalk that sparkled with her father's logo.

Walking through heavy doors, Savannah was suddenly angry that her father sent Chief to escort her to his "big surprise," and she wondered why he had chosen a man she considered her enemy. She had visions of seeing the few endangered animals left in the world being tortured. She even had a fleeting thought that she was slowly walking toward her own execution in four thousand dollar heels. Chief walked precisely two feet behind her, whistling an eerie tune, shoes clip-clopping down the long hallway, and she couldn't help but feel like she was being followed by her future assailant. She turned back to make sure David was still there. He always was.

They entered a grand room that had been used for a rotating exhibit. The glass cases were covered in thick velvet curtains. She thought she could hear her heartbeat echoing against the walls like a screaming child.

She stood in the middle of the room. Chief had disappeared. She heard clapping, and her father appeared out of nowhere with his TV smile on his face.

"Dad, what's going on? Is Chief going to come out here and spray us with bullets?" She was only half kidding.

"Shhhhh." Her father looked around quickly like he was afraid. She believed, incredulously, that he was. She wondered how many of those whispered conversations between her father and his most trusted advisor were actually threats or scare tactics or worse.

"I will not be quiet!" She raised her voice, and he grabbed onto her arm so hard it hurt. She could feel David move in her direction ever so slightly, and she wondered for the first time if he would have to protect her from her own father. And if he would do it.

"You'll scare them," her dad said desperately in a hushed voice.

"Scare what?" She glanced around nervously, wanting to see what was behind the curtains. Needing to see what was behind the curtains.

Her father flashed his award-winning smile again and slowly raised his arms. The curtains lifted with them like he was the host of a maniacal game show.

At first Savannah saw feet or even whole bodies at the bottom of the cases, writhing. The horror that had been sitting in the frontal lobe of her brain now released and exploded throughout her entire body. She didn't know what to feel, think, do and believed her adrenaline could have powered the entire Republic.

All around her, surrounding her on all sides, were people. Human beings. Some were kicking their feet in pain, rolling around on the floor, trying to escape their own bodies. They were frothing at the mouth. They were trying to release a devil of their own making, and it was clear he would never leave no matter how desperately they wanted him to.

Some of them were staring out into a world only they had visited, some chewing on an invisible piece of food, almost thoughtfully, unaware of what the others around them were going through: the comedown.

Her father was staring at her face, trying to read her reaction. In his typical fashion, he contorted how she was feeling into a neat little box that fit perfectly on the shelf of his agenda.

"You love it!" he told her. It wasn't a question, and she knew the difference.

"Dad, what have you done?" she whispered. He either didn't hear her or decided not to.

"They're my prizes! The biggest players in the Resistance. I thought I'd put them on display, and the great people of the Republic can come to see them and learn more about them." He had his hands above his head in excitement, almost pumping his fists in the air.

She suddenly felt like someone was watching her and turned slowly to see Chief holding a small video camera. Despite herself, she flashed a brilliant toothy smile and then immediately scolded herself.

"Cut!" Chief yelled and put down the camera. He shook hands with her father in congratulations.

"Does J.J. know about this?" she asked. Her husband had been distant, and she hadn't seen him in a week. She wanted to tell herself that there was a way to forgive him if he'd known about this new exhibit and hadn't told her about it.

To her horror, the Dictator pointed at her as if she had guessed the winning answer. "He helped me plan it!"

131

Savannah looked around, wondering where J.J. was now. She assumed he had guessed what her reaction would be, and she wouldn't see him for another week or two. She had married a coward, and if things had been different, she would have pulled out her phone and demanded a divorce. But it had already been announced that J.J. was next in line for the Dictatorship whenever her father decided he was done or couldn't do the job anymore. She couldn't leave him now, even if she wanted to. There was nowhere to go.

Her father grabbed her hand and led her around the exhibit, as if he was a child proudly showing off the paintings he had created with his fingers.

"This one was a fighter." He pointed down to a placard at the bottom of each display case, telling the different stories of the Resistance. "She led the movement in New York that shut down all the subways. But we got her!"

The woman was having a spasm, her eyes rolled back in her head.

"Dad, she's suffering. Help her. Please." Savannah pulled on his sleeve a bit as if she could convince him to suddenly have empathy for anyone who crossed him.

"That's the fun part, Van. They're all on different cycles now, but we're working on getting them on the same comedown schedule. We let the drugs leave their system and just when we think they can't take it anymore, they get a big dose." The Dictator clapped his hands together, a little boy at a party just for him.

A buzzer sounded and tubes lowered down into each of the glass cases. Large white pills were released into metal bowls that Savannah hadn't noticed before. The Resistance sleepers all made their way to their lifeblood by way of crawling on elbows or staggering against a pane of glass, arms outstretched.

The sleeper next to Savannah didn't move. She was staring out of her glass cage, shifting back and forth on her toes. She didn't seem to be staring off into space, either. Savannah felt like this woman could see them.

Savannah looked over at her father and Chief who were patting each other's backs and discussing the exhibit's expansion. Keeping her gaze fixed on them, she carefully made her way toward the display, pretending she was interested in her father's prizes.

The woman's eyes followed the Dictator's daughter as she walked slowly to stand right below her. Savannah glanced down at the placard: *Sarah Montgomery, Leader of Purple Nation. Captured, 2017*

Savannah had heard all about Purple Nation. They had staged protests and sit-ins across the country and had even been accused of taking a low-level advisor hostage. They had been all over the news. Every single day. Until they weren't anymore. They had all seemed to evaporate into the atmosphere.

She put her hand against the glass, and immediately Sarah dropped to her knees. With steady eyes and a purposeful palm, the sleeper put a shaking hand up to meet Savannah's. Their gazes locked, and Savannah could tell it took a tremendous amount of effort for Sarah to keep her pupils focused. Her other hand made a flicking motion as if she was shooing away a fly—it was almost as if by controlling her eyes, the rest of her body was forced to fidget.

"Are you OK?" Savannah mouthed. She didn't know what else to say. It was the first time she had seen a sleeper regain consciousness, even if it was just a little bit.

Sarah nodded, head jerking in short sharp motions. Savannah smiled. Someone was really in there. This woman had woken up.

Taking the deepest breath, Savannah held up a finger to the woman behind the glass, and mouthed, "I'll be back."

She gathered all the courage she used to feel before her father had initiated the end of the world. She tried to remember how she felt when she mattered or wanted something or cared about anything at all. She pulled at emotions deep inside her and carefully placed them at the tip of her voice box. Then she bravely marched over to her father and began to speak.

"Daddy, I have a request." She gave him a smile she hoped he could not resist, and he immediately smiled back, his veneers threatening to escape his mouth.

"What's that Van? Anything for you."

"Well, I was thinking," she began, thoughts racing. "And, if it's OK with you, I'd love to have an aide. A woman who can help me get ready for events and manage my schedule."

The Dictator looked confused for a moment, but just then his phone rang. "Of course, Van. You could use some help. Chief can find someone for you."

"David's going to help me!" she shouted without meaning to.

Chief looked angry, but her father was already distracted by his call. "Sure, David, sure." He put his hand over his phone and hissed at Chief. "We have to get back to the office."

Savannah tried her best to pretend Chief wasn't there as she took in a deep breath.

With that, they scurried out of the exhibit, and Savannah and David were left alone with the sleepers.

David stood at complete attention, eyes fastened to a specific point in the wall. Savannah walked over to stand right in front of him.

"David?" she said gently. He broke his stare and looked down at her with soft eyes.

"Yes, Ms. Savannah?"

"We are going to save that sleeper. I need your help."

"Anything, Ms. Savannah," he answered without allowing even a breath between request and answer.

"I need you to go to the factory on the edge of the Republic and find a sleeper that looks like her. We don't have a lot of time."

David looked torn. "But I can't leave you, Ms. Savannah," he said in a quiet voice.

Savannah glanced back at Sarah who was fighting every cell in her body to stay awake and not grab for the pills and throw them in her mouth and mash them down with her hungry jaws.

"OK," she finally sighed. "You're right. Let's go together."

She walked over and put her hand up to the glass again. "I'll come back for you," she mouthed. Sarah nodded, jerking her head in every direction.

Savannah's heels thundered as she walked quickly out of the exhibit, David so close, she thought he might trip over her.

"We don't have much time," she said again without turning around, and together they raced toward the waiting car.

2031, PORTLAND, MAINE

Elena had become a target. She watched out of her side eye each morning like a vulnerable rabbit exposed in the woods. Darren always arrived at the factory right on time. He held up his wrist to have his chip scanned, proving with a noble salute that he was a loyal servant to the regime. He clocked in at precisely 7:55am like the dedicated worker he was.

Every time she heard the beep of his chip scanning, Elena instinctively felt her breath quicken, and she had to work harder than usual to slow it down and keep it steady. She knew what was coming because it had started happening every day.

Her body ached from her late night adventures with Elliot and her daytime assaults from Darren. If this was the real world that she was supposed to grow up in, her loving parents would have never let their privileged daughter be assaulted—if it did happen, they would have had the best lawyers locking her predator up forever. They would have shaken their heads and subtly reached for each other's hands had she brought home a man like Elliot, one from the wrong side of nowhere whose mother had destroyed her life and his by way of lethal injection. But she had not grown up in the real world. From the moment the militia had taken her mom to prison, she had been in an unexplainable hell, which now included a detached love interest and a brutal post-lunch rapist. Some days, when Darren wanted to get an early start, his episodes even caused her to miss her gravel shake, and she felt precious ounces disintegrate from her body and into the polluted air.

She moved a can from one section of the assembly line and placed it onto the next. It was the most advanced job at the factory, requiring just slightly more brainpower than pushing buttons or pulling levers, and she was awarded such a task a couple of days after the first rape. She considered it her consolation prize, and it made her wonder if Darren really thought he was doing his sleeper girlfriend a favor by making her work harder than the rest.

After four hours, the buzzer sounded and every sleeper stopped what they were doing in unison. They all hung there, as if suspended in space, a slight waver to their posture. Guards walked up and down the assembly line with assault rifles at attention as if they were in charge of hardened criminals and not people who had been drugged and conditioned into human worker bees. Elena concentrated on shifting back and forth slightly, the sign of a functional sleeper waiting to be told what to do next. Elliot had taught them all how to perfect the move during one of their first meetings, and the group of them had practiced for thirty minutes. At the time, it felt like a sorry excuse for an aerobics class, but during moments like these, she wanted to bow to Elliot in gratitude. He had taught them how to make it look like their eyes were glazed over or how to hang their limbs just right. He was the most prolific student of the addict because he had lived with it, slept with it and breathed it in. It was all he knew.

Another buzzer sounded, and they marched in line to get their gravel shakes, holding out their hands and grasping onto metal cups. They sucked them down through wide straws and dropped the empty cups into a large plastic bin. The clang of the metal made Elena want to jump out of her skin. Every empty cup clanking around in the bin meant she was closer to that time of the day.

They made their way back to their stations, and she felt the now familiar tug on her arm. The sleeper behind her got confused and tried to follow her as she was pulled in a different direction, but Darren gently guided the line back into formation. Elena stood there waiting, *back and forth, short and slow movements, like you have to go to the bathroom, but not as frantic, like there's an itch you have to scratch but you have all day to do it, back and forth, back and forth.*

She could feel Elliot's rage rather as Darren dragged her back to the office. He pushed her body down in a chair, and she sat there staring as he darted around to sit behind the clear computer screen. So much information was streaming all at once, the messages and feeds almost seemed to be going haywire. Darren put on a pair of glasses and stared at the screen. He started nodding. *The glasses helped him understand the data.* This revelation was probably worth what was coming next, but there was even more intel to come.

"You gotta hold on a bit," Darren said in her direction as if someone in her condition would have noticed or cared. He picked up what looked like a phone and punched in some buttons.

"Yah, we got some sorta signal coming in down here at 59118. Says here that yous want to transport some of our sleepers?" He looked nervously over at Elena, and she realized that he had come to think of her as some sort of girlfriend, however sick that was.

"Well, we need 'em. We gotta good crew over here. We don't want them young folk. Theys a pain in the ass to train." Darren stopped talking and swallowed hard. "Yes ma'am. No, I didn't mean to sound disobedient. I just...Alright ma'am."

He hung up the phone and took off the glasses. He looked defeated, as if someone had stolen his prom date.

"Well, honey. We might not get much more time. Not sure if they gonna take you, but they want the high functionin' ones for they new factory outside the Republic, and they want the Jane Does like you, sugar. I has a feeling you gonna be on that rail. I better enjoy you while I can." And with that, he tore her pants off so violently, her button popped off and her zipper cut at her skin. She wanted to scream in agony, in joy of the possibility of gathering so much information in one single minute and of the possibility of getting closer to the Republic. The thought of it kept her sane as he pounded away at her until she felt like she would burst into a billion tired, angry, sore pieces.

When he was done, Darren gathered her up like she was his living doll and rocked her back and forth singing her a song. She felt droplets of water on her head and realized that he was crying. She thought about the sight they must have made sitting there on the concrete floor, him in his military fatigues weeping from what could have been with his sleeper lover; her completely naked from the waist down, with small trails of blood escaping from where the zipper had snagged her.

Finally, he pulled himself together and wiped away his tears. He shoved her onto the cold, hard ground, and she wanted to wince as her bones hit the concrete. He pulled himself up, brushing off his pants. Then he roughly dressed her and marched her back to her post.

She was grateful that Elliot was nowhere near her in line and enjoyed her last couple of hours moving cans. She told herself over and over that there weren't too many more times she'd have to endure this. Something new was coming. She was sure of it.

* * *

Elena had to wait until the next night to tell anyone her news, and her leg bounced nervously in the old cellar of Boone's Oyster House. The floor was littered with oyster shells of all sizes and shapes as if the people who worked there had enjoyed a fuck all shucking extravaganza upon learning that the world was ending. When she walked on them with her hard boots, the sound reminded her of days at the beach during low tide, walking on crackly shells in rubbery water shoes and finding treasures for her bright orange bucket. Sometimes her dad would carry her all the way back to the house because she had left all her energy in the ocean, orange bucket swinging and hitting his chest with every step.

She leaned down and picked up a few of the shells, breathing in a time when the waters were swimmable and the shellfish edible. She wished she had tried some of the things her parents always told her she would love: clams, scallops, oysters, mussels, lobster. It all seemed gross to her at the time, but she knew they were always right about what she would like. Sometimes it made her so angry with herself, all the chances lost, but she'd just as quickly release it, telling her young self that she had done the very best she could.

She'd found a stack of old paper menus, still in tact, and the nub of a pencil most likely used for scribbling down the night's order. She held the pencil in her hand and it felt foreign and it felt so completely familiar like it had always been a part of her, like she had never not held one for all those years.

The pencil touched down to the paper, softly at first and then more purposeful until it was sweeping across the page. It wasn't the most effective tool, but soon the nightmare she was living came alive on the page in short bursts of emotion. She drew a large eye, and factories erupted out from the lid where the eyelashes should have been. She was adding herself and Elliot reflected in the pupil when she heard the sound of oyster shells crunching.

Her pencil lifted up off the page, the spell broken. It was Elliot. He ran over to her, sliding a bit, and hugged her with all his years of wanting someone to love and to love him back. Elena quickly slipped her drawing onto a shelf and opened her arms to his fierceness. She might not have welcomed it on any other day, but in that dank, briny cellar she needed human touch in the highest dose possible.

They all gathered on worn wooden chairs, and Elena, spilling with her news, decided she would go first. She picked up a shell and held it in her hand, rubbing the smooth part with her thumb as she talked.

"I heard something, well, something extraordinary today," she began.

No one moved. She was worried that everyone had stopped breathing, and she needed them now more than ever. They had never heard her talk with such a sense of promise.

"I was in the office at the factory." She glanced quickly at Elliot, afraid he would be staring at the ground or out the window, ashamed for her, but he met her eyes bravely and did not look away.

"And this guard saw something on his screen, and he put on these glasses, these see-through glasses, and then he could interpret what the data was telling him." The others turned to each other and whispered for a split second, but then quickly quieted down and turned their attention back to Elena.

"He saw something that interested him, and he called someone on this flat silver thing that I didn't even know was a phone," she said laughing a little while everyone sat stunned because they had never seen her so lighthearted and charming.

Most of them had never heard her laugh before.

"And then he said…" She paused and smiled, and Elliot marveled at how beautiful she was when she was handed just one jagged shard of joy. "That they are moving some of us to a factory outside the Republic."

She looked at each of their faces, but they didn't mirror her excitement. Silver spoke first.

"But what does that mean? Who are they moving?" Her lower lip trembled like a small child's, and Elena wanted to reach for her and coddle her, but she knew it was better to let her wade through her emotions, even if they knocked her down.

"Darren said that it was going to be the high functioning ones." She saw Elliot's eyebrows raise as she used her rapist's name, but he still didn't utter a word or break his stare. "And he also mentioned something about Jane Does. So I assume I am going to be on the rail from our factory. Probably Elliot, too. The rest of you, I don't know."

"How the fuck do you know if you and Elliot are going to be on the rail? We could all be on the stupid rail!" Silver's voice was a high-pitched shrill, and Lana sitting next to her reached over with a firm squeeze on her shoulder to both comfort her and remind her to lower her voice.

"Silver." Elena took a deep breath. "We've talked about this. There are some things that are completely out of our control. Mostly everything, really. But this is a chance to get close to the Republic. I don't know for sure if some of us will go or all of us or none of us. But this is huge."

Elena went over and knelt next to Silver, grabbing both of her hands. "Silver, look at me." She shook her friend's hands, and finally the young girl looked her hero in the eye.

"What if I get left behind?" Silver asked like a soon-to-be orphaned child. "What if I never see you again?"

"Then that is what happens. We have to be strong and united in every way we can. This is our chance to get close to the Dictator and maybe even the Controller."

"We don't even know where the Controller is," Silver said, looking up at the tin ceiling.

"No. No, we don't. But it's a chance. We have to take it. We don't have a choice." Elena stood up, stripping off her maternal façade and zipping up her warrior one. She turned to the group.

"Listen everyone. We might not get a chance like this again. Most of us have been stuck in a hamster wheel at the same factories for years. They've never transported a group of us out of here before, and certainly not near the Republic. We have to be organized, and we can't slip up. We have to be tough." She looked over at Silver. "Understand?" The girl nodded.

"It sounds like we have a week. I will report what's happening to the Controller tonight and get our protocol. Then you all have to be fully prepared in case it's one of you. Got it?" They all nodded. Despite Silver's distress, there was a beautiful electricity in the room that Elena could see in full color. She felt like she could reach out and touch it. It was a string of lights on Christmas; it was a group of friends holding hands. It was hope. They all drank it in and pulled at it with their fingertips.

The group stood up and embraced, holding each other tight in a magnificent cluster of promise. Silver was in the middle as if she needed cushioning all around her from the impact of what was to come. Soon, they were collapsing all over each other and laughing, shells cracking beneath their boots, and even Silver couldn't help but be swept up in the possibility of it all.

2018, PENNSYLVANIA TO NEW YORK CITY

The small, abandoned girl decided to make her way up north. She trekked through the woods until she reached a highway with an overpass. In her past life, she would have never been allowed to cross it. Today, she squared her shoulders bravely and waited for the light like she had been taught to do. Then she marched across six lanes of traffic to get to the old diner.

The bell jangled when she opened the door, and a woman looked up from her phone.

"Yes?" She stared at Elena over drugstore glasses. She had stringy bangs and her hair was pulled back so tightly, it gave her a cheap facelift. Her eyes were outlined in the thickest kohl imaginable and crowned by a swipe of bluish eye shadow. The middle of her two front teeth was caked with some unexplainable black soot—a permanent shadow cast inside her mouth. Elena cocked her head to the side, staring at her. In her hyper-liberal privileged life, she didn't come into contact with people like this very often. To her, this woman seemed like a piece of art that had been a mistake.

"Hi. I need a bus ticket to New York City," Elena said without any hesitation or awareness of her age or appearance.

"Son, they stopped going to the City. We can get you to Jersey, though. You lucky. This is one of our last rides." She looked down at her screen for a second. "Nah, kid. Actually this the last one." The woman started punching buttons on an ancient register.

Elena was stunned. Son. She reached up and touched her hair and realized she looked like a boy. Her face flushed with embarrassment, but she told herself that she didn't have time for vanity. Then she felt her heart plummet as she realized that was something her mother would have said.

"Why aren't you going to New York anymore?" Elena's brain was mentally scanning the handwritten sheet her mother had left her. Her safe house was in Greenwich Village. Without a phone, she was already worried about how she would get there.

"Ah, son. They putting that city on lockdown. They handing out the assignments. I got mine. Militia." The woman beamed as if someone had made her the queen of something. Elena didn't understand what "the assignments" meant or why they were putting the city on lockdown (or even what "lockdown" was), but the fact that this woman seemed pleased with the state of affairs put Elena on high alert. She pegged her instantly for what her mother used to call "scrapers"—the have-nots who scrape at nothing to believe in something. The scrapers were the reason the president won the election in the first place. He was acutely aware of their raw underbellies and painted them a future so painstakingly perfect that they would have leaped off bridges or clawed their way up walls to get a taste of it.

Elena stood looking at the scraper with her muddied eyes and knew she had no choice. There was no home to go back to, and even if there was, they'd surely come for her soon—whoever they were. When her adult self looked back at that moment in the dingy diner, roaches crawling on walls above the front counter, the smell of bacon fat hanging forever in the air, she wanted to hug that little girl and her bravado. *How naive! How perfectly brave and hopeful!* If she were lucky, her grownup version might someday be able to grab at even a pinch of that resilience.

"Well, I'll take a ticket anyway. As close as you can get me."

"Your choice. That'll be forty dollars." The woman smacked her gum and pretended to look aloof.

"Forty dollars! It says twenty on the wall." Elena pointed to the sign.

"Well, these are desperate times, ain't they?" The woman finally met Elena's gaze and her shoulders fell. "Oh fine, you smartass kid. Just give me the money."

Elena felt around in her go-bag for the hidden pocket and reached small fingers inside. She was careful to pull out only the bill she needed (her mother had taught her over and over again to never show how much money she had), and handed a twenty to the woman.

"There you go. Godspeed," the woman said, handing her a ticket.

"There is no god," Elena responded automatically. She hoisted her pack up high on her shoulders as she went to wait at the front of the line.

The bus pulled up after fifteen minutes, and she was the only one to board. A lucid man sauntered down the stairs and asked for her ticket. She felt the hairs on the back of her bare neck stand up tall as his eyes, at half mast, gazed at the slip of paper she handed him.

"You going to New York, are ya? I can take ya to New Jersey, but I can't get ya through the tunnel."

He slapped her on the shoulder, and she flinched a bit. His words were slurred like her father's in the kitchen that day, the last day she saw him. She knew he had taken pills like her parents or some other debilitating drug, that he was dependent on it, and that he would vomit on the floor of his surprisingly clean bus if he did not take more of it on time. She knew what drugs did to parents, to people, to kids, and she knew that when her father had started taking them, he was barely capable of walking up the stairs to his bedroom. She, a small ten-year-old girl, had done her best to help her father, and she knew what bearing the weight of a grown man felt like as he took one step at a time. She knew that this man who was trying to read her ticket through blurred vision was not truly capable of driving her the hour and a half to "close to New York City," but she knew that she had no choice. He was the only way to get near the safe house.

She climbed aboard and sat in the very front seat. There was one other passenger asleep in the back.

The driver made his way to his seat, stumbling a bit. After a couple of minutes, he seemed to find his wits and started the engine.

"What's your name?" Elena asked loudly as he pulled out of the station.

"Lyle," he said back. He turned his head slightly and swerved into the other lane.

"Great!" Elena said, too enthusiastically, as if the octave of her voice could steer the bus back in the right direction.

The driver was quiet for a second, concentrating. Then he asked, "What's yours?"

"Elena," she said quietly.

"You're a girl?" She nodded, scowling a bit. "That's a nice name, Miss," Lyle told her.

She kept talking to him, keeping her voice low and steady, asking him questions at strategically placed intervals along the way. She quickly found his rhythm. It was choreography an addict could understand, and her

144

questions were like calming commands to keep them safe and between the lines of the road.

After exactly one hour and twenty-eight minutes, they arrived three hundred yards from the mouth of the Holland Tunnel. Militia were strewn across the entrance bolstering machine guns.

"Why aren't they letting anyone in, Lyle?" She was proud of him for getting her all the way there. She hadn't believed that he could, and he made her feel like anything was possible.

"Don't know, Miss Elena. They letting people out, but no one can go in. They says it's too full, and the protests was too much. The Dictator don't like that. Lots of people getting in trouble." Lyle laughed a strange laugh, but Elena decided he didn't mean it.

"I know," said the young girl whose mom had gotten in trouble and was put to sleep and taken from her. The word "Dictator" sent her heart galloping around in her chest, but she thought better than to press him on it. The notion of people doing things "the Dictator don't like" had cost Elena everything she had ever known to care about.

"OK." He carefully pulled into an abandoned gas station and Elena squeezed her eyes shut as he got too close to the gas pumps and ended up missing them by just a couple of inches. She believed that her mom or some external force was keeping her safe, and she bowed her head in gratitude.

"This is as far as we go, Miss Elena." Lyle put the bus into park and turned to look at her. She could tell he felt a bit fatherly toward her and that this old man cared about her, even after their short bus ride.

"Lyle? Why did you start taking pills?" she asked gently. For some reason, she had to know.

Tears welled up in his eyes and spilled over the infinite folds on his cheeks.

"Well. Miss Elena. My son died." He inhaled what seemed to be the most painful breath, even though Elena knew for certain that the pills took all the pain away.

"I'm sorry," she said, quietly. He reached back and patted her thoughtfully on the head.

"They put up one of them pill stations right in my neighborhood. They made my son take them pills and told me I was assigned to the militia." Lyle sniffed and buried his face in his rough palms. "My son mighta been a goddamn liberal, but he was a smart boy." He gazed out of the window. "Maybe he was too smart for his own good."

Lyle looked her in the eyes as best as he could, and she nodded for him to continue. "One day, I found him in his bed. He had gotten into the pills and taken so many of them. So I decided to take some.

"When they find out what I did, they won't let me in the militia. They want the militia clean and alert. And anyways, you can take the pain away. You can dull it real good. You can make it so it don't really matter, not really. But after a couple of hours, I just see his face again, and it all comes rushing back."

Elena got up from her seat and walked around. She hugged him. A hat with the Dictator's campaign slogan on it slid off his head, revealing a bald mottled scalp. "I hope you find some peace, Lyle." He attempted a heavy smile.

She turned away from him and pulled the lever of the door, walking down the steps of the bus and out into the mayhem.

It was dark, and the lights from the police cars were blinding. She felt like she was walking toward an end of the world film. Her dad used to watch them late at night, and she would creep downstairs to catch a glimpse from the hallway beyond the living room. The movies never scared her; they opened her eyes to unthinkable fears that only existed in runaway imaginations. As she glanced at the tunnel, she felt like they had prepared her. If aliens suddenly descended on the city, she wouldn't have blinked.

She placed her palm on the glass of the door as Lyle shut it. She peered through the pane and saw him pop a handful of pills and slump over his steering wheel. It was as if he had decided to get Elena, his precious cargo, to her destination before he released himself to the pain the only way he knew how.

Elena took stock of the ten or so men and women standing guard in front of a single tunnel that divided the real world from the city she had once described to her mother and father as the "center of the Earth."

It doesn't matter, nothing matters but you getting there. It doesn't matter, nothing matters but you getting there.

She knew that a ten-year-old marching up to the entrance of the tunnel would send off a mass hysteria, and she was worried that they'd snatch her and put her into some sort of foster care if that sort of thing still existed. So she hugged the wall of an abandoned building and slowly made her way toward the opening. She was small and wearing all black. She flattened herself against the side of an abandoned truck and tried to summon some of the fire her mother always told her she had inside her.

The blackness of night used its heavy hand to shield her as she watched and waited. Watched and waited. She heard one of the guards shouting to the others, and they all gathered around a screen he was holding. Elena could hear the faintest voice of the Dictator as they gaped at his promises on the small device. She quickly moved to a wall right before the tunnel, then slipped her way inside.

No one noticed her. She walked through an empty tunnel, almost skipping because she had made it, *she had made it*, and she imagined giant hands made of black soot patting her on the back and guiding her along.

But she was terrified of what was on the other side.

Elena emerged from the opening of the long underwater snake that had spit countless visitors into the belly of TriBeCa and looked around in shock. She had visited with her parents only a couple of years earlier, sitting, eating, people watching, feeling the sun on her face and soaking in the infinite buzzing around her. Now it was a ghost town with only military vehicles on the road. The taxis were gone, the stores and restaurants closed down. Once in a while she saw a sleeper who hadn't been picked up yet, but she knew to not be afraid of them. She could outrun them, push them over, scream in their faces and get no reaction at all.

I'm not afraid of them, she told herself, but she flattened her body against the sides of buildings and crossed abandoned streets quickly so no one would zero in on her determination.

Elena leaned against a red brick building that used to be an organic market, looked up at the sky and asked, *Where are you?* She suddenly felt like a small, lost child and needed her parents more than ever. In the less than twenty-four hours since they were taken, the memories of them as drug addicts had faded away and all she remembered was her mom and dad. *Why did you leave me?* She wiped angrily at her tears as they ran down her face. They made furious rivers on the back of her hand, which was covered in an ominous dust.

She stood there for twenty more minutes, gulping the heavy polluted air into her hungry lungs and trying to find her chutzpah. She did not belong in an apocalyptic version of Manhattan, yet here she was. She squinted her eyes and there it was: a sign for Sixth Avenue. With a forceful push off the wall, she trudged on.

After walking uptown for what felt like another fifteen minutes, she saw the entrance to the subway. The air was so thick, it made everything look like it was covered in a layer of grit, but she could make out the bluish-grey circle with a large "E" in the center. Her small hand gripped the filthy railing. The stairs led to blackness, maybe to hell, or to the bottom of the end of times. She reached into a pocket in her pack and took out a miniature flashlight. Holding it at her hip, she slowly descended into the depths of the underground.

One, two, three, four. The counting helped her stay calm as her foot connected with each step. *Five, six, seven.* She felt her sneaker slip. The ground went out from under her, and she landed hard on the step. She wanted to scream out in pain, but she bit her lip until she tasted blood. She could not draw any attention to herself.

Finally, Elena determined that she wasn't seriously injured and slowly stood up again. *Eight, nine, ten, eleven, twelve.* She was at the bottom. She felt the flat surface with the tip of her toe and shuffled forward a couple of feet. Her flashlight barely cut through the deepest dark. A high-pitched squeak resounded off the subway walls, and she remembered her dad telling her, laughing, how big the rats were down there.

"I saw one the size of a cat once," he had said, holding his hands up, and she had gently punched him in the chest to stop kidding her. Now she wasn't so sure.

She shuffled forward some more and didn't hear anymore squeaks, and kept going, going, going, shuffling, back against the wall like the instructions had said, shuffling until she felt the wall disappear behind her right hand. She carefully stepped one foot down a narrow stairwell, then the other, then turned to face a door. It was open just the slightest bit.

Elena quickly pulled the instructions out of a pocket in her pack even though she had memorized them—even though she knew them better than her own name and birthday and the pledge to the flag and the soundtrack from her favorite Disney movie that she had made her parents watch millions of times (despite her mom's protests about "princess culture"). The flashlight beam found its way to the bottom of the page, the part about the door. *Knock three times, then kick three times with your foot. If no one answers, sit down on the floor and wait for someone to return.* It did not say anything about the door being open or what to do if it was.

She slid to the floor out of exhaustion or maybe a little bit of defeat and thought about what she should do. Then, as if it had a mind of its own, her black sneaker pushed the door all the way open. Her body, led by curiosity and childlike stupidity, lay down on its stomach, and its elbows starting pulling her through the opening. She reached out her left hand, the one with the flashlight, and shined it as far in front of her as she could reach. A man was curled up on a blanket on the floor. He was covered in blood.

* * *

Elena woke up with a burning sensation on the side of her face. She reached up and touched it, recoiling from her own fingers. For a minute, she didn't know where she was, and then it came back to her in a series of rapid memories that rammed into each other like a pileup: *bus, tunnel, streets, stairs, door, man, blood.* She squeezed her eyes shut and longed for her childhood bed and the glow-in-the-dark stars on the ceiling. But when she opened them again, it was all still there.

With shaking hands, she reached for her flashlight that had fallen to the floor and slowly stood up. She walked on tiptoes and knelt down next to the man. He was exactly as the instructions described, although she had imagined someone more professional looking. His hair grew in every which way, threatening to overtake his face, and there was a distinct odor about him—one that she had never smelled before.

She reached down and placed two fingers on his neck, having to burrow under layers of unwashed locks to reach surprisingly warm flesh. Her fingers snapped away when she felt a pulse. She hadn't expected him to be alive.

This young girl suddenly needed him to be alright; he became her sole reason for existing and carrying on with this stupid adventure. Elena shook the man hard, putting her mouth up to his ear, almost gagging on the smell, shouting, "Please wake up!"

149

He opened his eyes and jumped up when he saw her.

"Who are you?" he asked, putting his hand in front of his eyes as if her presence was blinding him.

"You're awake!" She couldn't hide her little kid joy, but quickly checked her excitement and reminded herself to be cautious. Her mother's general rule was to trust no one until they cared enough to earn it.

"I'm Elena. I'm Sarah Montgomery's daughter." She watched as the man's face changed from annoyance into an expression of disbelief and even awe. She was used to this type of reaction. To hundreds of thousands of people, maybe even millions, her mother had been a national hero.

"Elena. Your mom talked about you sometimes." The man smiled at her, and she decided it was sincere.

"She did? Did you know her?"

"I never met her in person. But we were good friends online before everything happened." He pointed up to the ceiling referring to the world above them. "She's an incredible woman."

"Was," Elena corrected him.

"Yes. I'm sorry. I heard what happened." He bowed his head in respect.

"It's OK," she said, even though of course it wasn't. "What is this place? What happened to you?" She had been waiting for what seemed like days to find out why her mother had sent her here.

The man ran his hands through his hair and looked as sad as she felt. "This is my lab. I was meeting a friend to get an important package sent out of the City, but they killed her." Elena could tell that he was trying to tell the absolute shortest version of the story, and she didn't blame him.

"I'm sorry. So you're not hurt?"

He looked down at his arm covered in sticky blood as if he had noticed it for the first time. The sight of it seemed to devastate him, and he closed his lips tightly around a cry.

Elena put a hand on his other arm, and they sat like that for a couple of minutes. Finally, she asked, "What was in the package?"

"My work. I've created a serum that acts like an antidote to their pills. When you take it, drugs don't affect you." He chuckled a little, even though his eyes still looked very sad. "Even if those barbarians find me, they can't drug me." He looked down at the blood soaked floor and whispered, "They can't get me."

They were both quiet for a moment as Elena absorbed everything he had just told her. Finally, she asked, "What's your name? There was no name in the instructions. Oh, and I'm supposed to ask you a question to make sure it's really you. I just didn't expect to find you on the ground."

"It's Benny. You can call me Benny. What's the question?" He smiled at her, and she was worried that he thought she was silly.

"What's the symbol of Purple Nation?" she asked.

"Ahhh. That's an easy one." He held up his wrist to show her his tattoo. "The purple star."

"Right," Elena said quietly, a little embarrassed.

"Well, can I offer you something to eat? Some tea? Water? I have a feeling we have a lot to catch up on, and I'm starving." He chuckled again.

Elena was suddenly hungrier than she'd ever been and realized she didn't remember the last time she'd eaten. She scolded herself for forgetting one of her mother's rules: *Always keep up your strength.*

"I'd really like that, if that's OK," she told him quietly.

"Elena. You are the daughter of one of the greatest activists of recent times. And she trusted me with making sure you were kept safe and that you carried out her work. Of course it's OK."

Elena felt her body relax (just a bit), and she told herself that she was safe (for the time being) and accepted hydrated food and lukewarm tea as if it was a grand feast in a gold-plated room.

2031, PORTLAND, MAINE

Elliot worked the line for three days fueled by a frenzied anticipation. He knew that there wouldn't be an announcement as to who was getting transported, but he couldn't help but hope that there would be some indication. The group had been meeting every night to try to prepare for any possible scenario, guided by instructions from the Controller.

He carefully glanced down the line at Elena, who was moving her cans across a gap, and allowed himself to think the worst. What if he got chosen and she didn't? Or her and not him? It would take every last bit of self control to not run after her or drag her with him.

This was the first gasp of hope that he'd had in more years than he'd care to count and now it was tormenting him.

He tried to remain calm as he saw Darren bring Elena back to the office three times a day since he had heard the news. As Elliot pushed his button, he fought to catch a glimpse of her. Each time she returned to her position in line, she looked more shaken.

If it's not her, I can't leave her with him, he vowed to himself, to the universe. *But it has to be her, otherwise Darren wouldn't have increased his sessions like this*. It was true that the other guards turned a blind eye when it came to abusing sleepers, but Darren was setting a record.

The cans continued to cycle through the line, aided by the sleepers' drowsy hands, and Elliot's worries rolled along with them.

On the fourth day, when he believed he couldn't exist with his own racing thoughts any longer, the new guard, Maggie, grabbed him firmly by the crook of the arm like she had been trained to do. The pressure from her thumb inside the bend of his elbow was something he had felt so many times, it had become a part of him. After finding him the "right dose" at the clinic, he had been sent to training camp with the other sleepers. For hours and days and weeks and months, they were conditioned. A chorus of buzzing told their barely functioning brains what to do, while a series of tight holds and pressure on certain parts of their bodies guided them along to a specific place or task. Of course, they could always be prodded along with sticks or guns, but, as this young cadet knew, it was not protocol.

She led him down the hall to a room he didn't think he had ever visited. He kept his eyes trained tightly on the ground and his stagger loose as she brought him around to what looked like a dentist's chair. Pressing two fingers on his triceps and two fingers on his quadriceps, she lowered him down into the seat.

"OK, then," she said, looking up at a corner of the room. Elliot knew she was talking to a camera, and he wondered who was watching her. He fantasized for a moment that it was Dictator One, the same version that he had met so many years ago. Elliot was positive that the man who changed everything was still alive; he believed that they were inextricably connected to each other, and when the Dictator's heart stopped, Elliot knew he would feel it.

Maggie walked over to a table where a bunch of tools were sitting. She picked each one of them up and studied them, then placed them back on the shiny surface.

"OK. I am picking up the deactivator." She held up a short-handled device with a flat square surface on the end, almost like a metal stamp, then she walked over to Elliot and sat down on the stool next to him. She pulled a set of glasses from the top of her head to rest on her nose. They were so small and clear Elliot hadn't noticed them until now.

"I am within deactivation of the subject," Maggie announced to the camera, once again looking up to the corner of the room.

She placed the metal square over the center of Elliot's wrist, paused and looked up, "I am deactivating the subject."

Elliot remembered the day he had gotten the chip. He had arrived at the training camp fully immersed in his new skin. Every second alone, he had been practicing his craft of being a sleeper, dragging painful memories into his limbs to create movements that he knew would fool everyone. The day had been grey and windy, the salt water still wafting an inviting smell, even though officials were already warning those still awake not to ever jump in.

Entering the training center was what Elliot imagined prison would be like. He was stripped naked and every crevice was examined. Cold and desperate not to shiver, he stood under a freezing spray of water as a guard scrubbed him raw with a long handled brush. Then he was pushed along by the end of it toward the uniform station.

A man and woman had dressed each sleeper quickly, snapping pants around legs, pulling shirts over heads, shoving boots onto feet. Everything was black and unlike any material Elliot had ever felt. It seemed to respond to his cold skin and immediately warmed him all over his body.

He was placed on a moving walkway, held in place by clips at the bottom of his boots. He imagined a real sleeper tipping over and getting caught in the churn, hair tangled up in the moving rails. But unbelievably, they stayed upright.

They all reached the end, and their boots were automatically unhooked as they were prodded along to the end of the room. The mass of them shuffled along as one large blob of flesh and cells and minimally working brains, pressing against a wall as if they could get through. Elliot was in the middle of them, feeling like he was going to have a panic attack as bodies pushed against him from all sides. He tried to get in sync with their shifting back and forth, but he couldn't. It had no rhythm.

Nothing made sense about it.

Slowly, the wall started to rise, and they all spilled into a hidden room. A line of guards stood at attention herding sleepers along as if they were a flock of mindless sheep. Elliot realized, almost for the first time, like a grand revelation that had been in front of his nose the whole time, that they were.

Each sleeper was placed in a tiny padded cell. As Elliot entered his, he was able to glance around at his new home from under his eyelids. There was a small bed coming out of the wall and a kid-sized toilet.

A buzzer sounded and the doors all shut at the same time. It was the first of millions of buzzers he was going to hear in his life.

The guards had come around and implanted the chips that day, a team of technicians entering one padded room at a time. It was his first real test. The pain from implanting the chip was the worst pain he'd ever felt in his entire life, and the screams that had wanted to get out still haunted him from the inside.

Maggie sat there holding the deactivator above his wrist, and Elliot braced himself.

"Deactivating," she called out, eyes focused on her subject. When she clamped down on the invisible chip, an indescribable shooting pain went up his arm and seemed to pinch his heart. He wanted to tell her that she could cause cardiac arrest if she wasn't careful, but he didn't say a word. He felt like he was going to pass out, but he couldn't.

She got up and walked over to the table again to pick up another torture device. "Picking up the reactivator," she said to the camera.

She walked over to him again and just as she was sitting down, a screen flashed on. Music blared into the room, and it reminded him of when he had been locked in the clinic, the images of his mother and excruciating death metal music taunting him. He knew what this broadcast meant: it was a message from the Dictator.

Maggie pretended that nothing was happening and continued to speak out loud even though it was impossible for whomever was sitting on the other end of that camera to hear her voice.

"So, listen," she said, holding the activator above his wrist. "I know you're not like the others." Elliot felt his eyes blink involuntarily, but she picked up on it. "See? I knew it."

Elliot tried not to breathe or move, and he told his entire body, *"Stay still, sleeper."*

"I am not going to give you away. I am going to help you." Her lips were barely moving. "I can't get into it now, but I am going to reactivate your chip, and it's going to say that you're supposed to go on that rail, and everything will seem fine. But I am going to slip this deactivator into your boot, and you're going to use it to escape when the time is right. If, that is, you still want to escape." Elliot blinked again. Anyone else would have missed it.

"Reactivating patient," Maggie announced, her voice still completely drowned out by the Dictator's propaganda speech. As the searing pain shot up his arm once again, Elliot thought about how every word sounded the same as when he used to watch the news with his mother all those nights. It was the same promises over and over again for fifteen years as the world exploded with lies.

Elliot watched her subtly tap the deactivator with her finger as she leaned down to examine her work. It rolled onto the floor and she disappeared to get it, out of sight from the camera. He could feel hard metal being stuffed inside the edge of his boot. Maggie quickly emerged wiping some loose strands of hair out of her face.

"Clumsy me!" she said to no one because the Dictator was still going on about how he was opening a series of new factories outside the Republic.

Maggie carefully plugged her tools into the side of a computer to reset them, and then back into some small drawers in the wall. Then she grabbed him by the crook of the arm again, not bothering to apply the pressure this time, and led him back to his post in the line.

Elliot felt lighter somehow, as if Maggie had reactivated more than just his wrist and given him a fresh start. He pushed his button with a kind of glow he had not felt since Ohio. He channeled the boy who believed in something bigger than himself, and the fact that he didn't know what that was made him feel alive.

After sucking down gravel shakes into swollen bellies, and clanging cups into a pile of lost lives, he saw some movement down the line where Elena was passing her cans. He assumed it was Darren again, and he felt the same sick punch he always did around this time of the day. But as he forced his eyes to look as far over as they could without being noticed, he saw that it was not Darren at all.

Maggie was grabbing Elena by the crook of the arm and leading her down to the lab.

2031, THE REPUBLIC

It was Thursday, which meant it was her day to visit her father. Savannah stood in front of a full-length screen that acted as a mirror, but enhanced how she really looked. She remembered thinking they were silly when they were first invented, but then she realized everything was just perception really, and she soon embraced the concept. If she ever saw a real mirror, she thought, she would probably die from the truth.

She smoothed down her red dress and pushed her hair behind her ears, feeling Sarah's eyes on her. But when Savannah turned to look at her, Sarah's eyes were cast down at the ground.

"Do you remember the day I brought you home?" Savannah asked her aide.

Sarah nodded, slowly, still looking at the ground. "Yes," she whispered. After six days, Sarah had finally emerged from her room dressed in a clean military uniform, her skin flushed with life and her shaking finally gone. Her long red hair had been brushed and put into a bun on the top of her head. When Savannah saw her, she had smiled, and Sarah had attempted a small smile back.

At first, Savannah had treated Sarah like a grown doll she could dress and boss about. Sarah was only about four years older than her mistress, but in the previous world they would have never been friends. Sarah would have thought Savannah vapid and even stupid, and Savannah would have believed Sarah to be a snobby feminist. But it was not the old world, and it was hard to find a bit of light in so much darkness.

Savannah still remembered the day everything changed between them.

She had been crying on her bed, and Sarah had walked in on her.

"I'm, oh, I'm so sorry, Ms. Savannah." Sarah had quickly turned and started walking out of the room, fidgeting with the front of her pants.

"No, it's fine," Savannah had mumbled through her tears. "Come in. Really." She realized how much she ached for a girlfriend. She tried not to think about Deanna, but the memories were always there, and they always led her back to that day at her house.

Sarah had stopped and slowly walked back into the room. She started busying herself with tidying up the pillows on the sofa, and then laying out Savannah's clothing for the day.

"Do you think I'm stupid?" Savannah had asked her. Sarah paused, frozen in mid-air. Savannah knew that she had mobilized tens of thousands of people to resist her father and his administration, but the woman in front of her seemed timid and meek.

"No, Ms. Savannah," Sarah said. "But I've only been here for two weeks, so I don't know you very well." She fussed over the accessories for the outfit she had picked out.

"Of course you know me! You're Sarah Montgomery, leader of Purple Nation!" She mouthed the last part, never sure if someone was listening. "I'm sure you saw me on TV going to all those events like a little pawn. I'm sure you hated me." New tears sprung from her eyes, and she buried her head in her hands.

"I didn't know any of you people cared what people like me thought," Sarah said quietly.

"See? You people! I'm not a monster like..." Savannah's words hung in between them, but they both knew what she meant.

"I don't think you're stupid. I think you were born into your situation like anyone else, and you're trying to make the best of it. You saved my life, you know." Sarah turned to look at Savannah and was awarded a small smile.

"That's true," Savannah had sniffed.

It was eleven years since that day in Savannah's bedroom—when they had made a crack in the invisible wall that divided "people like them." Slowly, gradually, like a careful climb to an impossible peak, they started to like each other. As they stood together in the same room where they had spent countless hours talking, sharing, then finally plotting, Savannah believed this woman to be nothing less than a sister.

"I remember everything," Sarah whispered again. "Except the last couple of months with my daughter. That, I can't remember." She looked like she might shatter from heartache, and Savannah reached for her hand. The two women stared at each other for a long moment.

"Soon," Savannah told her. Sarah nodded, swiping at a tear that had not fallen.

* * *

The trip to see her father was always stressful, and Savannah clung to the edge of the private rail car as they neared his building.

David and another agent flanked her on either side, and Sarah brought up the rear as she marched into the decadent lobby and over to the glass elevator. It took three seconds to reach the fiftieth floor.

She knocked nervously on his door, and it opened immediately. Her father's aide, Gordon, didn't say a word to her. He turned on his heel when he saw her and silently led her back to the bedroom.

Savannah could see the sweeping grey city sprawled out at her feet from the floor to ceiling windows. It looked like a heap of garbage dressed up in its fanciest clothes—a metallic prison that everyone pretended they were lucky to be stuck in. She couldn't recall the last time she had seen a patch of green. She remembered feeling dirt between her fingers when she had volunteered at the Gramercy Park Garden Project. She could still feel the waves hit her calves in the Hamptons when she had decided to get up from her chaise to feel the ocean. How she wished she had gone in all the way that day, not caring how her hair looked or what her friends thought.

Sarah hung back as they made their way to the Dictator's room and went to sit in an armchair that had been turned to look out of the window.

"You sure?" Savannah asked her, and her friend nodded. Savannah knew all of Sarah's story by now, perhaps even those small details that fall through the cracks of the storyteller's memory. She knew it so well, it was as if she had lived it herself. She felt what Sarah felt. Savannah knew, as her loyal servant stared out into the dusty world, that she wished she had succeeded in her fight. Sarah would perch on the expensive chair and wallow in the irony that she was sitting forty feet from the enemy and had to remain silent. Savannah put a hand on her shoulder and gave it a squeeze before turning to walk down the hall.

The door creaked open to her father's room as if in protest of the visit. She was able to stare at him for a couple of minutes before he even noticed she was there. A nagging ache for her lost childhood pulled at her heart, but she shushed it away. It didn't matter now.

The man who had changed everything looked like the taxidermy version of himself. He was slamming his finger against a miniature screen and muttering to himself angrily. Now eighty-five years old, he struggled to walk around and refused a wheelchair, so he could often be found in bed or on a nearby couch. Savannah knew that it had shattered him to lose control over his body, and in some ways she felt sorry for him. She walked over to his bed and sat on the edge.

"Dad." She reached over and grabbed his hand. It was wrinkled and worn, but his face was smooth, more perfect than it had been fifteen years ago. They had erased every tyrannical line caused by every evil decision. The valleys of anger and hate and distrust were no longer visible, but Savannah knew they remained. They would always be there.

"What? Oh, it's you." He begrudgingly put down his screen and huffed at her.

"Hi Dad. How are you?" She got up and opened the giant curtains.

"Don't do that! I'll be blinded!" He turned away as if he were a vampire, but she ignored his pleas.

"Don't be silly. You need some sunlight in here. Besides, you can barely see the sun with all the smog." She walked back over and sat down.

"Your stupid husband is undoing everything I worked for!" he grumbled at her.

"Nonsense, Dad. He's making it worse. That's all. He's even more heinous than you ever were."

Her father smiled with what could only be understood as pride. It made her feel sick to her stomach.

"But he did give me a gift," she said. It was the purpose of her visit. J.J. had given her something to "make up for his mood swings" with the condition that she got her father's blessing. She thought of Sarah sitting in a chair gazing out at a wasted world, a taken world. It was up to Savannah to convince her father or she feared Sarah might someday curl into a ball and give up completely.

"What gift?" her father snorted. "You have everything you could ever want, thanks to me. I built this world for you, Savannah. For you and the children. I made it exactly like I said I would."

"Yes, of course you did," Savannah said sadly. She thought about how depressing it was that he still believed in what he had done. She thought about the day her sons disrespected her in front of her husband and how he didn't say a word. "But still. It's a gift. He's giving me a factory. We're opening it right outside the Republic."

"A factory?" her father laughed, and for a second she was nervous that he was going to think it was a frivolous idea and say no.

"Yes, to make protein shakes, Daddy. The women in the Republic are always looking for another way to lose weight, and we've got this great nutritionist…" she said, taking on a little girl's voice. She was fifty years old and felt like she was asking for a sweet from a candy store. *It's important, it's too important.*

"Ahhhh, yes. My little girl needs to watch her figure." He stared out the window at the disgusting world he had created. "Well, that's fine. I think you should have your factory. If that makes you happy."

"It does. It will," she said and leaned down to kiss his forehead. Her lips felt strange against his skin. They were both made out of plastic.

"Thanks, Daddy. I love you." She looked down at him, a demon lying in a pile of madness, and then turned and walked out of the door. He had already picked up his screen and was angrily pounding away.

Sarah turned to look at her as she walked back into the grossly overstated living room and stood up quickly as Savannah strode past, David at her heels.

After they were safely in the elevator and the doors were shut, Savannah could feel her aide looking at her again, and she gave a short, stiff nod. She could feel Sarah's sigh of relief, and she fought to hold back angry tears even though she had gotten exactly what she had come there for.

David pulled out a razor-thin gateway radio and sent a message so quickly, it barely existed in their dark world. But Savannah and Sarah both knew: he had just set the big, hopeful, rusty wheels in motion.

2018, NEW YORK CITY

Elena had been in Manhattan for five weeks. Every other night after the sun went down, Benny would lead her out of their hiding place and creep along the dusty stairs, ignoring the high-pitched shrieks of what she only imagined to be the largest rats in existence. They made their way up Sixth Avenue; it was the first time Elena learned to truly hug the shadows and become one of them. The two unlikely friends skittered about, in and out of bodegas and restaurants, stuffing their large bags with provisions.

There were times when Elena passed a place she had visited with her parents and the pain of it caught in her throat, threatening to steal her breath from her. It would sometimes erupt in visions from the past, and she'd get lost in their dull beauty, like she was paging through a forgotten scrapbook. But Benny would gently nudge her along, and she was forced to shove the memories and visions away.

All that mattered was survival.

Sometimes, Benny "got a sense" about something, and he was almost always right. One night, he grabbed her arm urgently, knocking a half-eaten candy bar out of her hand, and pulled her out of sight behind a store counter. Elena heard the sounds of a tank rolling by, crushing everything that was in its way, looking for leftovers like the two of them so the militia could send any strays off to their assignments.

At the time, she didn't know about the training centers or the factories—they were just getting started. She tried to imagine where people like her parents went. If it wasn't prison, and if they had already let her mother go from jail, then where would they possibly take her? Benny had ideas of his own, but to Elena, they felt like whispered ghost stories told late at night, and she knew neither of them really understood what was happening in the outside world.

She began to feel like they owned the city. No, owned the world. They were defying the system, the two of them, and no one would catch them, not ever. They were the largest rats the streets had ever seen, and their squeals of resistance could be heard echoing throughout the underground.

After one particularly brilliant haul, they sat in the lab assessing their stash. Elena was nibbling on some aged cheese thoughtfully, gazing around at Benny's equipment.

"You never really told me about your work," she said. "I have the basics, but I could use some details." She would sometimes open her eyes late at night to catch him cowering in a corner of the lab. Sometimes she'd find him asleep on a counter, surrounded by tubes and vials of what Elena liked to believe were magic concoctions.

"Oh, yes. My work." Benny chuckled, and Elena could tell the topic was laced with pride and sorrow and something else that she didn't quite understand. She had to know the real reason her mother had sent her there.

Benny picked up a can of baked beans and opened the flip top. He stirred it with a plastic spoon, trying to think of how to start.

"Well. You know what happened to your mother in prison?" he began.

"You mean that she was taken against her will and then drugged into becoming a doormat?" Elena responded angrily.

Benny laughed. "You're just like her! So much fire! Yes, that's what I meant."

Elena nodded, secretly pleased that he had compared her to her mom.

"Well, even someone as strong-willed and spirited as your mother isn't immune to addiction. The pills they made, that the Dictator had some big pharma company make...they're a powerful combination of two very addictive drugs. The first is one of the strongest forms of opiate I've ever seen. And the second is scopolamine, the "devil's breath," the brainwash drug, which enables complete and total mind control." Benny's eyes looked dreamy as if he was talking about a wizard making a potion.

"When it comes to controlling a population, they're obviously effective. If I was the most hated man in the country, and I was pure evil," Elena laughed as he made claws with his hands, "then I might have drugged anyone who opposed me, too."

"But I'm not pure evil." Benny grew serious. "I've been working my entire adult life on an antidote. A prevention. All of the above. It's a serum that blocks the subject from addiction. And if I'm not mistaken, my new serum will be able to work in reverse. If someone's addicted, it will 'cure' them. They'll go back to normal without any sort of comedown."

Elena stared at him in disbelief. In awe. She wished she had met him before or that her mother had been able to tell her about his serum sooner. But there hadn't been a sign, or any foreshadowing. It all happened so quickly. No one could have predicted the lengths to which the Dictator would have gone to rid humanity of its freethinkers.

"I remember the comedown," she said quietly. "I can't imagine anyone coming out whole on the other side of that. How do you know it works?"

"I know the prevention serum works. I tested it on about fifty subjects. But I only tested the cure on one person. Me." He smiled.

"And you seem completely awake to me," she said, smiling back.

"That I am. Anyway, when I was going to meet Clara..." She knew he got stuck in the moment when he'd found her. He had talked about her endlessly for the first week after Elena had arrived, but then it seemed like it tore him apart if he even uttered her name. It was as if he had used up all of his allowances to talk about the woman he believed he had essentially killed.

"....and, you know." He struggled. Elena nodded, trying to encourage him.

"I had just figured out how to make it duplicative. So, with access to the right facility and staff, I could make a large amount of it. Then, we could cure everyone who has ever been put to sleep."

"But you couldn't get the package out to your friends..." Elena said, piecing it together.

"Right." Benny looked over at the entrance of his lab as if the answer lingered there.

Elena nodded, thinking about the implications, the possibilities. She imagined finding her parents and giving them a glazed donut—the kind they used to get at the bakery down the street—laced with serum and watching them eat it and instantly come back to her, come back to their life. It was a fantasy she would hold onto for many, many years after learning about Benny's cure until the memory started getting tattered and broken and finally faded away into almost nothing.

"We'll get it out. Something has to give." The two of them sat with empty smiles, eating their loot with pipe dreams swirling around in their heads. They both knew that those were the kinds of things people used to say when there was still hope. Now, Elena struggled to picture a different kind of city, country, world. Her visions were a tangled cassette tape of uncertainty. But she mustered a brave voice and said, "So then we can save the world." Benny started laughing. Elena's smile immediately faded. She didn't like being patronized.

"I'm sorry," Benny said when he saw her face. "I'm not making fun. I just remember Sarah saying the exact same thing."

Elena allowed her heart to fill up with the joy of being compared to her hero and the hope of blanketing the country with a cure. She started laughing too. They laughed and laughed until Elena felt an overwhelming exhaustion come over her, and she fell asleep with her half-eaten cheese still in her hand.

* * *

When she awoke, Benny was standing over her, shining a light in her face.

"What? What are you doing?" she cried. She pulled the blanket up to her chin suddenly feeling vulnerable and a little bit afraid.

"Why are you awake?" He seemed frustrated and completely unaware of her fear.

"Because you're shining a light in my face!" she yelled at him. She wanted to run, but she had nowhere to go. She felt trapped.

"But I gave you a full dose of the opioid!" Benny seemed to be just as exasperated as she felt, and she wanted to scream at him, *You are not the victim here! You are the guy trying to drug a young girl at the bottom of the subway!*

Suddenly, he composed himself as if he realized how crazy he sounded. He took a couple of steps back from her, turned on a lantern and put the flashlight down.

Elena took a deep breath. "Benny. I trusted you. My mom trusted you. And you put that poison into my body. How could you do that?" She began to cry.

"I'm...I'm so sorry. I wanted to test the cure. I'm sorry." He looked down at his feet. She could tell that the actuality of what he had done was hitting him in waves. He finally looked her in the eye. She never had anyone look at her like that before, and she hadn't since. It was as if he was going to tell her the whole truth about herself in his next sentence. "Elena, you weren't affected by the opioid."

"What? Of course I was. I fell right to sleep."

"No," he looked even more embarrassed. "I crushed up two sleeping pills and put them in your juice."

"Benny!" she shouted at him, her mind racing. *What did this mean? What did it all mean?*

"Elena, if you were affected by the opioid, you'd be a zombie. Actually," he looked at the clock, "You might even be coming down by now. It didn't affect you."

"How did you give it to me?" she asked.

"Injection."

"Do you have any pills?" she asked, knowing full well that injection was a more direct way to get the drugs into her system than pills, but needing to see it for herself all the same.

"Yes. Hold on." He went back to his hidden lockbox and pulled out a bottle exactly like the ones her mother had come home with from prison. She swallowed back a web of painful emotions and held out her hand.

"Give me three," she demanded.

"Three's too many for your age!" Benny said, and caught himself. "OK, let's try three."

He handed them to her, and she popped them in her mouth. They tasted horrible, like a poisonous chalk that wanted nothing more than to kill her. He handed her some water, and she swallowed them down.

They stared at each other, waiting. He looked at the clock again. "It usually takes less than two minutes. For most people, it's immediate."

She nodded, and they continued to wait. Ten minutes passed. Twenty.

"Elena," Benny said finally. She nodded curtly. She was still angry with him.

"I'm sorry I went behind your back. I didn't think you'd agree to being a test subject, and it's not like I get a lot of company. I needed to know the cure worked on someone other than me."

Elena nodded again, but wouldn't look at him. She didn't want to let him off the hook that easily, but a huge part of her understood exactly why he had done it.

He walked over and knelt down next to her but she recoiled, and he moved back to the other side of the lab. "Elena, I need you to understand what this means. I need you to hear my words and let them seep into your brain and mull them over and then repeat them back to me. You are immune to this drug. The Dictator has created a drug to control people like us, and you are immune. You cannot be controlled. Say it! You are immune. You cannot be controlled." He was hopping up and down, not trying for a minute to control his excitement. "Say it!"

"I am immune. I cannot be controlled," she said quietly.

"Louder! Shout it!" he yelled.

"I am immune! I cannot be controlled!" she shouted.

"Again!"

"I am immune! I cannot be controlled! I am immune! I cannot be controlled!" She shouted it again and again until she was exhausted and laughing and the words filled her up with promise and hope and all the things one still believes in as a ten-year-old kid.

I am immune. I cannot be controlled.

I am immune. I cannot be controlled.

But it turned out, they were wrong.

2031, PORTLAND, MAINE

Elena waited anxiously in the front of the old wine cellar. On either side, she was surrounded by some of the most expensive wines in the country, yet their worth didn't really matter anymore because currency simply didn't work in the way it did before.

She had arrived a full twenty minutes before the rest of the group to gather her thoughts. The joy she had felt from being led into the lab by Maggie was made all the more visceral by the searing pain she had to endure from both the deactivation and the reactivation. She knew that her chip now read "transport" or something of the sort and that she would be going on the train to the Republic. Even though she didn't have a single insight into what would happen once she was there, it felt like a giant door had been opened and was waiting for her to pass through. She almost felt like she had died and the door to heaven was inviting her to finish her business on Earth so she could enter the nirvana she had been longing for.

Except she had stopped believing in such things like heaven when she was a child, and she knew as well as any waking person that nirvana or anything close to it did not exist. It made her feel sad, and she silently asked her parents why, why, they didn't believe in god and why they had taught her to oppose religion and anything related to it.

How she would have loved to believe in something without question. She considered this for a fleeting moment and then dismissed it: had she believed in god in the Waking World, she would have surely stopped by now.

Her thoughts were interrupted by the realization that Silver was standing in front of her.

"Silver! When did you get here?" Elena smoothed back her shaved hair. Silver was the person she was most nervous to see. "Sorry, I was lost in a daydream."

"A daydream about the Republic," Silver accused, hands on hips. "If you think I can't tell how you're acting, you're wrong."

"How I'm acting?" But Elena knew she was right. She felt different, more alive. More awake than she had since the day she left New York.

"You know. Like you have a way out of this hell. Like you have something to look forward to besides pushing buttons and being raped every day." Silver started to cry.

Elena gathered her up in her arms like she had a million times before, and her friend lay a blonde head on her shoulder. Both of their bodies shook with Silver's sobs, and Elena squeezed her as tight as the prison that had held them for so many years.

"Lannie, you're going to crush me!" Silver finally said, laughing through her tears. Elena laughed too and pulled back to look at the young woman's beautiful face, wiping her wet cheeks.

"I'm sorry. Yes. I'm going. They changed over my chip today."

"They didn't change mine," Silver told her, tears still streaming.

"They still could."

"Nah, I'm too stupid. Even for an awake sleeper. I'm as incompetent as the dopers." Silver sighed as if this was the worst fate in the world, and Elena knew that to her, it was.

"You're not stupid. You never were. You're smart and determined and bold, and you don't let a thing get to you. I'm so proud of you." Elena meant it all. When she found Silver, the young woman had survived the unthinkable, and now she was part of the movement that could change things. *It had to change things.*

"Thanks. I'll still miss you so much. It will feel like three fourths of my heart is gone." Silver sniffed.

"Only three fourths?" Elena asked, and they both laughed. "I'll miss you, too, but we need you here. Our work up north isn't over. OK?" Silver nodded.

The others started to come in, and Silver quickly took her seat on one of the broken bar stools.

They all sat there in silence as if their favorite movie was about to begin. Everyone knew that there was big news.

"Elliot, you go first," Elena said with a smile. She, more than anyone, was

169

anxious to get his report. She had seen Maggie take him by the arm to the lab and had estimated that he spent longer in there than she had. She'd waited eleven hours to hear what happened behind that thick metal door, and she was beginning to feel like she couldn't wait a single second more.

"OK," he said, wiping his palms on his black uniform pants. She could tell he was nervous. "So, today, one of the guards. Her name is Maggie. Anyway, she took me into this lab we have at the factory. To be honest, I didn't even know we had one. I'd never been there."

He paused and sipped in some air. Elena knew he was struggling and she didn't know why.

"So, um. She sits me down in this chair like the kind at the dentist." A few people snickered and murmured because they hadn't seen a dentist since the Waking Years. Elena knew that no matter what their memories of the dentist were, they would have given anything to see one now.

"And, well. She deactivated my chip." The group grew louder with excitement. Elena held up a hand to quiet everyone down. "And god, it was so painful. I didn't remember how horrible that pain was." Everyone nodded. They remembered too. "The whole time she was deactivating it, she was talking to a camera in the room, saying what she was doing.

"Then, the screen turned on and there was this loud music, and then the Dictator came on and gave his spiel." They sat in silence, waiting. "And Maggie went to get the activator, and she pretended like she was still talking to the camera, but she was really talking to me."

No one moved. Elliot took the deepest breath Elena had ever seen, and she saw miniature fireworks all around him, and she saw colorful sparks hitting the ground with a satisfying sizzle.

"And she told me that she knew I was awake." Everyone gasped. "And that she was going to help me."

"What?" Elena almost shouted. "But how do we know we can trust her? You remember the last time!" She was angry, excited and terrified all at once.

Elliot turned to look at his friend. The person he had started to love more than anyone in the world. "I know because she slipped a deactivator into my boot."

No one spoke. No one stirred. If wind had blown through the cellar windows, it would have swept them all away. Elena felt her door of hope swing wide open and get torn off its hinges.

"This is everything," Roger said. They all nodded, basking in it. Calling it up and spinning it around so they could relive it over and over.

Elena finally stood up. "Who else is going?" Three others stood up. Elena glanced at Silver nervously, but the woman met her gaze.

"I am going too," Elena said. "This is our chance. We have an ally, and we have a deactivator."

Silver stood up too. "I'll take over reporting to the Controller," she said. "If you'll have me."

Elena looked over at her, and this time the tears spilling down cheeks were hers. "Of course I'll have you. The job is yours." Then she walked over to Elliot and grabbed his hand. The sparks she'd seen when he was speaking now pinged between the two of them in a surge of every single moment they'd ever had to endure after the lights had gone out.

She squeezed his fingers and made a decision that was neither backed by intel or rational thought. But it felt right, and that was all she cared about.

"Elliot, give the deactivator to Silver," she said, squeezing his hand again. He opened his mouth to protest, but then closed it and reached down into his boot to pull out the small metal device.

Silver scrambled over and bowed her head as Elliot placed it in her hands.

The rest of the group moved toward them and they were one momentous blob of humanity, and it didn't matter who was going or who was staying or what happened next, really. It didn't even matter if they ended up pushing buttons for the rest of their lives. All that mattered that night in the cellar was that they had found each other and that they had been given one more chance. All that mattered at all was that they were still awake.

2031, THE REPUBLIC

Sarah sat in her quarters, staring into her full-length screen. She held up a remote control and switched off the "enhance" feature so she could really see herself. She had spent so many years in the Republic, she had grown both accustomed to and disgusted by tricks that distorted the obvious. People who lived there didn't know what was real and what was completely fabricated. But she figured they didn't really care any more than they had the first day they all pledged to stand by the Dictator no matter what.

She leaned in to examine her face, which looked completely unrecognizable from the day she had left her family to go to the rally in D.C. There were wrinkles that stretched from the corners of her eyes to graze her temples, and if she had to name each one, it would have been after something she'd lost.

An undefinable amount of time had passed since the day she arrived in the Republic, but in many ways, it felt like a hiccup. On a good day, she believed her little girl was still out there, small and alone where she had left her. For all Sarah knew, her daughter had stayed in their home, maybe finding a way to survive or maybe finding a nice family to take her in. Maybe she had found her way into the militia and worked day and night for the good of the Dictator. But from what Savannah had told her about the state of the country, she knew that there was almost no chance that she was still in Pennsylvania or even still alive. The best case scenario was that she was drugged and working at a factory, but the thought of it made Sarah want to scream and hurl herself through the floor-to-ceiling window that displayed, quite cruelly, what the world had become. She was a mother, and the day her daughter arrived had redefined her. It was her job to protect her baby no matter what.

She remembered giving birth to her daughter, the painful release of baby exiting and the sweetest weight of squirmy life being placed in her arms, staring up at her mama with alien eyes. *I made you*, Sarah had said, looking up at Ben for confirmation. It was her single greatest accomplishment in a lifetime of accomplishments. She had vowed on that day to take care of her little girl, to never leave her, and all the other blind promises you make when you stare one of the only miracles left in its sweet, wide-eyed face.

But she had failed her.

It was eight thirty in the morning and Sarah had thirty minutes until she needed to wake Savannah. She was grateful to her. She was. She had seen the Dictator's daughter on television time and again—a stupid puppet led around by her fascist father. She had called Savannah names, shouting and pointing at the TV. But she had been wrong about her, or at least the new version of her. It didn't even matter what she had been like before, or whether she had turned a blind eye to the abuse her father inflicted on the country. Sarah had no choice but to be grateful for a waking life because she had lived the alternative, and it was worse than death.

That day Elena and Ben visited her in prison, she felt like she was drowning in a murky fish tank. One of the most prolific activists of her time, she had been to prison dozens of times, especially before Elena was born. Ben liked to joke that their second, third and fifth dates were him bailing her "out of the slammer." She loved when he said things like that, like he was an old wise guy from a black and white talkie. It was one of his million stupid, innocent quirks that made her sit in the shower and sob. She ached for him.

The guards at the low security prisons had either met her before or heard of her, and they had always treated her incarceration as a joke. After all, she had never committed a violent crime, and her most serious arrests were for trespassing or resisting an officer. Many of the guards even admired her; some would pump their fists in her direction and tell her to "keep fighting" for them. She had become an unwavering voice for the people.

Her prison stay after the rally was different, though. The guards were hostile toward her and singled her out. They called her a poison of greatness, a resistance toward progress. They called her a baby killer and an ally of terrorists. They kept her in solitary confinement from the moment her bloodstained sneaker stepped foot in the facility.

He's stocked the prisons with them. They all work for him, every one of them, she had thought as soon as they threw her in a tiny padded cell. She'd felt a dread creep in through her toes and an admiration squeeze at her heart. *Shrewd move, Mr. President. Genius, really.*

The first visit from Elena and Ben had been agonizing—it was the first time her little girl had seen her in prison. When Sarah saw her daughter sitting in the hard green chair waiting for her mama, she wanted to run and hide. She needed to pretend everything was alright for her. It was the very last gift she had given her child.

The final thing she remembered before her deep sleep was being dragged down a hall, lights whizzing above her, strong fingers gripping into her arms, arms wondering if they would be ripped from their sockets. She felt a searing pain go up through her shoulder as she was thrown up onto a table in what seemed to be an operating room. Her legs and arms were strapped down so tightly, she felt like her body was no longer her own. Then a needle plunged into her arm, and her world went black.

Well, not black, exactly.

It was as if someone had placed a distorted lens over everything. She could make out shapes and very rarely something snapped into focus, but it was only for an instant and then it faded back into a blur. Her limbs were so heavy, it took all her energy to move them even a little bit, and lifting them was so difficult, she stopped bothering. Her thoughts scattered into dark corners of her brain, like a gunman had infiltrated the lot of them and started firing. Just when she thought she'd found one and tried to make some sense of it, it disappeared and she scrambled around to locate it again.

There had been moments, though. The time when Elena was brushing her hair and everything suddenly became clear and made sense, and she fought to hold onto it as her mouth tried to move to release its words. But just as quickly, it was gone, and she retreated to her underwater cave made of cotton.

During the transport from Pennsylvania to the Republic, Sarah had experienced one of her moments of clarity, and as they dressed her in a long velvet gown and pushed her inside a glass case, she fought to hold onto it. The pain and the shaking of her comedown threatened to gobble her alive as she gazed through a three-inch thick pane of glass at the man who had desecrated the Waking World. She wanted to howl at him and pound the barrier that separated good versus evil, but she knew that even if the glass suddenly shattered, she was too helpless to displace even a hair on his head. Sarah was so focused on the Dictator she hadn't even noticed Savannah come up to the glass until she was standing with her hand pressed against it.

Her brain had struggled to remember who she was. The nausea ripped through her body, but her mind became a shade clearer. *The President's daughter. Savannah. That's Savannah.* The thoughts tumbled on top of each other as she willed herself not to throw up in her cage. She could hear the pills tumbling down into her bowl, a familiar clank that a sleeper would recognize anywhere, but she was not a sleeper, *she was not a sleeper!*

Savannah had left her to suffer in between four walls. Sarah was caught in between hope and the pills that taunted her. They called out to her, cackling: *Take us! Crush us up! Let us lead you to salvation!*

It took four hours for Savannah and David to come back, and she lay on the floor and everything felt hot, and it was as if an iron the size of her body had pressed down hard on her chance at survival. She felt like she was dying. She wanted to die.

David unlocked the door to her glass case, and she tried to look up at him from the corner of her eye. She could feel hands undressing her, and she tried to scream out, but the devil had taken her voice away. Then she was lifted up into the air, and she wondered if there was a heaven after all and if she was on her way to it. Then she wondered why there was so much pain after death. She looked back at her glass box as she floated away and saw a red-haired woman clothed in the long green dress she'd been wearing and decided right then and there that she'd left her body and was looking down on herself.

But she hadn't. They took her back to Savannah's tower and lay her on a bed in a room that would become hers from that painful moment forward.

The comedown continued for four days.

"No pain meds," she heard Savannah tell David, as he looked down at Sarah in concern, and Sarah was both grateful to her and cursed her in between sharp breaths. She knew it was necessary, but the pain was so excruciating, she wondered if she was going to be torn in two.

She thought about her daughter, she thought about childbirth, of the sweet reward at the end of the pain. She braced herself again and again for the never ending dry heaving and wondered what else her body could want to rid itself of. She dug her nails into her palms until they bled and had to be bandaged by the Dictator's daughter, herself; she bit down on the plastic mouth guards David forced into her mouth, worried her teeth would disintegrate with the pressure.

On the fourth day, there was less dry heaving and the shaking had been reduced to a quiver, and she could stand up on her own for a small period of time.

On the fifth day, she accepted a bowl of soup and, with an unsteady hand, put a spoon into the bowl and scooped up the most delicious smelling broth and brought it to her mouth. She felt like she had eaten a mouthful of heaven, it was so good. She finished it like an animal and asked for another bowl immediately. They brought her one, and she finished it faster and with more fervor. Then she laughed a little because the old Sarah would have never been caught looking so out of control.

Her stomach steeled itself. It had not had real food in so long. But to her surprise, she kept it down, and her body rejoiced in its healing. She was beginning to feel whole again, even after all she had lost.

When Savannah came to see her on the fifth day, she was sitting up and looking out of the window. The shaking was gone, and she had a beautiful rosy color to her cheeks.

"You're awake!" Savannah said when she saw her. Sarah knew that this entitled woman didn't know how right she was, that she had probably never been so right in her life. Despite her coming to Sarah's rescue, the activist in her didn't want to side with the Republic or anyone associated with it for even a second. Especially not the President's daughter. Certainly not the Dictator's daughter.

"Yes." Sarah said quietly.

"I'm glad." Savannah clapped her hands together. Sarah could see that Savannah sensed her distrust and was trying to smile away the elephant in the room.

"Look," Savannah began. "I'm not my father. I am not a fighter like you. I'm nothing like you, really. I wish I were." She looked out the window too, losing her train of thought for a minute, then finding it again. "But I do think we share some of the same beliefs. If you give me a chance."

Sarah looked up at her and shrugged.

"If you'd like, I need an assistant. You'll get your own room and everything. And you'd get an allowance to buy some things for yourself. Although I have to OK anything you buy. You'd work for me, basically."

Sarah shrugged again, her stubbornness holding her resolutions to her like a straightjacket.

"If you don't, they'll send you to the factories. This was the only way I could get you out. No one can know who you really are." Savannah's voice grew desperate, almost whiny and Sarah cringed. She was sure it was just because she didn't want to get in trouble with her father.

"What happened?" Sarah had asked her that day, gesturing around desperately to their surroundings. It wouldn't be the last time she asked. She had been asleep for such a relatively short amount of time, but everything had changed. She felt like the pigment had been syphoned out of the landscape she could see from the window. The energy she remembered from right before she was arrested had been reduced to a stifled cry for help.

"He did everything he said he was going to do," Savannah whispered. Sarah nodded. It was enough for the time being.

In the end, she agreed to live in a golden tower with her new boss because she had no choice. She didn't even know if her family was still alive or where to look if they were. There was no phone line to call their house in Pennsylvania or Internet to do a search. Only the elite were allowed communication devices, and they were heavily monitored. It would have been like looking for someone in the dark ages, and this presumptuous woman was giving her another shot at life. She had to take it.

"OK. I'll do what you want," she finally said.

Their relationship was built over time, almost in slow motion. It was like sewing a gaping wound with a heavy hand, but gradually, they became closer. It took months for Sarah to begin to trust Savannah's stories of how she lived in a prison built by her father. She didn't buy it at first, but she slowly began to understand.

At first, she was forced to be by Savannah's side at all times, as if the Dictator's daughter was the Queen of England, as if she needed a lady in waiting at her beck and call. Sarah knew it was also to keep a close eye on her. Her room had a camera that followed her around wherever she walked, and she felt inclined to get dressed underneath her covers. Any possible object she could use to hurt herself had been removed and her door was locked at night from the outside and unlocked exactly two minutes before she needed to go to Ms. Savannah's room to wake her. To this day, she still didn't know who locked and unlocked her room every day. When she asked David, he didn't say a word.

The first time she found Savannah crying alone in her bed, she was dumbfounded. How could a woman of such magnitude, with such fascist blood running through her veins find any reason to be sad? But when she took a closer look, she began to see that Savannah lived in her own type of cage, and Sarah actually started to feel sorry for her.

"What's wrong?" Sarah had asked her mistress, who was soaking her silk sheets in her endless tears.

"Everything," Savannah had responded. Sarah rolled her eyes because this woman thought that being locked in a tower without a purpose was the worst thing in the world.

Savannah sensed Sarah's disdain and peered out from behind the sheets. "What? You think I'm not worthy of being sad?" she accused. "You think someone like me doesn't have feelings about what's happened?"

"I don't know, Ms. Savannah. It's not my place to judge." Sarah quickly picked up some clothes that had been thrown on the floor.

After that day and week and month and year and years, Sarah began to piece together what was happening. It was the firm but sometimes subtle suppression of a powerful woman who had tried too hard to play with the almighty men in her life. They had put her to sleep in a different kind of way than the Resistance—they suffocated everything that made her who she was.

Sarah began to stand with Savannah in solidarity. Quietly at first, then louder when it was just the two of them together. She never shouted at the Dictator or J.J. when she watched how they treated her, although her heart kicked at her chest with all the hateful words she wanted to say to them. As the two women began to see each other, they realized they were the same. They were comrades and confidants, and they grappled for each other's hands behind closed doors, if only to give a squeeze and remind one another that they had a kindred soul in the world.

It was 8:58. She heard the door unlock with severe punctuality. She quickly opened it, but as usual for the past eleven years, no one was there. Her heavy black boots echoed down the hallway in their thirty-two steps to arrive at Savannah's door at the dot of nine. She nodded at David who was standing like a statue and gave her usual light tap.

"Come in!" she heard, most likely from underneath the covers, and she punched her code into the lock pad outside the door.

There was never a worry if Dictator Two would be there—they hadn't shared a room in over a decade. Sarah estimated that Savannah saw her husband a total of two hours a week, sometimes more if there was a silly event meant for the elite to further congratulate each other on what they had created. Sarah had gone to one of the events once and then asked to never go again. They had served food that, even in her waking years, she hadn't had the chance to eat. Although she knew the food wasn't real—it was made of pure chemicals that most likely gnawed at their organs from the inside—it smelled like the best meal she had ever tasted.

She had watched them all toast each other and had watched Dictator Two give his repulsive speech to a crowd of minions. She had watched the crowd cheer, then erupt with an uncontrollable intensity, and she had looked at the double doors and seen an aide wheeling Dictator One in on a gold apparatus that made him look like he was floating into the room. She had wanted to run toward him and knock him over, to pummel him until he cried for mercy, to tell him, words tumbling, spit flying, that he had taken everything, *everything* from her, and she wanted it back. She wanted him to use the power he had over everyone to put her back in her living room in front of the fire braiding her little girl's hair.

But of course, she would have been detained and put back to sleep, so she didn't do a thing, and instead she suffered in silence. Then she quietly asked if she could wait outside at the next event.

When she walked into the room, Savannah was, in fact, under the covers. Her eye makeup had run down to the peak of her cheekbones, and her lashes were stuck together in unattractive clumps. Sarah smiled a bit as she opened the curtains to let the bleak world in, and Savannah squinted in protest.

"Good morning, Ms. Savannah. The sun isn't shining. The birds aren't chirping. We have entered the phase when the Earth will surely implode in on itself." Sarah had been saying the same greeting for as long as they both could remember, and it got a laugh every single morning.

"Mornin'. Let's get me dressed, and then we can talk about next steps. The first wave of them should be here in a couple of days." Savannah suddenly became all business, and Sarah was grateful. The factory. Their secret project. It had given them both a reason to wake up in the morning. There weren't visible cameras in Savannah's room, but that didn't mean they weren't being watched. They plotted the intimate parts of their plan masked by the din of a hairdryer or while Sarah vacuumed a section of the room.

It was the closest they had ever come to finding Sarah's family. If they were out there, they would be recruited for this new factory. She was sure of it. Sarah believed in the possibility of it, and it sat heavy on her chest at night. But the chances of it happening the way she imagined it might were so small, it sometimes made her cry out in pain. Savannah knew it and Sarah knew it, and yet they never mentioned it to each other. Her Elena would be twenty-four. Twenty-four! Even if the recruitment worked and Elena ended up working in their new factory, she wasn't sure she'd even recognize her little girl. It was possible her daughter was so completely asleep that she might never wake again.

Sarah picked out Savannah's outfit for the day: a red dress with red shoes. It was always the same, every single day. The woman's entire wardrobe was red to represent the Republic and what it stood for. She knew it made Savannah sick to wear it, but she knew better than anyone how essential appearances were.

Their plan was too important to dismiss the charade now.

2031 PORTLAND, MAINE TO THE REPUBLIC

The day had come when everything would change, or so they hoped. Thanks to Elena's surveillance during her dreaded sessions with Darren, Elliot knew they were going on a different train this morning—a high speed rail that was said to go even faster than their commuter rail. Elliot couldn't wait to feel his stomach lurch into his throat with excitement. He felt quite literally like he was running to the edge of a cliff. He was more than willing to launch himself into a new start, convincing himself it wouldn't end with him crashing hard into the ground.

The buzzer sounded, signifying the mass shuffling out of pods and toward the breakfast gravel shake. Elliot gulped it down, ignoring his gag reflex and his human desire to scream at the guards handing them out: *This is inhumane! We can't breathe when we're drinking cement!* But of course he did not say a word because this day could be his chance at something. If someone had put a gun to his head demanding him to guess what that chance was, he could not have said.

Another buzzer rang throughout the housing facility, and they all began to move toward the rails. As each sleeper reached the door, their chip was scanned, and they were shifted by a series of metal barriers that moved to guide them in the right direction like cattle. Elliot's chip was scanned and his barriers moved all the way to the left—to a position he had never been in before—and his heart soared. He shuffled toward the silver train, so shiny, he could almost see his reflection. He had avoided it until now, but he faced it head-on today. Peeking from under his eyelids, he saw that he was now a man. He was shocked. His loosely strung together memories always painted him as a growing boy. Suddenly, he wanted to lean close to the metal and study the hairs on his chin and see if he had laugh lines sprouting from the corners of his eyes like his mother had.

But instead, he shuffled right past the man he had become and slowly made his way down a narrow aisle. He was pushed down by a guard who was making sure the sleepers flowed into the appropriate seats, and a buckle automatically strapped itself around his waist. He knew Elena was sitting catty-corner from him. Her excitement reached out and tugged on his ears; it grazed the back of his neck. Her emotions were mirror images of his, and he would have given anything in the world to reach out and touch her hand and pull her into his lap or at least into the seat next to him and put his arms around her as they watched the coast race by. There was nothing before them but bleak toxic hopelessness, but it was thrilling nonetheless.

The train made its way out of Portland, down, down, down the coast and into what used to be Boston, where it stopped to pick up more sleepers. Elliot saw an old ragged billboard for the Boston Marathon out of the corner of his eye. It must have been pasted up ages ago, yet bits of it still remained as if they refused to leave no matter what. The rest of the city looked like a wasteland, and Elliot half expected zombies to start stumbling out from behind the crumbling buildings.

They continued on to the next stop and the next until they reached New York City. Elliot had never been there until now, but Elena had told him about it during their nights near the dock, hands lacing together, experiencing what it was like to be human for a few captured moments.

He shut out the sights and tried to imagine Elena's city from when she was very young with its bustling crowds, and then the other version when she lived with a mad scientist in the underground. He wondered what she was thinking right now as they passed through, and if it made her want to get off the train and pick up where she had left off or hide her face in her hands to shut it all out. He imagined it was probably some of both and wished he could protect her from the memories, whatever they were.

The train pitched a little to the side, and Elliot peeked out from the edges of his eyelids. A mass of sleepers were coming out of alleyways and slamming into the side of the train, a giant wave of broken lives.

"How many?" one of the guards asked another.

"We only picking up 'bout twenty or so," she responded.

"Then why all them other sleepers coming out of the woodwork?"

The guard put a hand to her ear, listening to her headset. "The power went out in one of the factories, and they couldn't contain 'em. I ain't never seen sleepers act like that, have you?" Elliot could hear a bit of fear in her voice, and he thought it was funny that guards carrying some of the most powerful weapons known to man were scared of a bunch of pill heads who probably didn't have the wherewithal to walk up the train's steps.

"I ain't never either. They sure is a lotta 'em. How they gonna get them sleepers back into formation is beyond me." The other guard sounded scared, too.

The group of twenty were finally loaded on the rail and strapped into their seats, but the crowd had started swarming the train from the other side. Elliot could feel it shake with the bodies pushing against it, and he wondered if hunger and disease and addiction and hopelessness could knock a whole train off its tracks.

"Go! Go!" he heard over the speaker, and the train lurched as it tried to break free from the crowd. Sleepers were grabbing at its sleek exterior and aimlessly trying to push through the doors, not by mindfulness, but by sheer force of body count.

Elliot could see just a tiny wrinkle across Elena's nose, indicating only to him that she wanted to scream or cry or jump up and stop the train and help every one of those people—those who she considered to be *her* people, her mother's people—climb aboard and be saved.

The train began to inch forward, finally picking up a tiny bit of speed as it strained to accelerate and balance. Then, like a rubber band that had been stretched beyond its limit, it snapped free.

Bodies and blood and limbs went everywhere and sprayed the train and pounded the windows, but there were no screams because there was no pain left inside these people who were being pulled and smashed to pieces. Elliot wanted to crawl under the seat to shield himself from the sight of the human rain, the bloody downpour, but instead he tried to keep his eyes on the floor and feel nothing.

They reached full acceleration and once again he felt the glorious pull of speed. Water poured down the windows in a self-cleaning sprinkler system, and soon all evidence of the incident was erased.

Except it would never be gone for the people who were awake on the train. The human rain would bloody their nightmares for years to come.

2031, NEW YORK CITY

When Elena spotted the familiar buildings from under long lashes she knew they had reached Manhattan. It made total sense why they were there, yet she hadn't expected it. Somehow she thought it had sunk underwater completely or that one of the explosions they had heard in the infinite distance had decimated the city. But she was wrong, and there it stood.

She felt a sharp pain in her abdomen, one of several over the past couple of days, and ignored it, blaming the brilliant sight of the city she'd left behind so many years ago. There were no words for how she felt when they pulled up not far from where she'd been taken.

That night had been like any other: they'd gone on a run the moment the sun melted into the river, except on that particular evening, Benny had wanted to go farther than they'd ever ventured before.

"There's an Italian market up near Madison Square Park. It's huge. You could get enough cheese to last you a week," he said, nudging her arm.

She smiled, but just a little. She hadn't quite forgiven him for trying to drug her, but she also realized that things were different in this world than they had been in the last. In this world, it was alright to drug a young child to save humanity. Right? She had settled on eighty percent yes. There was more to it too. Benny had discovered something extraordinary about her, and she would have never known she was different without his experiments.

"We can take blood samples from you and figure out how you developed this immunity. I'll be able to take my work further than I ever imagined," he'd said, and while she didn't love the idea of being a test subject, she felt powerful, like she had a great gift to give. She thought about handing her parents that serum-laced donut and then, after they'd been cured, telling them the news—that the regime could never hurt her.

But Benny was also very clear about one thing, and Elena never forgot that it had saved her life. "If they ever get you and give you pills," he said to her one night in their underground hideout, "you have to pretend you're asleep. That the drugs work on you. Got it?" She nodded, but she was confused. How would she do that if they didn't?

He saw her brow furrow and took her by the shoulders. "I'm serious,

Elena. You can't let them know, or anyone know that the dope doesn't affect you. Not ever. Do you understand?" She could feel his grip get tighter, and she knew how important this was to him. Maybe it was important to her, too.

She nodded. "Can you help me?" she asked. Her mother had always taught her to ask for help when she wasn't sure of something. *How else can you become an expert if you don't ask help from an expert?* she would say. She had seen her mom tear off her hero cape and humbly admit that she wasn't sure when she wasn't, that she had more to learn when she did. It only made people look up to her even more, as if humility was one of her superpowers.

"Of course. I've been studying sleepers my entire life," he said with an empty smile. Elena thought about how they'd probably had vastly different childhoods, but had ended up in the same exact place.

The night of the Madison Square Park run, she'd been practicing being a sleeper for only four days. They had sat across from each other in their little bunker, and he'd given his instructions in a clear and steady voice. Ever the perfect student, she had followed them precisely. Benny knew every nuance of every movement (or lack thereof) of an addict, and he was as much a brilliant teacher as she was a pupil.

When they reached the enormous market, Elena put her hand on the door, pausing.

"What?" Benny asked her.

"I came here with my parents. I remember it. I got lost in here." She smiled. It had been both scary and exhilarating to be on her own. She'd run through the rows of pasta, touching every single one (something her parents would have never let her do), and climbed up on a barstool at one of the counters to spin around as fast as she could go, watching the rainbows of her imagination spew from every turn. That's where they found her, and they hugged her tight and scolded her all at once, her mom crying, her dad throwing his hands up in the air, and she'd laughed her infectious little girl laugh until the three of them were all laughing. Then they clung to each other in the simple joy of having found each other again.

What she would have given to have been found in that deserted market that day with Benny.

"Let's go," he said finally. "We can't take any chances lingering out in the open."

They walked inside, crunching on some broken glass in the entryway. The smell of smoked meat hung in the air, and she drank it in with greedy breaths. Her family rarely ate meat except when her father took her on an ultra top secret run to McDonald's (*Don't ever tell your mother about this*), but she would have given anything to have it right then.

"I'll lead you over to the cheese section," Benny whispered, winking. "And I'll go get some pasta and maybe find some jarred sauce. We'll have a feast!" She smiled, thinking how perfect it would be to taste marinara and pasta and cheese. She decided that they could live here in this city forever, just existing, surviving, until the world righted itself again. It didn't sound so bad to her in the least.

They came to a large sign in the aisle, and Benny pointed her in the right direction. "Meet back here," he told her sternly, suddenly sounding like her parent. He did that from time to time, and it gave her such a warm sense of comfort, she could drown herself in it.

She quietly made her way to the cheese, her mouth watering at the thought of an aged parmesan, ignoring the fact that it might have gone bad because things like that didn't matter much anymore. Stepping over old packaging strewn on the floor, she neared the bar where her parents had found her twirling happily on barstools. There it was, just around the corner, just four steps around the corner, but suddenly she smacked into something. It was soft; it had been moving. It was clothed in military gear; it had an assault rifle strapped to it.

"Solomon!" it said in a hushed voice, grabbing her by the shoulder with a piercing grip, and Elena tried to pull away, to kick at it, but it picked her up around the waist and ran with her as she kicked and pushed against its arm.

"Solomon!" It found who it was looking for. A man stood up, leaving a twirling barstool in his wake, and smiled slowly.

"Whaddywe have here?" he asked.

"It lookie like a little mouse," her captor responded. Elena could tell in the dull light that a massively tall woman with a bleached crew cut was holding her in an airtight grip.

Elena wanted to scream, but she didn't dare. She wanted Benny to stay amongst his rows of pasta, touching each one thoughtfully, deciding what they should eat for dinner. She wanted him to suddenly notice she had disappeared like that day with her parents, and spend forty-five minutes looking for her in every corner using a hushed voice, and then finally decide she must have run away. She did not want him to find a girl hanging helpless in a strong grasp. She wanted him to be safe, to go back to their underground home and finish his work and save the world.

"She don't have a chip, RoRo," Solomon said to his partner. She immediately grabbed Elena's wrist and examined it as Solomon shined his light for her to get a closer look.

"Well, I'll be damned," RoRo said. "We got to get her to Command, and get her assigned. And get some pills in her, 'course." They both laughed.

They snuck out of the store without a sound, despite their enormous sizes, and slipped out into the night. Elena breathed a sigh of relief. Benny was spared for the time being.

"*I'm sorry, Benny,*" she said to him silently. "*I will be OK. I will be OK. I am immune. They have no power over me.*"

She felt a rocking, and her mind snapped back to the present. She gave a sly peek and saw that sleepers were surrounding the train, thousands of them, more than she could count. They were reenacting the scariest zombie movie she'd ever seen as they haphazardly clawed at the side of the train, a hoard of desperate cats. She wanted to squeeze her eyes shut at the sound, but she didn't dare because guards were pacing up and down the aisle trying to figure out what to do.

"What these sleepers think they doing?" one shouted.

"I done know, but I think they trying to get in," another said.

Elena heard them shouting on the loudspeaker and then felt the train pull with all its strength to free itself from human despair.

The sleepers were separated from limbs as it rained, rained, rained, and it took everything Elena had inside her to not cry out, an animal, in fear that this sight would eat her alive with its gruesomeness.

I hope you're not out there, Benny. I hope they didn't get you and drug you and put you to work at a factory, and I hope you're not trying to get inside this train and I hope you still have your arms and legs and guts, and I hope you've left or stayed underground, and I hope you somehow know that I'm OK.

The water sprayed away the mess they had made, and the shiny train sped its way out of the city.

Goodbye city, cruel city, grand city. Goodbye Benny, goodbye last breaths of freedom. Goodbye.

2018, NEW YORK CITY

Benny had been stuffing his duffel with eighteen-dollar bags of pasta, his mind racing as usual. He felt like he had a message to shout, but no one could hear him, and he wasn't sure if they ever would. He didn't know who was left out there or if there were pockets of people like him who hadn't gotten assigned yet and who still believed in a Resistance. He often thought about Patti and Jonah, and he fretted about them and their family. Had they gone into deeper hiding when his package didn't arrive? Had they been captured and reassigned? What then? Sometimes, it was all too much for him to consider and, like the memories of Clara, he pushed his friends into an underground place in his brain where thoughts of them couldn't hurt him.

They had seen more militia on their runs lately. They mostly remained uptown from what he could gather, near their headquarters, but he worried that he had taken Elena up too far with his silly idea of an Italian dinner. An uncomfortable energy crept into his bones once they crossed Fourteenth Street (not letting himself even glance in the direction of Union Square and Clara's remains) and grew to a frenzy as they neared Twentieth. Elena didn't seem to notice, but he could feel it. He almost told her to turn back, but her kid-like excitement stopped him.

He felt awful for slipping her sleeping pills and then opiates. Injecting opiates into a child! But he didn't regret it. He had never met someone who was completely immune to the effects of such a powerful drug, and now he observed her as if she was a magical unicorn he had discovered in the gutters of Manhattan. The implications to his work were unimaginable, and his thoughts tumbled over each other as they tried to make sense of these new findings and what to do with them.

Benny found some jarred sauces and inspected the expiration dates, allowing himself some leeway given the circumstances. He stuffed three into his bag, making sure the pasta cushioned them so they didn't make any noise.

He stopped. Something was wrong. No noise. He could feel the desolation as intimately as the rumbling of the military tank he had felt earlier. His work had made him so in tune with the human spirit, he believed he could sense a heartbeat from three city blocks away.

He detected none. The air was dead and still except for the panic clawing at his chest.

Maintaining his silence, he crept around the market, heading back to the crossroads where he had left Elena. He followed the path to the cheese, but she wasn't there.

"Elena," he hissed. The silence could be felt, and it caused the hair on his neck to quiver with quiet realization.

He wandered farther into the belly of the market and hissed again, "Elena!" this time louder and more desperate. There was nothing.

Benny spent the next two hours searching and hoping and wondering if she'd run away and left him forever or if she'd been taken and where she'd go next. Maybe she'd decided to give up like her father had that day and travel up the thirty blocks to the cluster of pill stations and factories and stuff her face full of drugs to escape it all. Then he realized she couldn't.

He knew it was late, and that he was too close to the towers on 56th Street. With one last look at the market, he hoisted his bag up on his shoulder and walked out of the store. He couldn't risk leaving a note, and even if he could, he didn't have a pen.

The walk was long and hard, and he almost didn't care about staying hidden in the shadows. Elena was gone, and it was his fault.

"I'm sorry, Sarah," he said to his long lost friend. *"You trusted me to watch over her, and I didn't. I'm so, so sorry."*

He neared his subway entrance, and a thought occurred to him: *She's here! She couldn't find me and went back to the lab.*

Slipping on dust and grime, he ran down the stairs, bag banging on the backs of his legs as he rushed toward the hidden door, careful not to smash the sauce on the subway wall. Now that he knew she was inside waiting for him, he wanted to make her the greatest meal she'd ever had as an apology for taking her so far uptown.

He pushed open the door and saw what he knew in his heart to be true: that Elena hadn't returned at all. That he'd left a ten-year-old out there alone in the bleak city. That she might not be in the city anymore by now.

For Benny, it was the last straw in a series of too-short straws. He fell hard to his knees and began to cry.

2031, THE REPUBLIC

There were a couple more stops before they reached the Republic, but to Elliot they had all started running together. He fought to stop himself from being lulled to sleep by the moving train—sleepers closed their eyes when they were told, when the sleep buzzer sounded and never before. He would draw too much attention to himself if he gave in, even though it would have likely been the most restful sleep he'd have since arriving in Portland as a boy.

He could sense that they were near the Republic before he could catch a glimpse of it. His stomach felt a sharp tug to the right as they rounded a bend, gliding around what looked like a fake mountain peaked with gold-dusted snow. The sparkles glittered even without the sun and Elliot half expected a golden eagle to soar out from behind it, spreading its wings in a sweeping welcome. He wished Elena could see this mountain made of fairy dust, but she was facing the other direction and would have had to turn her head to take it all in. Then he remembered that this was eye candy created from the evil mind of the Dictator, and he vowed he would never tell Elena how stunning it was.

They came to a tunnel and it swallowed them up, making the train dark for just a moment. Red overhead lights flashed on, bathing them in a sinister hue. Just as quickly, they were spit out the other side, and the dull grey light from a diseased sun tried to shine once again through their windows.

They had arrived. Nothing, not a mountain dusted with gold or a world spurred into chaos, could have prepared Elliot for the Republic. Everything had changed since he had seen it in its infancy. Even in the smoggy light, it glistened and glittered with its gold and silver and shiny red buildings that stretched so far up into the sky, he was sure they were acquainted with the clouds. There were so many of them, Elliot wondered if the city ever ended or if it just stretched all the way to the ocean. The thought that there were enough people to occupy those buildings made him feel incredibly small and helpless as he realized just how many followers had stood by the Dictator out of fear or love or admiration. Elliot felt like he was going to be sick, like the thought of how completely fucked the world had become was finally tugging too hard at his gag reflex. The Republic was gross and ostentatious and careless and beautiful all at the same time.

They pulled up just to the edge of the city to a cluster of buildings that seemed tarnished compared to the rest. He was grateful to be there. He couldn't stand a single second longer of anticipation. A buzzer sounded and their belts released. It was time.

2018, NEW YORK CITY TO PORTLAND, MAINE

The blonde woman carried Elena all the way back to the military Jeep that was waiting five blocks up the street. Elena had stopped fighting and began preparing for what she imagined was coming next. The woman, RoRo, opened the door and shoved Elena inside, sliding in next to her. RoRo held her wrist tight, but she wouldn't have tried to escape anyway. She knew she'd been caught, and she knew she wasn't as strong as even one of the guards. *Know your limitations,* her mother had always told her. *It's the only way to build on them.*

They drove up the street, hitting potholes that sent the Jeep flying, until they reached the hub of the city. Elena leaned toward the window to take a closer look and couldn't believe what existed only forty blocks away from her and Benny's hideout. There was a series of large buildings surrounded by militia who carried giant guns. People resembling the latest versions of her parents were stumbling in formation through one of the oversized doorways and when the last of them staggered through, the thick doors closed behind them.

She searched for her parents, wondering if they had somehow ended up here. She imagined how she'd drag them down to Benny's lab and how she'd get them fixed up and how they'd escape New York and even the country and go live somewhere as they were meant to be. Just the three of them.

RoRo dragged her out of the car and led her to the tallest skyscraper she had ever seen up close. Elena watched as a sensor scanned the woman's wrist and flashed an alert that an unassigned person was entering the building. She assumed it was her.

They walked down a long dark hallway until they reached what felt like an operating room. RoRo tossed her up on the metal table and strapped her wrists and ankles down.

"We found a loose one," RoRo told the technician who looked annoyed.

"How'd you find a loose one? This city's been scanned a million times. I thought we'd got every last one of those stupid revolutionaries." They both laughed.

"I dunno. She was in that market down the way." RoRo shrugged her giant shoulders.

"Well, who knows? Let's get her fixed up," the tech said. Elena couldn't believe how they were talking about her like she wasn't there, like she was a pet that had to be put down. She suddenly became a little bit terrified.

"OK, first I'm gonna drug her. It's the humane thing to do. I put one of these here chips into someone before I drugged 'em and man, did they howl. I was numbed up myself when I got mine, so I dunno, but I think it hurts real bad." The tech was prepping a large needle.

"I bet! I woulda loved to see that! That's what they get for crossing Dictator, eh?" RoRo slapped her leg.

Once again, the word Dictator hung in Elena's guts like a virus. She was happy that her mother was asleep and didn't have to witness how their self-appointed ruler had gobbled up the souls of everyone who stood in his way and had become the most powerful person in their country's history. She was in so much shock, she almost didn't see the needle coming toward her.

She tried to move away from it, but knew as it found its way to her skin that the time was now. The tip of the needle pricked her, then plunged into her arm, and she screamed as it burned all the way down her right side and spider webbed throughout her entire body.

But just as quickly as it spread to her limbs, her chest, her head, it receded. Her cells chased the poison out, away, and she had no idea where it went. In an instant, she felt fine.

She grabbed at her wits and told herself that she had to implement Benny's instructions now, now, now, and she told her body to shut down its basic functions, to stop fighting, to go limp.

"She drugged up real nice, Esther," RoRo said in admiration, and Elena felt like a child who had performed perfectly at her recital but her parents hadn't been there to see it.

"Yeah, she is," Esther responded. "Now for the chip. Thank god she won't feel this. I tell you, the last one howled real good."

She walked back over to her tools and stood there for a minute preparing everything. Then she returned, holding a long silver rod capped with a square end.

The implant punched into the thin skin of Elena's wrist, and she wanted to cry out in agony, but instead she retreated to a place inside her that only she knew: holding her mom's pinkie in the park, tugging on her father's scratchy coat and wrapping her little arms around his neck when he lifted her up high enough to touch the sky. The day she started kindergarten and cried, stuffing her face in her mother's hair and sniffing in just a bit of her strength so she could be brave enough to walk through the doors.

She thought of waves at the Jersey Shore, learning to read, wearing a bright blue sundress and drinking pink lemonade with fresh strawberries at the bottom. She thought of every glorious moment of her idyllic childhood and piled them up to block out the pain and did not, would not show these two unbelievably putrid, brainwashed women that she could feel a thing. They had to believe in the rawest parts of their insides that she was a sleeper, as they called them. She had to believe it herself.

The pain sucked at her small wrist like it was drinking her blood, but, almost like she willed it to, it eventually subsided. She told the tear clinging to her eyeball that now was not the time nor place for it to give her away. It stayed put. Everything about her body was frozen in time.

The two women were still chatting and laughing as Esther cleaned her tools and typed some notes on a computer that looked more like a transparent piece of floating paper.

They left the room, and Elena stole the minute to catch her breath, but she knew they were probably watching her.

"They're always watching," her mother had said after her parents discovered that their phones and their smart TVs and the Bluetooth in their cars were listening. "Don't think for a second that you aren't being watched and your every move recorded."

Elena let her body relax even more into the hard cold metal table and tried to assess her situation. She didn't have her pack on her at the market, so they wouldn't be able to find out her identity or see her mother's handwritten instructions. She breathed a tiny sigh of relief. She didn't want the instructions to be the reason they found the lab.

Everything else, she figured, was out of her control. She was in the system now, but there was no prior record of her, and she was still awake. She'd just have to keep up her ruse for a little while, maybe a couple of days, and then she'd find a way to escape.

Trying to push away thoughts of how to tear open her skin and pull out her newly implanted chip, Elena felt an overwhelming exhaustion. Her eyelids were made of steel; she had no control over them. They shut with an inaudible thud, and the last sliver of light disappeared behind them.

2031, THE REPUBLIC

Their project began a year ago, right after Sarah had confided in Savannah—something she just blurted out in conversation, and Savannah had been obsessed with the concept from the moment she heard it.

"But how does it work? How exactly?" she asked, and Sarah patiently told Savannah what she knew about the antidote, which was very little and much of it speculation.

"I only spoke to him online, so I don't know much. But he published his findings to a small group of us," Sarah smiled a little. "I guess it wasn't such a small group toward the end." She found herself stuck for a minute, remembering how it felt to lead, to unite. Oh, the protests they had! The marches, the rallies! Oh, how intelligent every single member was, how talented. She had really believed that they could do anything with their brains and their will.

"What I know is, if you take it, you can't get addicted to narcotics. And he was working on the next iteration of it before I went to prison. He called it a 'cure.'" Sarah chuckled a bit, but Savannah looked excited.

"Imagine. A cure for all this." She swept her hand in the direction of the window, her voice barely audible above the hairdryer Sarah was pretending to use. "We could put it in their shakes and reactivate the masses." She clapped her hands like she'd heard the dreamy end to a fairytale.

"It sounds romantic. And silly," Sarah had said, poking Savannah's arm with her finger. She used to do the same thing to her daughter when Elena was little, and she'd adopted the move with her mistress.

"Not silly! We could recreate it! Or find him. That man who made it." Savannah's voice was getting higher and higher with excitement.

"Find Benny? In this madness? Now I know you're crazy. Now, what should you wear to this luncheon?" Sarah changed the subject because she thought it was dangerous to dream. Savannah's guts weren't ripped out of her body like Sarah's. Her world wasn't taken from her in such a final swoop that she didn't even realize it had happened. She wasn't separated from her family and left to wonder every single second of every day if they were alive or dead or stuck in the middle.

But she persisted. Savannah became fixated on the idea and talked about it incessantly every time they were alone. Sarah answered her questions curtly, and finally she stopped answering at all. Then one day, Savannah said in a whisper as Sarah was tucking her in, "What if I send David to go find him? We'll pretend it's a tour of the New York factory."

"Go find who?"

"Benny." Savannah smiled.

Sarah had felt an anger rise up in her, one that had been dormant for ages. It felt so strikingly similar to the one she'd felt the day of the election. As everyone wallowed in their sadness, she had allowed it to elevate her out of the darkness to fight.

"Savannah. He's fucking dead! Everyone's dead! Everyone I ever loved because of you people, you stupid, demonic people!" Sarah stopped and looked around, confused. She'd felt possessed. Savannah was staring at her with her mouth open.

"That was awesome! I love this Sarah. We leave tomorrow."

Savannah had crawled out of bed and took her friend in her arms. She towered over her by almost a foot, and Sarah felt cradled, and she felt loved.

The Dictator's wife pulled back and looked at someone who was broken, but knew deep inside that there was still some fight left. "Tomorrow?" she asked.

Sarah nodded. "Tomorrow."

They had decided Sarah should stay, "Just in case." Sarah didn't really mean what Savannah meant when she said that—it was one of the many times she found the woman silly and juvenile, especially for her age. But Sarah agreed even though she knew from the last time her lady had taken a trip that the minutes felt like they were barely ticking by and the days seemed to stretch into weeks. She was so terrified that one of the other government workers would recognize who she was in her past life that she kept mostly to herself when Savannah wasn't there. In every way, Savannah was her protection. Her lifeline. Her friend. Her only friend.

The morning of the New York factory trip, Sarah had helped her get ready, packing a small suitcase with red and black clothing for whatever the weather decided to do in a given moment. There were ponchos and sleek jackets and skin tight pants that resisted water and wind.

The two women stood together, and Sarah remembered that she had wished Savannah luck and thought how odd that was. For what? Savannah was going off to find Sarah's long lost Internet pen pal who claimed he had a cure for addiction.

But find him she did. Savannah arrived back in the Republic two days later. Sarah got an alert the moment she crossed into Republic territory. It was written in their secret code.

"Meet me at the hospital."

Sarah had grabbed her things quickly, running down the hall to the elevator and out to a waiting rail. She sat down and felt the familiar pull of the strap hugging her body. Then a velocity that gripped at her heart spit her to the hospital entrance in under two minutes.

Savannah was waiting for her in the lobby, looking eight feet tall in sparkling heels. Sarah had never been to the hospital. She walked to the entrance and stopped short before her boot took its first step inside.

The hospital glistened and glittered with jewels that caught the light of an imaginary sun. There were faded etchings on the walls of America's past, of great Presidents, of civil rights leaders, of people who had fought for something better. It was a world she'd dreamed of, that she'd begged for at her most vulnerable, and the sight of it, even faded into extinction, made her want to cry.

They went up to the sixtieth floor together, and Sarah felt like she had a caged animal pacing around inside her body. Savannah had given her no real indication as to what had happened, and she didn't dare ask in a public space.

Savannah was all business as her heels resounded down the long hallway, which was painted in a deep charcoal. She pushed open a door, and Sarah almost stepped on the backs of her ankles, she was walking so closely behind her friend.

"Sit down." Savannah was maintaining a ruthless poker face, but Sarah could sense she was excited. More excited than she had ever seen her.

Sarah took a seat in front of a control board. The room they were in had a two-way mirror and leather seats and almost resembled the other side of an interrogation room. She looked over at Savannah to try to get more information out of her, but she only offered a sly smile.

They heard the heavy door open in stereo over the speaker system in their room. David walked in, dragging something.

He sat a man down in a chair, but the man quickly dropped to the floor on all fours and retreated to a corner. He cowered there like a feral cat, like the lights were too bright and the surroundings too foreign. He had a beard that attempted to reach past his chest, twisting and knotting in the most extraordinary way, a gnarled tree that had been alone in the forest for ages without any human contact.

His hair was so long it seemed to eat its owner alive with its madness. His clothes were tattered, but not as much as his other attributes would indicate. As Sarah sat there staring at this person, she struggled to try to make sense of what was happening in the next room.

She tugged on Savannah's sleeve and Savannah turned to look at her. "Is that him?" Sarah asked. "Is that really him?"

Savannah grinned like a lioness, like a person who had gotten everything she had ever wanted, and this was one more notch on her belt. She nodded slowly.

"But. How did you find him?" Sarah asked.

"He was exactly where you said he was. We followed your instructions to the underground lab. I didn't go down there, of course, but he was there! He fought David. I think he tried to stab him with a syringe, but David got him, and we also brought some of his equipment. He tried to smash it before David nabbed it, but he salvaged a bunch of vials."

Sarah had so many questions that she could barely formulate one. "How did he survive down there all this time? Almost fourteen years!" As she whispered it, she wanted nothing more than to go into the room and gather the man in her arms like he was her child. She couldn't imagine such dank solitude, such permeating loneliness, and she believed a simple bout of human contact could be what he needed to feel like a person again.

"I don't know. Supposedly it was pretty crazy down there. Empty, moldy cans of food and lots of potions. It was like a witch's den! A homeless witch." Savannah clapped her hands together, and Sarah tried to extinguish a moment of hatred for her. This stupid woman didn't know what it was like to suffer or need or be crushed by the world that her own tyrannical father had built with his smooth entitled hands. But then she remembered that Savannah was on her side, and she needed her. She loved her, even if she said all the wrong things sometimes.

"Does anyone know who he is? Or why he's here?" Sarah asked cautiously, almost inaudibly.

"No, no one saw us. No one comes to this hospital anymore anyway." Savannah waved her hand like it was no big deal, but suddenly this man in the other room, this person from Sarah's past, was more important to her than anyone or anything else.

"Can I talk to him?" Sarah asked.

"Yes. I've cut off the feeds to these rooms, and David is keeping watch in the hallway. I'll call him when it's time to move him."

Sarah nodded and got up slowly. Savannah grabbed her by the wrist as she turned to walk out of the door.

"Sar. Be careful, OK?"

Sarah gave her a look as if to say: *Like it matters?* but nodded anyway. She walked down the hallway and David opened the heavy door. Benny moved as far as he could into the corner—if he could have gone through the wall, he would have. He looked beaten and exhausted and done with this life. She didn't blame him. She had felt that way, too, and she hadn't even been awake the whole time.

"Benny," she said quietly. He didn't respond. She wondered if he'd heard her as he kept trying to get away.

"Benny!" she said just a little bit louder. He stopped scurrying for a second. He was completely still.

"Hi. I don't know if you remember me. I'm Sarah. Sarah Montgomery. We were friends. Are friends." She forced a laugh. "We never met of course, but we were friends online. In my group. Purple Nation. I led Purple

Nation, and then I was arrested at one of our big marches in D.C., and then they drugged me in prison, and then they drugged everyone!" Her voice sounded foreign to her own ears and like she was nervously trying to make friends with a person who didn't understand a word she said.

"Anyway, the Dictator's Wife rescued me, she was Dictator One's daughter at the time, Savannah, and now she's Dictator Two's wife, and anyway her father had me in this exhibit, which is another story for another time, but she saw me, and she put me through detox, and she saved my life." Sarah turned to look at the two-way mirror through which she could not see. Speaking directly to it, she said, "Yeah, I've never really told her, but I owe her everything. I owe her my life."

She turned back to Benny and noticed that he was watching her. He was listening. He had slid his back down the wall and was now sitting against it. His shoulders were slumped over a bit in resignation, but his head was cocked in what she hoped was understanding.

"Sarah?" he finally asked. His voice croaked with all the years he hadn't used it.

"Yes. I'm Sarah. Your old friend. Hello." Sarah reached out her hand and noticed it was shaking.

He stared at her for so long, she was worried he had fallen asleep with his eyes open. But finally he asked again, "Sarah?"

She nodded.

He leapt up so fast and grabbed her hand, pulling her toward him with such force, she could have sworn it came from something greater than them.

"Sarah!" She heard Savannah's voice over a loudspeaker, but held up her hand bravely, signaling she was alright.

Benny had pulled her so close, her face was just inches from his.

"I thought you were drugged or gone, but now you're here and now I can tell you what I've wanted to tell you or anyone so my body can be released from the guilt that has crippled it for so long." His eyes were wild, and she was terrified, but she squeezed his hand and nodded again, urging him to go on.

"Elena found me. She followed your instructions and took one of the last buses up to New Jersey. It was right after you and Ben were taken."

Sarah's hand rose to her mouth without knowing it.

"She walked through the tunnel and uptown by herself. She was only ten years old, Sarah." He pulled her closer. "To this day, I don't know how she did it or why she wasn't scared. It was kind of like because you told her what to do, she could do anything."

Sarah grasped his hand tighter. Tears poured down her cheeks, careening around her open mouth.

"She found the subway entrance and walked down those steps, and she found my lab. I was sleeping, and she waited for me to wake up. She woke me up," he said. Sarah thought she detected a small bit of amusement in his voice, but she couldn't be sure.

"She stayed with me for months. We foraged around the city. She was a good friend. A hard worker. I was obsessed with my work, with that stupid antidote, so one night I decided to drug her."

"You what?" Sarah yelled at him, trying to pull away. He wouldn't let her. His grasp was unbreakable; they were fused together.

"I had to. Or so I thought. I needed another test subject to try my cure."

"You monster," Sarah spat at him.

Benny smiled, and it seemed unfamiliar on him, like he was trying on an old coat that didn't quite fit anymore. "You're right. She said that, too. She was really angry with me."

"Did your stupid cure work?" Sarah asked.

"I don't know. Because we discovered something incredible. Elena is immune to the drugs. She cannot become addicted. Not ever. We tried ten more times. I gave her pills. I injected her full of opiates. Nothing worked on her."

Sarah looked up at the ceiling as if it offered a clue. She'd had such a specific belief that Elena had been asleep in a factory all this time, but now she felt like her grasp of reality had been unraveled.

"What happened to her, Benny?" Sarah felt like a small girl watching a sad movie, hoping against hope for a happy ending.

"She was captured. At least I think she was. On one of our runs. It was my fault. I shouldn't have taken her so far uptown. I'm so sorry, Sarah."

Sarah slid down next to him, not knowing what to say or feel. She was angry and proud and terrified all at once because this man next to her had just pried open the most unfamiliar feeling of them all: hope.

Benny turned to her, balancing on one knee to grab both sides of her face and force her to look at him.

"I believe she's still out there, alert and aware, fighting quietly for our cause. I think she's hidden among the sleepers, pretending she's one of them. I know she's OK, Sarah. I know because I saw it with my own two eyes. I know she's still awake."

* * *

Sarah watched Savannah fuss with her red pants for the millionth time and walk nervously around the factory floor fixing this station or that. She had never seen her friend like this—nervous and unsure—and yet they were about to attempt something unthinkable. If they were caught, Savannah had promised to take all of the blame. But while Sarah trusted her as much as she could in this situation, she knew that it would be the servant who would be punished, not the wife of the Dictator.

Savannah put her hand on Sarah's shoulder, and she jumped.

"They're here," she said. "I just heard the train pull in."

Sarah stood up. They had recruited all the Jane Doe sleepers in the Northeast and a group of men so it didn't seem suspicious. They had found every woman who didn't have a background or who couldn't be linked with a past.

"Let's go," Sarah said. And together, squeezing each other's hands, they went to greet their new workers.

2031, THE REPUBLIC

Elena's belt unhooked and a buzzer signaled for them to stand up. The doors opened and another buzzer instructed them to get off the train. She shuffled forward with the group, feeling like this was a new start. She tried to pretend that it was her first day of college, an experience she had been robbed of, or day one of a new job.

They made their way, slow as mud, down the stairs and through the opening. They all crowded in a holding room and stood as still as they could, some of them bouncing around a bit in their own bodies and some of them swaying subtly from side to side.

A woman walked into the room, and Elena could hear her before she could see her. High heels resounded off the concrete floor like a jackhammer demanding attention. Careful to continue her zombie dance of shuffling back and forth, Elena snuck a peek from below her lashes.

She saw red shoes, red pants (with tiny black lines zagging up the sides) and a tight black shirt. She dared to continue her pupils upward and glimpsed the ends of long blonde hair, followed by a defined chin, pouty mouth, perfect nose and big, gaping eyes.

It was the Dictator's daughter. Savannah. Even so many years later, Elena recognized her from every broadcast she'd ever watched, her parents screaming at the television.

What is the Dictator's daughter doing here?

She realized Savannah was picking sleepers out of the crowd.

"Her. Her. That one. Right there." Elena felt pressure on her elbow crook, and she felt herself being pulled to the front of the room and then out the door.

Savannah led the pack of the all-women group that had been chosen. Each one was tugged along gently by a military escort as they filed down the hall behind her.

They were brought into a small room and lined up side by side. A buzzer sounded that signaled them to stand still.

Elena's heart was pounding and her mouth felt dry, but she reminded herself not to lose her wits. She felt like they were in a police lineup or the target of a firing range, and she had no idea why these seven or so sleepers had been singled out or why they were all women.

They stood there for about five minutes until another buzzer sounded, and they all turned to exit.

One of the women was pulled out as she was leaving. Elena felt a tug to the right. She was being pulled out as well.

They were taken into another smaller room, pushed down into chairs and left alone, a thick door shutting behind the guards. Elena would have given anything to talk to the other sleeper and ask her if she knew what was going on, but the woman was only semi-conscious and Elena had to face her searing thoughts alone.

The door opened again and three pairs of feet walked in. Elena recognized Savannah's red heels, but the other two people were wearing black boots like hers. She guessed one was a woman's feet and one a man's. She didn't dare look up past their calves.

The feet stood there in silence for a couple of minutes.

"That's her. I think that's her," the woman with the black boots said. The voice sounded so familiar, Elena felt a deep ache in her heart that she had somehow forgotten or buried forever.

"Guard!" yelled Savannah.

The door opened, and a guard rushed in.

"This one," Savannah told him, and the other sleeper was quickly dragged out of the room.

"You're sure we're safe?" the familiar voice asked.

"I only told you a million times!" Savannah responded, exasperated. But Elena could tell she was joking and the women were friends.

"OK, OK."

"Are you sure it's her?" Savannah asked.

"Of course I'm sure," said the voice.

The woman knelt down in front of Elena so her face was in line with her downcast eyes. Elena continued to pretend she didn't notice. She wouldn't let herself believe what she knew, with every increasing second, to be true. If it wasn't, then she would die right there from the most devastating thing that ever happened to her in an endless avalanche of devastating things.

"Elena?" the voice ventured. Elena had heard the same voice say her name so many times it was part of her.

"Elena, it's me," the voice tried again. Elena couldn't speak. Her voice was lost, and she worried that she wouldn't be able to find it in time.

"Maybe he was wrong," the voice said to Savannah. "Maybe they found a way to drug her."

The woman shook her gently, trying again, voice layered with a hint of desperation. "Elena. It's me. Mama. It's your mama."

The word broke Elena in a way she never thought she'd know again, and she was scared it was a trick, that she would finally look up at the face and it wouldn't be her mom at all but someone who sounded just like her, and Savannah, a woman she had always known to be evil and hated by her parents, would laugh and call a guard to drag her out and lock her away forever. She was worried it really was her mom, and she'd reach for her and embrace her and her hero would disappear again, maybe into thin air. The fear tore at her, wide gashes that she felt to the bone, but her irreparable aching for her mother was greater than anything she'd ever felt before. In the end, it won.

"Mama?" she said, finally looking up. "Mom?" It was her.

"Elena!" Her mom grabbed her and pulled her up and held her close like she had when Elena was little except now she was taller than her mom. They pulled apart and laughed through their tears, and Elena could see miniature sparkles surrounding them.

"You're tall!" Sarah told her, brushing away her daughter's tears.

"You're the same. Exactly the same," Elena said back. "How?"

"It doesn't matter now." Sarah glanced at Savannah, who had tears streaming down her face. "It's a long story. I want you to meet someone. This is Savannah. Van. My friend."

Elena narrowed her eyes and bowed her head just a little in respect.

"It's nice to meet you, Elena," Savannah said, swiping clumsily at her tears.

"This is David," Sarah said, gesturing toward the man who stood at attention. David glanced over at her and gave a deep nod, a small smile on his lips as if he was seeing an old friend after a long stretch of time.

"Listen, my love," Sarah said. "We don't have a lot of time. I can explain everything, but for now, we have to get you to your sleeping quarters while we figure out our next step."

"OK." Elena felt breathless and overwhelmed. She didn't want to let her mother go, but she trusted her. She had never stopped trusting her.

"Elena, Benny told me that you can't become addicted," Sarah began.

"Benny? You've talked to him?" Elena wasn't sure she could take much more news.

"Yes. I'll explain that later, too. The others like you who are immune to the drugs—are some of them here with you?"

Elena felt her guard instantly go up even though the woman in front of her was her mother. What if they were making her mom say all these things? What if it was a trick? She felt like she was at the edge of a golden tower with one toe hanging off. In the end, she decided she had nothing left to lose and took a running leap off of it.

She turned to look her mother in the eye and felt like everything could finally be alright again. She took both of her mother's hands in hers and squeezed them tight and opened her mouth and said in a big, brave voice, "There were fourteen of us in my sector. Some of us are here. I know there's more. There's a Controller I report to. I don't know where they are or who they are." Elena felt lightheaded from the confessions and closed her eyes for a moment hoping she did the right thing.

Her mom turned to look at Savannah who didn't look surprised, which left Elena feeling like she was a helium balloon floating high above her own body. She was starting to understand something unbelievable except the pieces refused to snap into place. She wanted to take a damp cloth and swipe at her own comprehension, but she didn't know how and the important bits remained blurry. Sarah turned back to Elena and spoke slowly.

"I want you to tell us where the others are, and how we can tell they're still awake."

"OK, I can do that. I know everything about them. Mom, what's going to happen?"

Her mom looked back at Savannah who nodded. David's five percent smile grew to twelve, but he was so still, Elena wondered if he was still breathing. Sarah took a deep breath and pulled her daughter close, stroking her hand like she used to do when Elena was little. Then she leaned in and whispered in her ear.

"Welcome to the Command Center, darling. We're building an army."

Made in the USA
Lexington, KY
24 October 2017